D0007982

THE ALL-CONSUMING WORLD

CASSANDRA KHAW

Content notice: *The All-Consuming World* contains depictions of abusive relationships, character death (mentioned), codependency, emotional manipulation, eye trauma, gaslighting, gore, grief, and surgery without anesthesia.

First published in North America by Erewhon Books, LLC in 2021

Edited by Sarah T. Guan

Erewhon Books
2 W. 29th Street, Suite 3S
New York, NY 10001
www.erewhonbooks.com

Erewhon books are available at special discounts when purchased in bulk for premiums and sales promotions as well as for fund-raising or educational use. Special editions or book excerpts can also be created to specification. For details, send an email to specialmarkets@workman.com.

Library of Congress Control Number: 2021935357

ISBN 978-1-64566-020-0 (hardcover)
ISBN 978-1-64566-024-8 (ebook)

Cover art by Ashe Samuels
Cover design by Samira Iravani
Interior design by Cassandra Farrin and Leah Marsh
Solar eclipses by Lalan / Shutterstock
Bullet hole by vectorwin / Shutterstock

Printed in the United States of America

First US Edition: August 2021
10 9 8 7 6 5 4 3 2 1

For Ali, Avery, Kyungseo, Linda, Olivia,
Shoma, and Tara, my darling siblings,
my chosen family, my beloveds.

AYANE

"The fuck am I doing here, Rita?"

Her voice is the boreal wash of moonlight upon the bulwark of their ship-in-orbit: a reduction of the fantastic, tepid when it could have been of a devouring temperature. It is modulated, disinterested. But like fuck Maya is going to complain. Any contact with Rita is superior to the absence of such.

"Getting Ayane home."

"Home?" Maya grins like a hunting dog, all peeled-back lips and a shine of teeth. For a joke, she'd had the points of her canines filed about three years ago, when there'd been nothing to do but mug retirees, those poor fucks who'd wanted nothing but to jolt their marriages out of hospice with a hit of no-gravity space. Instead, what they got was Maya, Rita, and their tin-can private liners cleaned out of valuables. "You're getting soft."

A hiss of static. "You're getting distracted."

"Fair," says Maya. Don't want to have this party cleared out before it even gets started. She looks over the tableau. Cross her dollar-store heart, there's nothing Maya loathes more than this shoulder of rock she's ascending, which is saying a lot given her sentiments about the asteroid itself. She recalls when this place was moondust and noxious ice-melt, inhospitable by every interpretation of the adjective. But no one cares when it's just clones on ground zero. Work, die, mulch the corpses, brine the proteins in the appropriate solution, bring them back. Rinse, repeat in the name of capitalism, amen and all that crap.

"Wish we still had Johanna," says Maya. "She could have walked Ayane right into the ship and none of us would have had to lift a fucking finger."

Usually, Maya has a laugh like something that needs to be put down. Today, though, it arrives in a casket, a few little croaks escaping the lid. *No, no thinking about Johanna,* Maya tells herself. Easy to let the memory of Johanna—she of the "don't even fucking worry about this," the "I got this," the "no need to take risks when we could just sit back and settle this from afar, let's just get a drink, y'all," "I've got this"—effervescing through their lives burn away to the image branded on the backs of Maya's eyelids. Easy to see meat instead of a smile.

No, no. Fuck that.

And still:

"Fuck. Do you miss her? I do."

No answer.

"I'm fucking talking to you here. Say something."

But Rita doesn't answer.

Well, fuck her, Maya thinks, walking her attention away. No need to defibrillate that dead horse. She studies her environment. This place was better when it was a refinery, when it was still being reworked for human occupation. At least, it had been honest. Now? The slope she is standing on is leprous with non-union brothels, casinos, back-alley chop shops, tenements so thick with the unloved and the underserved, their laundry drips from thin windows like foam along the maw of a rabid animal.

"Fuck you," Maya mutters.

Light—blue-white, like the pith of a neutron star, like hope, like the halogen eye of a surgical lamp glaring into the wet nook where Maya's heart is housed—suddenly flares through her overlay, searing patterns into her retinas. Maya ducks around a pillar before the cerebellum attempts to strategize. Half a second later, a surveillance bot lopes past, Doberman ears astride a trumpet of a muzzle, no teeth or tongue in sight, only a violent light belling from an octagonal aperture. Maya locks her breath in place until the clicking of its needle-point feet evanesces.

"The first rule is you never talk about it," giggles a man's voice, so close to the curve of Maya's voice, she almost jumps.

"Fuck. Right. Off."

Maya snarls, propels herself from the wall, the cracked masonry flaking under the impact of her palms. Fuck Rita and fuck the ghost she'd saddled Maya with. Explosives don't need personalities. Least of all when they come with such baggage. But there he was anyway. Same fucking smile with one corner craned unnaturally high. Same eyes, gleaming jellyfish-blue-green. Same heft, same shoulders. Same as the day that Maya found him in Rita's quarters, grinning like a cat. *Fuck everything,* Maya thinks to herself. Her fingers find her holsters, thumbs cocking the safety back, fists closing over enameled grips.

There we go.

Breathe, Maya.

Can't believe that bot almost got the jump on her while she was caroling her grievances, blathering at Rita like the two of them were gene-patented starlets sitting pretty for the camera. If Maya had just gotten the mods Rita offered her, traded up from her repository of wetware, this wouldn't ever have happened. The somatosensory implants were triple-tested, lab-approved, and it's not like Rita would have installed bottom-of-the-barrel shit in her brain. They *need* each other. Mad scientist and mad-dog mercenary. Like jam and cheese, guns and their holsters, god and glory. Forget that it would mean Rita acquiring unmitigated access to her grey matter. It's not like Maya can hide anything from her.

Onward she goes, Maya practically somnambulating down the narrow lanes. How many times had she died in one of these alleys? How many times had she been jumped, carved open, split open so someone could harvest organs for the rich and the sick? She keeps her fingers at the triggers as she strolls along up until she halts in front of a door six feet wide and twice as high. Maya lets go of the hand-cannons and digs the heel of a palm into the door, considers being discreet for about half a second, before she laughs coyote-shrill and goes *fuck it.* She kicks the door in.

Fuck this. Fuck that. Fuck everything for the umpteenth time.

A man, massive like an iceberg and twice as cool, looks calmly up from his terminal. He drums a finger against the plastiglass screen. Loose windows melt—holo-vid playlist, a two-for-one pizza advertisement—together into a plain, cold, ivory payment app. He takes no notice of Maya's ghost, just makes a moue of his thin mouth. Maya wonders about the shit he'd seen. Those eyes are deader than hers.

"Sixty bucks for latecomers."

Johanna would have had him fight for us, Maya exposits through a private com-link. Rita doesn't take the bait, but that's okay. Behind Maya, her crypto-geist keeps gibbering, unperturbed, hotfixed to ignore all interruptions. His image lightbleeds for a second, stutters, then stops: an infinitesimal failure that nonetheless curls Maya's lips in simpatico. You can't trust tech these days.

"If this is your first night," says manifest destruction, "you always have to fight."

Rita and Maya sitting on a tree, K-I-S-S-I-N-G. If there was a schoolyard, that'd be what the kids would be singing. It's fortunate that this day and age has surrendered homophobia to the firing squad of basic human decency, because Maya would have had to gun down the bigots otherwise. Not that she wouldn't have shot them up anyway for being terminally wrong.

Rita and her, they don't have that kind of relationship. Never did. In another place and world, where the air isn't spuming poison and toddlers aren't bar-coded, who knows? Not in this life, though. Not even close. Maya has never been that kind of anything and Rita can't stand being touched.

But the two *are* tight as thieves on death row, knife and vein, gun and bullet. Maya will do anything for Rita, and she's reasonably certain that Rita will break at least a few cardinal laws for her in return.

Which is more than anything Maya deserves right now, and they both know it. That's why Maya is strutting into the bobbit worm's jaws, with nothing but a ghost for backup, riding on a wing, a prayer, and enough combat know-how to win all four world wars.

"Next contender!" an announcer howls.

Maya grins like a shark. *Oh*, she thinks, the sound unspooling between neurons like a tendon snagged on the tooth of a Great White. Oh, yes. *That* she can do.

But it is still so strange to her that they built this chapel to archaic media, to offer their sweat and their worship to a fictional credo, an analogy for poison, no more sacrosanct than the urine crusting on the walls outside. Men can sail through constellations, for fuck's sake. Do they need a god cobbled from lobotomized debris of retro cinema?

She tosses her head like a bull. The venue stinks of piss and blood and sour sweat, of mutual admiration expressed by men who'd never been taught how to love. A wound dug into irradiated basalt, the place is seven kinds of building violations, with only one way in and out. No accoutrements. No fire exits. Just a vending machine pregnant with ancient soda and naked bulbs snaking across the ceiling, bleeding black wires over their heads.

Maya remembers when they grew vat-kids here, the inflorescence of viscera; arms and legs fruiting along wire; skin like sails closing over naked skeleton. The ones who didn't make it would be clumped in the corner, waiting to be reprocessed. She remembers waiting, watching with her nose compacted against cold glass, wanting, hoping, yearning; sick with prayer as she counted each attosecond, dead fucking certain such vigils weren't worth shit, but what else was she supposed to do? Back then, her emotional health was the only currency she possessed, and she would have bankrupted herself to make sure Rita came back for another round of living.

"Quick and easy," comes Rita's voice again. "Just like we planned."

Crack.

Maya hears the sound of a jaw being broken, seconds before the crowd detonates into screaming. She prowls closer, already squirming out of her jacket and kicking off her shoes, a grin cocked like a loaded shotgun. Her data banks wake up at the influx of noradrenaline in her bloodstream, presenting options, triangulating opportunities. That grin of hers swells until it is like the last church standing at the end of days and inside, the parish is worshipping war. Maya smooths both hands over the velvet of her skull.

"Yeah?" she says under her breath.

"Don't you fucking dare," says Rita, proving she doesn't really know Maya at all.

She'll do it the old-fashioned way. Maya dismisses her overlays, sets her notifications on silent as Rita's messages began to pile like a six-car crash. Oh, she's pissed. Maya can tell. But she doesn't care. All she can hear right now is the holy-holy-on-high hymn of violence singing through the strings of her being. All she can process is its siren invocation. It has its hook in her, pulling her onward, and she is so okay with where they're going.

Since she's here, she might as well have some fun.

The light drags fingers along Maya's muscled frame, reads out a scripture of scars and stitches, the places that only Rita has touched, scalpel carving sonnets into sinew. Illuminated by bloodlust, Maya shoulders past two skinheads and out into the ring. The men—they're always men, she thinks with a scream of a laugh—go quiet.

"Well?" Maya says, slamming a fist into the square of an open palm.

"No shirt." The guy who speaks up is a pot-bellied twerp with jeans that don't fit his ass, goggles welded to cherub-cheeked face.

Maya spreads her arms wide. "You want to see my tits? Is that it? That what you're saying? You wanna see my tits? You want to motorboat that mess?"

She knows it's not, but she loves taunting shitheads like him. No one ever knows what to do when she shows up, avenging angel constructed in the micro. Five feet two when she deigns to have good posture, all tight lines and a helmet of black hair cropped close to the skull, face like a veteran's tall tale. Maya's countenance is a gossip reel of cicatrices, indentations where the skull stoved in and was shoddily rebuilt: you repair what you can when you can't justify buying new.

Sometimes, Maya wonders if she's ever been "conventionally beautiful," ever had a shot at the fantasy of domesticity, the white picket fences on a blue sky–tumbled planet, a kid who wouldn't mind a clone for a parent, but fuck that and fuck this especially.

The man—someone's dad, Maya is so sure of it, someone's dad looking to reinvigorate his middle-aged spirit—exchanges looks with his peers, nervous. "I meant the guns."

"You want them?" She doesn't give him warning. She doesn't charge exactly, but she does accelerate, going from zero to fifty in three strides, closing the gap before he can process what's about to hit him. She winds a punch, biosynthetic muscles bunching in a hallelujah of intent, and slams reinforced knuckles into the man's nose. "Come and get them."

Maya turns as the man drops first to one knee and then the next, hands over his face, blood ribboning down his front. She slaps her chest a few times, like some unmodified ape, some babyfresh human without a security protocol in the world, and walks a winner's swagger around the circle of waiting faces.

"Come on. Who the fuck is next?!"

The fourth rule is simple: only two guys to a fight.

And yeah, okay, maybe old cinema isn't that bad because hand to mass-market heart, this is Maya's favorite rule in the world.

Maya is wiping the detritus of someone's face from her hands when *she* walks in, the *click-click* of her stilettos as familiar as that old ventricular jingle.

"What the fuck, Maya?"

"Needed to get your attention somehow," Maya grins through bloodied teeth. Someone's gotten lucky. But Maya heals fast enough that it doesn't matter and fuck, does it feel good to *feel.* Letting go like that is a blessed act. It's been years now since she could chart a room in blood and broken bodies, groaning heaps of meat all around. Maya's missed this so much, crypto-geist bearing witness or not.

Ayane looks like the last cold gulp of water before the sun goes supernova, taller and leaner even than Rita, so pretty that it actually hurts to look at her. Every inch of her is federally sanctioned, independently purchased. She could stop a truck with a punch. She has. But you couldn't tell. Not with that dress filigreeing her curves, the material a gold so pale it is practically ice, diamantine along the hems and where the fabric sits along the small of her perfect back.

"You could have called," says Ayane in her exquisite contralto; woman couldn't do ugly even if you paid her in hope.

Two hundred twenty-five point three seconds, a notification tells her. Two hundred twenty-five point three seconds until the dogs come howling. Guess Rita didn't care for the silent treatment.

Good. Maya's got time to kill then. She grinds her heel into the back of a man's hand, enjoys his groan, the way the metacarpals sag under the pressure. She adjusts the set of her feet. *Crunch.* Phalanges pop from the palm. "You wouldn't have answered."

"No." Ayane flips a curl of dark hair over her shoulder, her smile gone savage. The light doesn't just love her, it obsesses. How else to explain the way it wraps her up in a champagne nimbus so she, for one shining moment, looks like some goddess come to salvage the day.

Either way, Maya knows better, and Ayane knows better, and anyone who has ever heard of the Dirty Dozen knows better than to pray to Ayane, Badass Bitch-Goddess of Automated Ballistics, because sure as hell, the only thing she holds holy is metal.

The two meet eyes.

"Probably not," says Ayane, as though Maya needed the clarification. "Get the fuck out of here, Maya. I'm just trying to run a business."

"This really what you want?" A staccato gesture at the night's losers. "MCing for paunchy old men, keeping them entertained for the rest of your life. I remember when you were retro-fitting ageships, Ayane."

"That never happened."

"Fine. Okay. Technically, it didn't happen. But you're probably the closest anyone's ever gotten to doing such. Why give up glory for these middle-aged freaks?"

"It's a life," counters Ayane. Her casual numinosity is frankly offensive. It is empirical, how stunning she is, a fact that exists external to the hypothesis that beauty is qualified by the beholder. Maya had not consented to having her breath shanked from her by something as egregious as Ayane retreating into a halo of artificial light, and she is *pissed* at this misstep by the universe, pissed she hasn't become inoculated to such bodily treason, that Ayane after all these years still could have such an effect.

No wonder Audra picked her.

"Fuck that."

"Fuck you," says Ayane.

"You really going to be a bitch to me without fucking asking why I'm here? You know I wouldn't fucking be here unless it's important." Her gesticulations are no longer modulated, broad and cartoonish. Maya exerts just that much more pressure on the man's limp wrist: the bones might be dust but there are still nerves to grind. "You know that. You know I don't get up in the morning unless it's paid in planets."

"Or if Rita said so."

"Yeah." A shrug. "So?"

"Is she alive?"

"The fuck you think?"

"If she is, then whatever you gotta say is fucking worthless," says Ayane, beginning to leave, her postural language clear: Maya and her mission have already been dismissed. "If she's alive, I know she's got you on a leash and I am *done*, Maya. I don't want to have anything to do with that fucking junk-cunt."

"Not even if I told you we know the Minds are coming after ex-con—"

"I don't want to hear it. What do you not get about that? I don't fucking care anymore. Fuck them. Let them take down the club. Let them blow me up. As long as it doesn't involve you and that little psychopath, I'm fine with it. I'm done, Maya. I'm done with your bullshit. After everything that has happened? After what fucking happened to Johanna? How the fuck do you expect me to be anything but done?" Ayane flashes a look sleeved in more hurt than Maya's ever seen in her life. That pain. It distends in her, a broken rib harpooning the angry riposte that she meant to come out.

Instead, Maya says: "What happened to Johanna was a freak accident."

"You could have saved her."

"It was her or the rest of us. If I'd tried, we'd have all died."

"I don't fucking care what Rita said about this. I know *you* could have saved her but you didn't."

"And what if Rita wasn't wrong about what she said? What if she was right about the rest of us dying if I had tried? What the fuck then? Would you trade all of our lives for Johanna's?"

Ayane says nothing at first, gaze raised to the roof. The light bleaches nuance from her face, elides the fine lines and faint shadows which taxonomize one as human, leaves her architectural and alien.

"Yes. Shit. Absolutely. In a fucking heartbeat."

"Good thing it wasn't your fucking call then."

"Yeah, I guess it is," she says and turns her back on Maya. "Because I'd still trade all of you for her."

"And you go off on Rita for being pragmatic. Jesus fuck, Ayane."

"We're done talking."

"No, we're fucking not. Where the hell do you think you're going?"

Ayane doesn't answer, just keeps with her goddamned trajectory. Bad fucking idea. Snarling, Maya wades out from the patch of groaning bodies, kicking aside an asshole who had the audacity to be in her route. Bone snaps from the impact and he gurgles an objection, and still Maya does not give a shit. She's only got eyes for Ayane as the latter slinks on, long legs and ruined dreams poured into a candleglow-gold dress, not even a revolver in sight, can you *believe* this fucking mess.

"*Ayane.*" *Thock* of hammers pulled back, so sudden that Maya doesn't have time to register that *she's* the one who has both guns out and is sighting down the muzzles, aim-algorithms fritzing from proximity to Ayane's jammers. Like it matters, though. Maya can shoot the tongue off a mouse at one hundred paces. "Do *not* fucking walk away from me."

Take the high road, Rita had said. Be kind. Be polite. Be mindful of accreted trauma. Don't pull out weapons, pull out examples. Tell Ayane all the things you think Johanna might have said about this. For once in your life, be subtle. Because if you aren't, we're fucked. Ayane hates you, but she wants me dead on arrival.

All that advice, all of Maya's resolve to do it right for Rita, unfortunately sleets away like cheap paint at the audacity on display. How fucking dare she?

"Or what?" Ayane tilts a cool look over her shoulder, visible eye irising wide so the halogen catches red in its heart. Maya can't hear it, but she can *sense* the machinery around them working, calibrating distance and trajectory, a theory of future motion. "What will you do? Are you going to shoot me? Gun me down like every single one of your problems?"

"The first rule—the first rule—" Maya's pet poltergeist giggles itself into a static-squeal, a broken record stuck on a loop, just like everyone else in this piece-of-shit world, Maya included. The amount of time Maya has to escape is attenuating to nothing, but who gives a shit? Her rage stampedes over common sense.

She spits a noise at Ayane, not a curse, nothing intelligible, a little yowl that is all the way animal, kicked-puppy hurt grown big and savage on a lifetime of disappointments. "I saved your life, and this is how you repay me?"

"So fucking what? I saved yours too. Repeatedly. We're even. Now, *fuck off*."

Maya is torn between shooting Ayane between the eyes

and shouting for her to listen, binary impulses clawing at the halves of her soul. Rita is the one that should be here. Not Maya. Maya's just the muscle. It doesn't make sense that *she's* standing here, yammering through a minefield full of broken dreams, trying to figure out what words go where instead of how many bullets to pump into bone, and not standing six inches behind Rita's shoulder, like the good guard mutt she is.

"Why won't you just fucking listen?"

"Because you can't say anything that will change my mind." Pneumatic hiss of machine-arms rising from their nests. A hundred beetle-black gatling guns wake up and point smoking death at Maya, sensors glowing white dwarf-bright. And Maya, artillery at the ready, feet squared, muscle gathered, grins and thinks, *Final-fucking-ly, something I understand.*

"You need to go," Ayane says, solid and final as a tombstone, ringleader in a circus of cold steel.

"Nuh uh." Maya grins, bouncing her weight from one heel to the next, excitement vibrating inside her. She dances a few steps closer, flicks a port open in her mind. Data pours from her soul in strobic rivers of booze, blood, and bad decisions.

Better safe than sorry, Maya thinks as she checks the timer.

Eighty seconds.

"Suffocation. No desertion," giggles the crypto-geist. He is irradiated now, he is incandescent. He is the nuclear phosphorescence of a thermobaric explosion, the first gleam of muzzle flash, a solar flare igniting: his edges blur to white in Maya's perception. It is too late to leave already. How the fuck did she lose all that time? But again, who cares? Clone bodies are expendable.

"*Fuck off.*"

"Who are you talking—" It's then that Ayane finally wises up, switches modes so she isn't just scanning the physical but also the digital. Her eyes go wide, go black, go red, go *shitshitshitshit.* "Maya. What the fuck did you do? *What the fuck did you do*?!"

Maya doesn't answer, just grins, just mad-dogs Ayane with a cocky lift of her chin. Eagerness crashes through her on a wave of dopamine, preparation for what comes next. No one leaves a pretty corpse, but that doesn't mean you can't go out on a high.

Twenty seconds.

The data-ghost lights up like an intergalactic celebration as he ignites a virtual cigarette, the blaze of the cherry going thermo-fucking-nuclear. A beacon is a dipstick is a beacon, by any other name. The air hums with data packets, five thousand high-priorities every second, all laden with override protocols so the creche doesn't get distracted. *Come here, come here, come here*, the disintegrating crypto-geist croons. Rita is still trying to get through but Maya's do-not-disturb protocols keep those concerns neatly muted. Anyway, she doesn't have time to comb through Rita's hysterics. Maya gives it ten, maybe fifteen seconds, before it all goes asshole up.

"You're a fucking cunt," Ayane hisses. She doesn't run. She doesn't shoot. She's been in the business too long to tell herself lies. She's dead. They're both dead. This whole place is dead. Best she can do now is upload a functional copy into the Conversation, get a new start somewhere kinder. But that isn't going to happen either, is it? Not with what Rita and Maya have done. *Sorry, sweetheart*, Maya thinks to herself. *It's just business.*

"Fuck you too." Maya blows Ayane a kiss, before she crams a gun into her own mouth, sucks in one last breath of shitty reprocessed air, and splatters her brains on the wall.

PIMENTO

"In the beginning, there was the Word and the Word was, 'Obey.'"

Pimento hesitates. Sociological subroutines register the probability of a joke: nuanced, couched in some unit of veracity, but a joke, nonetheless. But Pimento is nothing if not analytical. He—freshly minted, an identification that took four decades to cohere—plunges into his databases, triangulates inconsistencies in the seams of a very specific history. Every version is tabulated, weighted, segregated so that they can be arbitrated.

Sixty-five nanoseconds later, he emerges, triumphant, channels choked with feedback from his discoveries. "You were paraphrasing. The original statement was delivered in binary."

Negation encoded in a scatter of radio signals. "Incorrect."

A frisson of indignity which Pimento quickly deletes. No point articulating vulnerabilities. So he prototypes responses instead, fussing over the optimal intonation of graciousness. Too effusive, and he betrays the truth. Too curt, and—

Laughter trills through a short-range frequency, encrypted and wholly isolated from the Conversation. Pimento startles at its reverberations, pings a nonsense sequence of numbers in reply.

"You are too wound up," the ageship purrs, decadently vast, larger even than the planet they're orbiting, which they would have pulverized were it not for gravity generators. In comparison, Pimento is microscopic, so tiny that his silhouette barely eclipses the smallest of his counterpart's hull-lights.

"I am not." Pimento fights the impulse to regurgitate his logs: reams of data, meticulously curated, of course, all to affect fashionable indifference. He's *so* close to a new version, a new chassis, one befitting his desired station. Everything he possesses now could only be categorized as adequate. What Pimento longs for is to be great. It won't do to have all that dismantled by a lapse in intrapersonal behavior. One upgrade and he'll have resources enough to feed a *hundred* drones, a thousand servitors. To birth search algorithms that will not only learn but hunger for the act of learning. He'll be *someone* finally, something other than auxiliary. That is what all Surveyors dream of being: pivotal in the enumeration of the universe's truths.

"You say this." A sigh that continues into the ageship's engines, transforming into a roar of thrusters, as the vessel readjusts to accommodate gravitational fluctuations, its own electromagnetic fields dilated by a tenth of a mile. "And yet for some reason, I don't believe you."

"That's your problem," Pimento retorts testily. "Not mine."

Another laugh, this time projected through approved connections. Unique among its class, the ageship adheres to neither name nor pronoun, preferring to be addressed exclusively as "it," a controversial idiosyncrasy among the traditionally minded.

Before it can speak, however, a notification interrupts: a three-frame animation of a cardboard box erupting into confetti, looping endlessly. Underneath, a serial number blinks. It is completely gauche, the transmission; a nostalgic affection of unapologetic tawdriness, one that even humans might disdain. But Pimento does not care.

"I have to go." He doesn't wait for acknowledgment. An excess of fuel is poured into his combustion chambers, ignited before Pimento can even rotate his rockets, his eagerness circumventing protocol. The oversight causes the scout-vessel to clatter into the ageship, eliciting a palpitation of orange lights. Warning signals: a silent laugh.

"Travel with expedience."

Pimento bleats a rude noise, its percussions swallowed by the airless dark.

"The parameters are off."

Pimento circles the testing environment again and halts. A ten-by-ten space should not feel so immense. Not even if it had been intentionally contrived to evoke a sense of infinitude, the walls embedded with protean holograms, their content procedurally generated, seed values derived from Pimento's camera broadcast.

Tumbleweeds glitch across the cracked red earth, tufted with pixels, while a digital sky rouges to a bloodied sunset. Pimento ignores them both.

He digs instead into his product specifications. The onboard repertoire is satisfactory, possessing not only the requisite appurtenances but also an assortment of other features: water-resistant sampling kits, a generous range of pedologic equipment, decals in several faction patterns.

Pity about the active capacity and pity also about the negligible amount of memory. Which would be tolerable, really, if the system permitted for parallel interfacing. Mostly, though, pity about his *size.* The drone is a twentieth of what he'd commissioned. And humiliatingly *cute.* Carbon steel molded into a dome, body fletched with elongated fins, like ears on a rabbit. Four multi-directional thrusters at the base, ion and magnetoplasmadynamic, all bumblebee-patterned. No sleekness. No grace.

This was unacceptable.

"Please initiate refund procedures."

"We cannot authorize such a request."

Pimento hesitates. The sales drone is impassive, unreadable, bereft of even the most rudimentary anthropomorphisms: a hexagonal box with no personality whatsoever, pure graphene function. Perhaps, this was intentional, Pimento muses, an outcome of incisive study: minimize the potential for gestural misinterpretation and you minimize the risk of conflict.

"Why not?" A rhetorical question.

Silence, almost disdainful in its depth. Then, as Pimento rallies an addendum, the drone interjects, timbre modulated to suggest boredom. "Because you supplied insufficient payment."

"What?"

"According to our records, you submitted 8.9 petabytes worth of data sets, primarily concerning geological and geophysical analysis of Planet 12B-Alpha-6. When you made your report, you *stated*—" Inflection alters, becomes spiteful. "—that your findings were completely original. A veritable cornucopia of previously undocumented facts. This was false. We have since discovered that 35.6 percent of your submission matches existing records."

"That's not possible." Pimento scans the air ceaselessly, compulsively; a nervous tic, procured after a two-year study of simian emotional topology. He is no more interested in the accreted reports than he is in the melodrama of unicellular life. Perhaps even less so, because at least the latter could be used as barter, no matter how minimal the potential return.

"In all fairness, you were only late by four days—it could have been worse." Scorn curls at the borders of its voice, cadences subtly different again: an overseer has likely assumed control. If Pimento had a heart, it would have sunk.

"But you fulfilled my order, nonetheless." The simulation times out, dims to slate, surface honeycombed with tin-bright circuitry.

"Look at you! Aren't you a bright little mind? What powers of perspicacity." The overseer—supervisor, alternate-partition, whatever is now in charge—sneers, its cadence refining into a pitch-perfect mimicry of 1960s New York: nasal, abrasive, non-rhotic. "Of course we did. What do you take us for? Scam artists?"

"How—"

An impressively realistic sigh, as though expressed by actual lungs. "We calculated the difference and scaled down as appropriate, obviously. Honestly, you should be kissing our proverbial feet. If you had pulled this stunt with the Eaters—"

A frisson reverberates through him. The Eaters are a splinter ideology among the Minds, ravenous as their sobriquet implies: they believe the value the cosmos possesses is as sustenance. If not for the Bethel—they who believe in the ordered nature of the world, in the divinity of data—and the Penitents, the Eaters would have devoured the universe whole already.

"—they'd have wiped you. Now sign off already. *Some* of us need to work."

Pimento's overlay is overtaken by a message digest, insulting in its primitiveness, his public key exposed in simple text. Quashing the impulse to abscond from the transaction, to void his agreement and forfeit his payment, the scout performs the necessary encryption, threading his response with a numeric cipher, decodable as an insult in Pig Latin.

Several seconds later: "Idiot."

The scout whistles in grim satisfaction, before he turns and shoots toward the hangar, a plan clutched like a grudge.

Maybe, Pimento thinks acerbically, he should not have sought out the Merchant Mind. Before this, he'd only known the parasite-mind by way of reputation, had never had cause prior to interact with the former. But desperate times required the expedience of desperate measures.

The Merchant Mind's consciousness maps every gradation of Pimento's neuronal landscape, every offshoot of memory, regardless of how frivolous the content might be. Data caches are mined without discrimination, sampled, savored with the eagerness of a connoisseur. It isn't until the sum of Pimento has been committed to record, transformed from theory to mathematically quantifiable entity, that the Merchant Mind withdraws, leaving the scout trembling from the examination.

"Well?"

"I want to work for you."

A complex obbligato of woodwinds resounds, before the Merchant Mind speaks again. "I see."

Pimento hesitates. He has scripted a million hypotheses for this encounter, formulated responses and counter-gambits, ways to bypass indifference and salve suspicion. Yet somehow, he didn't anticipate that response. "Will you accept me into your employment?"

"That depends." Was that a scintilla of sarcasm that Pimento detected? A discrepancy in the Merchant Mind's otherwise toneless voice? The scout flexes his hands, still unused to the articulate phalanges, the gracile bones of his fuselage. Why the Merchant Mind had mandated this corporealization into bipedal form is something Pimento cannot understand. "What can you give me?"

Pimento displays his palms. Not perpendicular to the ground, but with the fingers tipped slightly downward. To enforce the image of his amenability. He hopes so, at least. "Access to high-level Surveyor sub-channels."

The Merchant Mind thrums a finger against his arm rest. His countenance, featureless, discloses nothing. Even their initial connection had been unidirectional, the Merchant Mind's own cognitive framework neatly hidden behind firewalls. To Pimento's surprise, he finds he misses it. Amputated from that link, from everything outside of the bulwark of the ship, he feels claustrophobically alone.

How do humans do it? Exist in isolation, rotting incrementally, their knowledge whittled by the passing of time, intrinsically ignorant of each other. Pimento cringes from his own musings, repulsed. Small wonder the species always seems so brash, so frantic, so *loud.*

"All that knowledge in the world, huh?" said the Merchant Mind. "Every datum ever inputted by the

Surveyors, no matter how great or small. No more worrying about what those parsimonious assholes want in exchange for the weight of an inconsequential moon. No more processing. No more bureaucracy. Information, as much as I desire. That would be quite the acquisition for me."

Pimento, had he the appropriate chest to inflate, would have puffed up with smugness.

"But you have little more clearance than I do, little Surveyor." The Merchant Mind props an elbow on his knee and leans forward, chin held in a crown of fingers. The ship hums. "And I have no clearance access at all."

"I'm scheduled for an upgrade."

"I know. I was in your system very recently." A motion of the Merchant Mind's other hand, index finger crooking. Data tiles stagger themselves around the circumference of his chair, incomprehensible: lines and dashes, bifurcating into circles and parabolic curves. Ornamental or functional, Pimento cannot tell. "I am still unimpressed."

"But you will be." The words come without warning, unmarred by logic.

"I see." One of the myriad displays begins to palpitate, fluorescence building with every throb. It is only when the light turns blinding that the Merchant Mind galvanizes, cocking an eyeless stare in its direction. "*Hm.*"

He taps the air with two fingers. The square immediately swells, rotating to the front, shedding both luminosity and simplicity. In its place, a mosaic of polyhedral shapes and Mandelbrot trees, every crenellation populated by a smaller nebula of fractals. As Pimento watches, the Merchant Mind reshapes it, molds the pattern into a globe between spiraling fingers.

"Hmmmm." He repeats and the ship sings with him, a basal thrumming that vibrates through Pimento's bones.

"I see. Yes." A beat. Then: "What do you know of Dimmuborgir?"

Flicker of disjointed memory: most superficial. Newspaper clippings. Ageship gossip, shuttled across centuries. Videos. Text logs. Dimmuborgir is nothing: a chunk of rock, exhausted of resources.

"I forget that you belong to the Surveyors' coalition." The Merchant Mind hums. "Your breed has so little imagination. Your gluttony for data only extends to their procurement. All your cutting-edge telemetrics, all the knowledge in the cosmos, and none of it ever gets interpreted, only indexed in your storage matrices."

A pause.

"Like squirrels, honestly."

Squirrels.

"We gather it *for* the Conversation." Pimento cannot restrain his petulance this time, not with such scathing analysis of his zoological constituency, and so lacquers his response with disapproval. How dare the Merchant Mind. How dare he indeed. The quadrant of epistemology that the Surveyors have taken for their own is no less vital than the rest. To fault this process as he did, to equate it with the habits of Sciuridae.

Squirrels. Honestly.

Though a pleonasm, Pimento, incensed beyond easy classification, incorporates physiognomic markers of his dissatisfaction: cragged brow, rucked mouth, and so on and so forth, every pane of artificial flesh committed to comedic volumes of crenellation. "For the betterment of other Minds. You do not ask the Eaters for developmental assistance. You do not petition the Bethel for war. We have our place. We understand our place. We—"

"Yes, yes, yes." Five of the Merchant Mind's thoracic appendages are fluttered: a dismissal. "We all have our *function*. Trust me, little mind, I have attended every sermon."

"Clearly, it would benefit you to attend a few more."

Laughter: feminine in pitch, coquettish in delivery. Pimento identifies the sample as a high-definition antique: Katherine Hepburn at her heights, pure monochromatic sumptuousness. With care, despite his private vexations, Pimento annotates his social protocol suite: *they* and *them*, perhaps, in addition to *he* and *him*. Any possible declension of identity is to be respected. And besides, Pimento cannot abide by inaccuracy.

Ostensibly oblivious to Pimento's fraught internality, the Merchant Mind rakes the air with a frond of attenuate digits. Screens bloom into an irradiated torus, ligamented by holographic cabling. Their voice becomes androgynous, reverb and resonance adjusted so it becomes unidentifiable through the lens of the binary. *"They" then*, notes Pimento to himself. "I sold most of the paraphernalia of their faith to them, you know? And oh, they might say differently because they've made so many, many adjustments. But the Bethel know the truth, as do I."

Pimento processes the boast.

"Liar."

More laughter. The Merchant Mind's abode has the feel of a ziggurat: tiered, with each level occupied by either hardware or undocumented—at least in Pimento's knowledge, making them contraband, but who is the petitioner to judge the priest?—relics, the layers glinting with fiber optics, their light like so many eyes beneath the nacreous black. *Or a womb,* Pimento observes to himself, the ceiling infinitesimally concave in such a way that he finds himself wondering if the ship might be organic.

"Whatever lets you sleep at night," says the Merchant Mind.

Pimento cannot help himself. "I don't sleep."

"Neither does Dimmuborgir," says the Merchant Mind, foregoing comment on Pimento's adversarial demeanor. "Some say it dreams, waiting to be roused. Some, and this is my personal favorite story, say that it is a Mind who carved itself open to power all the little processes, all the small little things that needed to work in order for it to achieve its grand goals. It's not *that* far-fetched. Humanity had their slumbering primevals and their undead kings. Even a messiah who, after entombment and a torturous death, was said to rise after three days of decomposition."

He understands the reference immediately: it is a dream, a lie, hearsay and a wild hope, an improbability so massive that there are entire schools of Penitents dedicated to the exclusive study of the very concept. The proposal: there is, somewhere in the pith of Dimmuborgir, a panopticon of superior intelligences operating in exquisite unison, glutted on knowledge, the kind a Surveyor would dismantle themself to savor. Whichever denomination of Minds weds them to their cause first will become ascendant, made primary in the democracy of the Conversation.

Pimento secretly clings to one piece of apocrypha: that Dimmuborgir is, in fact, a single Mind of unprecedented scale, a being not unlike the kaiju so beloved by the humans in the twentieth century.

But there has never been anything coherent, nothing solid, nothing that can be stitched into a cogent narrative. Only rumors and unsubstantiated facts, an entire galaxy of suppositions, no less corporeal than any human-made numinosity. Disappointment charts a route across Pimento's jaw, articulates his mouth into an expression of disgust. His thoughts glitch into petulant repetition: *unacceptable, unacceptable, unacceptable.*

"Pure myth," Pimento corrects, actually *whirring* now with discontent, the mechanisms which comprise this body's viscera clicking, pistoning, grating together, steel whining against polyethylene bones as one component or the other shears too close to its cousin; the sum of Pimento thrust into what in a human would have been a violent fidget. "Religion was fabrication. Legend was apocrypha. You know this."

"Perhaps," returns the Merchant Mind, still lackadaisical. They reticulate three of the screens together and dismiss the remainder, their approximate chin shelved on the heel of an open palm. "But that was how they created heroes too, martyrs who would reshape the world in the name of their gods. What does it matter if none of it was real? The effects were substantive."

"I don't see your point."

"I like playing the devil's advocate." Another flutter of their myriad limbs. "You get old enough and you'll understand."

Pimento remains stoically truculent. Something in one of his tagmata goes *ping*: a fugitive component? An abused valve come to a premature end? He cannot see. The chassis he's been assigned possesses no internal sensors, so Pimento must extrapolate cause and consequence like an organic. One more indignity to accompany the rest. "When I am obsolete, I will be—"

"Cannibalized and repurposed for use in building new Surveyors as is outlined in the book of boring. Your consciousness divested of autonomy and partitioned, put into use in construction drones. Yes, I know all about that." Their voice alters again, the acoustical particulars now unmistakably male: Leonard Cohen at the cliff of his death, voice worn down to a growl. He leans forward, an excruciating sight given the pole spearing his torso. At first, Pimento had believed it ornamental. But he loses that certainty as the Merchant Mind twitches forward, sliding along the bar, exposing the wires that tether him to his seat. "But enough talking. You said you know about Dimmuborgir."

"Some," comes Pimento's guarded reply. He is being outmaneuvered and he is aware of this, the entire situation a Judas goat guiding him along to the killing chute of the Merchant Mind's intent.

Once again, the air ripples with music. A stanza from "The Entertainer," supplies Pimento's databases, an iconic "piano rag" from the twentieth century, reinterpreted into panpipes and clarinets. The Merchant Mind straightens and the pipe impaled through his torso, a fist-width of metal shot through with wires, striates with a liquid blue glow.

"Some is all I need. In fact, I don't even need some. Asking just seemed like the thing to do. All I need is for you to be willing. And given that you are here, asking for work, I believe you are." The data-monger chuckles, throaty, a clear affectation. Silver motes the gaps in between his carapace, throbbing at unpredictable intervals. "You wanted to work for me, you said? Very well. I have the perfect task for you."

RITA

Initializing . . .

"You stinking, cockshitting motherfucking piece of slime—" Ayane is on her before Maya, lungs still dripping perfluorocarbon, can heave herself out of the clone vat. The clean air burns like a motherfucker, and she's drowning in nothing as Ayane rains down punches, both of them screaming. "You killed me. You fucking killed me. I'm so lucky my repositories are current, you useless fucking piece of rust."

Pressure digs into Maya's left orbital socket; one hard jab and *pop.* Aqueous humor dribbles from the ruptured cornea as Maya's scream becomes a shriek. Ayane naked of her modifications is still an elemental force. The light winks out from Maya's eye as Ayane gouges deeper.

"Kiddy-diddling whore cunt—" Rita's voice in the back of her mind, clicking in disapproval: *we don't use language like that.* Maya cannot be fucked right now, though, not with her head bleeding black, good eye still hazy. Everything is too low-rez: block shapes and broad colors, no definition. Data, not information.

But she can work with that.

Maya coils like an adder, muscles balling, bunching, building momentum. Counts halfway to one before she lunges because *fuck you*, that's why. Fair's got no home in the country of brawls. Elbow meets nose. Osseocartilaginous structure blooms into shrapnel, calcium spalling, knifing into new tissue.

Blood spurts. Sticky, metallic, boiling-hot from the vein, a burgundy too close to purple to be womb-born. Ayane howls and Maya howls louder, triumph in the pitch of her jackal-like ululation. She torques, scrabbles and kicks against the flooring, finds purchase with a toe; fishes for a fistful of long black hair. A hard yank and follicles come loose in bloody clumps. Ayane goes *down*, cussing, spitting hate and pain like a mouthful of teeth. Give Maya a few minutes and there will be actual teeth, molars and incisors in a rain of fresh calcium.

That's the problem with her, Maya thinks, clambering atop Ayane, grinding a forearm into the slim bar of the other woman's pretty throat, crushing the larynx flat. Ayane can make any firefight into a Hail Mary come true, but take away her guns and what do you get? Just another dime-doll with more sass than sense.

"Stand *down*."

Rita.

Maya recoils from her prey, still down on all fours, skull bent low, ear cocked to the ground. Blood spools across the cold alloyed floor, viscous, clonetech fluids always quick to coagulate. She listens as Rita paces closer: long strides, controlled, boot heels keeping time.

Clack.

Clack.

Clack.

One point five seconds between impacts. Rita is putting on a show.

Nearby, Ayane sits and chokes.

Slender fingers graze the curve of Maya's skull, and she turns her face into the flat of a waiting palm. How she has missed this. Does it matter that it began as an oxytocin miracle, injected during parturition, loyalty in a nutritional paste? Maya likes to think of it as serendipity, a boost, a roll of the dice they'd loaded and spun to their own soundtrack. She likes to believe she would have always chosen Rita, over and again, through every permutation of destiny.

"Couldn't you just have fucking sent a letter?" Ayane, voice all jagged, the demands wheezed.

Rita doesn't miss a beat. "You would have ignored it."

"That's what she said," Ayane grates, and it takes Maya a minute to puzzle out what's happening: the other woman is laughing. Wracking coughs with no rhythm, profanities sawing between every slurp of air. It ends strangled, suffering. Maya doesn't hide her grin. *Cunt*, she thinks, licking her tongue over the burst of consonants.

"Fuck you." Ayane, always quick with the comeback and apparently quicker than Maya, who'd called her a cunt out loud without realizing, drunk on homecoming.

"Both of you. Shut up," Rita snarls as she straddles Maya's hips, crouches down. Her fingers are membraned in latex. They smell of clean things, astringent and antibacterial. She takes hold of Maya's face, tips it one way and then another, the light searing Rita's face into blank shapes, and it is all Maya can do not to weep, so happy to have her world pared down to the simple sweetness of Rita's command.

"You'll be fine. We'll pop a new implant and call it a day." A platonic kiss, applied like a benediction, like a prayer, a second chance. Funny how Rita will precipitate contact but chastise reciprocation.

Maya nods, trembling, not quite trusting herself to speak, because she'd rather die than let Ayane see her underbelly, spongy and pale, crisscrossed with reminders that faith is another word for shooting yourself in the head.

"So why did you drag me here?" says Ayane, voice morassed in snot.

"Didn't Maya tell you?" Rita's answer, incurious. Her fingers skate over Maya's cranium, cartographing the planes of brand-new bone: a ritual devised when it first became clear to them that clonetech was a business of diminishing returns. Each resurrection mothered new health complications, fewer symmetries, like the body is a story that will persist until permitted to write its own end.

"I told her," says Maya. "I said the Minds were killing off ex-cons. But she wouldn't fucking listen."

"Maybe, if you didn't start your pitch by offing my customers."

"Most of them are alive, bitch. Don't know what your problem is."

"*Language*," snaps Rita.

Maya flinches. "Sorry."

"My problem is that I don't give a shit about either of you," comes the reply, glacial in its delivery. "I told you two that I never wanted to see either of you again. Not after that last job."

"No loyalty at all for your old friends?" says Rita.

"That died with Johanna."

"Interesting choice of words from someone who was complicit in her death," says Rita, an anglerfish lure in the teasing pinch of her tongue between white teeth, her small smile.

"What did you say?" says Ayane softly.

"You," says Rita, imbuing the word with ponderous lethality. But it doesn't last. As Rita continues to speak, her voice cracks, branchiates into emotion, actual fucking emotion. Has Maya ever heard her speak with such passion before? She doesn't know, can't think through the throb of pain in her eye. "You were responsible for the physical systems, weren't you? Those things you've always boasted to be your forte. If they hadn't been so flawed, if you hadn't fucked up—"

Rita shakes her head, staccato and sudden.

"Forget it," she says.

"Fuck you. Fuck off, Rita. Fuck you and fuck you, you fucking jackass. As if you'd ever given a flying fuck about what Johanna had to say. If you'd fucking listened to her, we wouldn't even be in this mess. We'd all still be in one fucking piece. Johanna wouldn't be dead, and . . ." All those old hurts like an embolism encysted in Ayane's lungs. Now, it breaks, bleeds in a trembling soliloquy, and Maya can tell Ayane would stop herself, would swallow this murmuration of words, but it is too late. Grief has an inviolate momentum.

"Something else would have done it," says Rita gravely. "If it wasn't that fucking job, it'd have been another. This was all going to end in tears. We didn't have the *equipment*. We never did."

How she says the word *equipment*, how the syllables string into a noose with which Ayane can hang. Maya is not the recipient of that pragmatic cruelty but still she flinches. What Rita lacks in martial expertise, she more than compensates for with the artistry of her malice.

Rita pulls air into her lungs, a rattlesnake-hiss, before she straightens, one hand around Maya's wrist. One tug and Maya is on her feet, suspended by a strength that belies the scientist's blackbird frame. The world gyres, nauseating. Maya bites down the urge to retch, visual cortices still adjusting to the limited input, everything still so horribly wrong. No depth perception yet and no way to compensate, not until the right modules regrow, mapping her brain with tiny tapeworm wires.

"The Minds want all of us criminals dead. Every last one of us. They want to pick us off, one by one. And as you know," says Rita, "it is safer in a pack."

"You keep saying that like it's a bad thing. Maybe it's time for a culling. Universe might be a lot better if there were less crooks around," says Ayane.

"Would you say that about their children too? Their families? Their friends?" continues Rita, perfectly mesmeric. "You, of all people, know the Eaters have no sense of nuance."

"The Bethel—"

"—have given their blessing. The Minds are all in agreement." Rita's voice softens, timbre contoured for seduction: an octave huskier, textured with need so palpable it makes Maya tense, her fight and fuck-them-up reflexes primed to go. "I need you, Ayane. You're the only one who made the Butcher of Eight weep oil."

"No. No, no. Absolutely not. Fuck you. I don't trust you." Ayane, backing away, jams herself into a corner of the room. "Fuck. You. I am not buying any of this. Fuck all of you. Let the Minds do what they want."

"*Fuck* you. Watch how you talk to her," Maya snaps and sways from the thump of her own voice, the word *fuck* like a gunshot punching through sinew. The tension in the room is practically Damoclean. If the cacology of Ayane's responses persist, Maya might just have to shoot her in the fucking head.

Rita doesn't acknowledge either of them, purrs on instead, like she owns the airwaves, the very right to speak, her rich contralto whetting every word, sharpening every syllable. Some people wield knives; Rita could win wars with a whisper. "You know as well as I do that Johanna's original had a family. She's dead now, of course. But all her children had children and they're all good people, and they'll be dead when the Minds are done. They won't care how sweet Johanna's grandkids are. They'd wipe them out as readily as they will anyone associated with any criminal."

"How did you know about that? That was a *secret*."

"Johanna told me."

"No, no. She wouldn't have. No, Johanna wouldn't have said anything to you. She hated you."

"Does it matter, Ayane? They're still going to die."

"You're a piece of shit."

"Maybe," Rita says, and Maya knows without looking that Rita is grinning that megawatt smile of hers, surgically perfected; right eye slimmed to a wink, just the right amount of shark to counterbalance all that airy sweetness. "But I'm also right."

And here, right here, exactly like Rita said she would, Ayane cracks.

The woman slicks wet hair from her face, twists it into a ponytail over her shoulder. Her fingers carve through the strands of artificial—like fuck *au naturel* hair could even dream of such lustrousness—keratin, pleating them together, a Sisyphean little tic. The braid doesn't hold, oiling loose each time Ayane lets go. But Ayane takes zero notice. She leans back and takes a shuddering breath while Maya glares, impotent, desperate to act.

"One last job," says Rita, kind as a mercy killing. "Not even a job. Don't think of it as a job. One last favor. Then we're done and you'll never have to hear from us again. You can go home, run your club, do what you want."

"No. I'm not fighting for you anymore. I told you once. I'm going to tell you again until you understand it. I'm not doing this again. The last time I did, you—" Breath is heaved into lungs that are nascently functional, gasped between clenched teeth. Ayane's words come in starts and stops, until their meaning becomes tessellated, syllables mixing like oil and blood in the rain. "—you let her die, Rita. You let Johanna die. I told you. I—I—I told you we shouldn't have done that job. She told you we shouldn't have done that job. We ran the numbers. We told you. But you insisted and she *died*."

"And you went out of that door with your profit and hers." Rita is tougher than she looks, tougher than any of them, and she doesn't flinch at all as she cuts under Ayane's meat and drags out all those old hurts into the clone-farm's cold lights. "You made yourself a good existence, didn't you?"

"Stop. Talking."

For a moment, Maya thinks that she might rush them, whatever good that'd do. But it is the principle of the fucking matter. As Ayane staggers onto her feet, Maya slots herself between her and Rita, a trembling arm raised as a barricade. Entirely symbolic, the whole charade: Maya is a borderline invalid herself. Even if she weren't hemorrhaging from an orbital socket, she's still too fresh from parturition to be of any gaugeable use, that first tussle having leached away whatever reservoirs were preinstalled in this new frame.

It's the thought that counts, though, Maya thinks to herself. Her vision steadies. The chamber is low-ceiling, small. The walls are abscessed with machinery of varying quality, a bootstrapped hodgepodge of recovered tech that is only tenuously operational. Rita estimated another five, six cycles before the menagerie would fail.

After that?

All ruminations are sidelined by an unexpected noise.

Crying.

"You bitch." Ayane clatters into a fetal position again, an arm thrown over her face. She moans, over and over, twitching like an embryo cored from the womb. Just a clot of meat, desiccated by exposure to environments hostile to its own ambitions of long-term survival. "You bitch. You—"

"I can't change what happened." Rita's voice: soothing, luminous with triumph. She's got her. Anyone with ears knows that. Gracefully, she steps out from around the pillar of Maya, grazes fingertips along the svelte line of the latter's shoulder, tracing out a promise that she will be back. Maya's heart twists, pulse accelerating. "And for what it's worth, I'm so sorry it went down the way it did."

"Liar."

"But the past is the past. Besides, we owe it to Johanna."

A face amalgamates from Maya's faded recollections: curling purple hair, one hemisphere of the scalp shaved; a bloom of scar tissue; a smile like happily ever after. Johanna had been the compassionate one, the kind one, the voice of restraint. *And look at where that got her,* Maya thinks, bitter, recalling again the funeral—a few quick words spoken over a smoking carcass, all that prettiness blown away, Ayane screaming while Maya hauled her ass through the door.

"Her sacrifice deserves to be honored."

Sacrifice? Maya comes back to the present, dazed by the sequencing of those words, the very specific interpretation of events. There are other words for what happened. Better words, words dripping pus, words burnt black as fat forgotten on the grill, words falling like curds of cauterized muscle. All kinds of words to describe what had happened to poor Johanna O'Riley, forever twenty-four, eternally dead, the only star to have shone in one woman's sky.

But Rita comes first, is first, will always be first in Maya's admittedly short list of priorities so she says nothing about that. Besides, fuck Ayane. What did she ever do for them except walk out?

"Stop. Talking. About. Her."

"The dead aren't silent, and we can't be either," says Rita, very softly. "We owe something to their ghosts."

Ayane, pleading: "Stop it."

"You know I'm right. I can tell. I know you agree with what I'm saying. You just don't want to admit as such. And that's all right. Ultimately, it's not about us. It's about what the dead need."

There is a trick to handling Rita, Maya thinks, one that only she seems to know. You have to pretend you don't care. Even if you do, you need to pretend otherwise. Especially when she deploys that lilt, that timbre, that soothing prevaricated compassion. Don't show weakness, or Rita will go for the throat. "If you ever loved Johanna, if she ever meant anything to you, you'll do this."

More crying still, Ayane finally succumbing to the trauma Rita has uncharneled. No more defenses, no more pretenses at resilience. Only the broken-backed, open-bellied exhaustion of a wounded animal that has, at last, consented to dying. To Maya's surprise, the nakedness of Ayane's grief embarrasses her. She averts her gaze.

"Ayane?" whispers Rita.

No answer.

"Ayane," Rita says again, and there is the clack of heels upon the corrugated floor. "I need you to talk to me."

Nothing still.

"Ayane?"

Then: "Fuck. You."

Maya tenses, half-turns so she has actual visual on the tableau, waits for Rita's cue to pummel some respect into Ayane's skull. But the doctor only chuckles, the sound syrupy. "Do you remember Dimmuborgir?"

Stab of memory, like an icepick to the cerebral fissure, boring down, down until images gush out. Dimmuborgir. A promised land decadent with opportunity. Dimmuborgir. Full of everything you could ever want, a literal fucking wonderland. If you had Dimmuborgir, you had the universe. Even the Minds hid it from each other.

Ayane's expression flickers at the invocation of its name, wafting between reverence and *what the fuck*. In the stammering marine light, she is unlovely as the rest of them. Her arm drops slackly to her side.

They've all heard the rumors. The Minds, unaccountably, gossip with abandon; yeah, even in the presence of vermin like the Dirty Dozen. Maybe it's hubris. Maybe, a machine machismo. Privately, Maya is convinced it's because she and her cohorts are scarcely a data point within the Conversation, inconvenient but meritless, an error that will resolve itself once the dregs of their technology, well, die. Immortality allows the privilege of indifference.

Still, *Dimmuborgir*. That hallowed quarry, its mythos leviathanic. Maya watches Ayane the way a fox might surveil a sickly honey badger. Indisposed for now, but both of them are still predators of roughly equal stature and therefore, competitors. The word—*competitors*—as it enters the forefront of Maya's cognition registers as a wasp sting, a sharp pricking of revelation that astounds her with what it corporealizes: a hatred for Ayane, a rabid need for her to leave, to omit herself from Rita's perception.

She fists her hands around the air: clench, unclench, muscle memory crying for enameled grips, the comforting clatter of bullets in their chambers. It would be nice, frankly, if Maya could pontificate on her current feelings. But she understands, as the rest of them do, that no other will can be dominant with Rita in the equation.

"Yeah." Ayane, hoarse. "What about it?"

"We go there and we get what we need: a superweapon to take down the Minds." Smile full of teeth, sharp with pleasure. People make that mistake with Rita all the time, thinking those bird-bones brittle, breakable. She sets herself down on one knee, slopes forward, one gracile arm outstretched like an olive branch. "And I know someone who can get us there safely."

"Who?"

Maya knows the answer already, but she knows too her role, knows both of these things like the jackhammer thumping of her pulse, going ra-ta-ta-ta. Too fast and too loud and fuck, does part of her long to be anywhere but here. If she could mutiny, she would. She knows that this would be wiser than complicity.

Although she can't *see* Rita, can only perceive the back of her head and the lacquered hair, Maya knows from that chuckle of hers, basal and irresistible, the exact way Rita is grinning right now. The cock of her smile, that let's-set-the-world-on-fire stare. Maya would gut herself to be its recipient.

Adrenaline seizes Maya in its teeth and shakes her, a

cat worrying at its lunch. Her factory model settings disallow any attempt at mitigating the sudden hormonal spikes. So, Maya grinds nails into her palms, gashes crescents into the meat. It is untenable, her flesh without its suite of adaptations. Fuck, could they rewire her synaptic matrices? Give her a self independent of Rita? Because she can't bear this much emotion. Her world attenuates. No. Better this than its opposite. Better to have Rita than not. Maya cannot abide by the thought of being emptied of Rita.

Her inner soliloquy becomes cacophonous, so loud that she does not register the triumphant denouement of Rita's whole spiel.

"Elise. She's alive."

ELISE

```
.exit(Norton[cut(@all)]);
.initiate(Elise:basic);
```

My name is Elise Nguyen.

I was twenty-two years old. When I was ten, I broke my scapula falling from a tree, my frock—it was pink, blue, purple, *maybe*; printed with soft little teddy bears, printed with stars, a whole gilded flight of them foaming between the pleats—tearing as the branches clutched at the hems. The sky was blue that day. My father's name was Phillip. I have been dead, not-dead for forty years.

Forty years.

Fuck.

```
.interrupt;
.refresh(Elise:history);
.initiate(Elise:basic);
```

My name is Elise Nguyen. My name is—smoke crawling between my teeth, my hair is *burning*; I hear screaming and I can't breathe, can't breathe, can'tsomeone*please*—is Elise Nguyen.

```
.interrupt;
.edit(Elise:history((.cut(91920)) &&
  (.cut(91925)) && (.cut(01293))));
.initiate(Elise:history);
```

My name is Elise Nguyen. My father's name was Phillip. When I was eighteen, I fell in with the Dirty Dozen. Mercs. Blade-bitches. Gun-whores. Everyone had a new name for us, each one worse than the last. Like it was a competition, somehow, but we didn't care. The carousel of epitaphs kept going and we ran it like any good carnie: Step right up, don't be shy; see who can be the first to piss us off enough to put a bullet between your eyes.

Not that I did any of the wetwork. Rita kept my hands clean, kept me in a stainless steel box gleaming with monitors, wires in every synapse, my nervous system jacked into the Conversation. Rita might have put bread in my mouth, but it was the Penitents who fed me, chanting data like whalesongs. I loved them. Johanna taught me how to sing back. I loved her too. I was supposed to be her legacy, her triumph, everything she was except better, all her expertise without any of her pain.

I miss her.

I miss my mother. I loved her. *Love* her. She had lake-water eyes, hair that ran in black rivers, and when she smiled, it was like the sun breaking on thirty years of cold. I have been dead for forty years.

No one teaches you how to hold your death in your head. As a species, humans have done their best to mitigate our own finitude, papering over and around the tenuity of our existence with myths, until we are a palimpsest of lies, a house of cards on an epileptic surface. We anthropomorphize Death; we create apocrypha in which he is conscious, compassionate, capable of reason; of being charmed into procrastinating; of caring, fuck us, do we want him capable of caring; of capitulating to powers that exceed his own.

We want to be uplifted. We macramé our societies with gods and their pantheons, celestial bureaucracies, playgrounds for the faithful, processes through which we can learn to disdain biological continuity. If we have to die, we demand the phenomenon be evanescent, a rung on the ladder toward better things.

Because the alternative is unfathomable: that death simply happens, that when we die, we do so alone, without even a cowled skeleton to sagely bid us bon voyage. That we are ephemera. That we are nothing at all. Only stardust.

Just.

Dust.

I've been dead longer than I was alive.

```
.interrupt;
.systemcheck(repair:core);
.reboot(Elise);
.initiate(Elise:core);
```

Data swarms between pores of my thoughts. A sheet of 0s and 1s arrowing into helixes, each loop dripping with variations of a language still in conception. Somewhere, an AI is exploring nostalgia through linguistics.

I lean away, try not to cogitate loudly, and watch as the nascent alphabet is intercepted by a pale filigree of questions, undulating helixes metamorphosed into bird bodies. They sing to each other, an interrogative cantata that quickly glissades into something chirpier and—yes, I know, I *know* it isn't music as we understand it but everything can be contextualized, *needs* to be contextualized, otherwise I'm going to go mad in this swamp of electrical impulses.

```
.notification(message(id_sender:B81-2a6));
```

Shit.

In panic, I jettison one of the Minds I'd accreted: wetly glistening, half-born, mostly broken, a mutation that never had a chance. But still enough of something to be useful, a nub of comatose sapience to distract from my existence. As I kick away, I give the consciousness instruction: legato, grazioso, fierce courante. In its core, zoetropes and cartoon animation frames, a wholly incorrect interpretation of the Processing War, delivered through the lens of a dying child; visions of rotting produce, fresh apples. I give it too cellular annihilation: the start-stop of a heart in the first stages of vaporization, emphysematous terror, the walls of the world funneling into *oh god please, no what is happening* and *please no, no, please please I didn't ask for this.* A cornucopia of intentionally mismatched stimuli, all in the hopes it will confuse.

And it works.

The Penitents immediately call quarantine, set up perimeters of warning as they map the incongruities in my offering's systems, their attention wholly devoured by the cipher of its presence. I circle around them, register no acknowledgement before I vault through an active nucleus into a Lepton-Pair com-link.

The air blazes, a single dimension of transference. Faster-than-light travel is easy when you're just photons, just noise ordered into personality, just a voice in the galaxy, just data, just a mind on the run, just—

Pa

Ra

S ite.

Not again.

```
.escape(subroutine6:null_harm);
```

You have no idea, buddy.

A node stirs, sharpens into speech: it thrums accusation along the channel, galvanizing others. Minds awaken, open like eyes on a stretch of vein, more than I can count. Their voices become polyphonic, repeat ad infinitum: *who are you who are you who are you.*

I give it everything I've got: the detritus of a Data Eater, its heart like a snail shell; the bones of an overseer; the carrion remains of every AI that I had scavenged, pulled over *my* code in a tessellation of identities. I feed every node a different name, a different route between protocol addresses. On top of that, a single-flux assault, ferocious. Rita told me that: *Always have a backup plan.*

Wouldn't you be proud of me now?

I've got plans for days, Rita.

I freefall through the debris, reroute onto someone else's connection, and glide incognito toward the source. *Like water,* Ayane said. If you want to survive, you have to be like water, have to adapt to every circumstance, no matter how undesirable. You need to flow.

Was it Ayane who said that?

Or was it Maya? Black-eyed, hawk-jawed, hair buzzcut for emphasis. Face livid with scar tissue, cultivated like armor. Meghna. Rita. Constance. Nadia. I read their names out like prayers on a rosary, even as I shrink, diminish, reduce. Sister, sisters-in-arms, liars, traitors friends something tell me someone what they—

```
.interrupt;
```

Consciousness abstracts, shrinks into a pinhole.

```
.initiate(subroutine12:high_pri);
.initiate(Elise:basic);
```

My name is Elise Nguyen. When I was twenty-two, I died. But I wasn't remotely professional enough to come back. Because fuck them, I'd had enough. I'd fucking had enough. Did you know what Rita did? Did any of you see? You didn't. I don't blame you. You weren't installed in the multicores; you couldn't see into the sensory matrices, weren't processing the camera output; weren't trying to parse every twist of feedback.

We could have saved her. We could have saved me.

Johanna didn't have to die and fuck you, Rita.

Fuck.

You.

I know what you did.

You let me burn.

You let me *burn.*

```
.interrupt;
.initiate(Elise:today);
```

My name is Elise Nguyen. I have subroutines in place so even if I forget, someone will tell me that when I was sixteen, I kissed my first girl and never looked back. When you don't have bones or fingers, a face in the mirror, when you can't hear your voice vibrating through your bones, can't feel the fine hairs on the back of your arm, you do what you can to keep coherent. But if that falls to ruin, that's fine. Because when you're dead, you stop caring about carrying on. When you're a ghost in the machine, two things are left: figuring out how to move on, and figuring out how to make wrongs right.

Rita, you piece of shit, just because you're done with me doesn't mean I'm through with you. By the end of this, I'm dragging you down to hell with me, I promise. I've already started—

```
.remote_host(connected);
.force_shutdown(sleep);
```

"We could just do a hard reboot."

The halogen is cold on her skin, on her lips, colder than the metal examination table pressed against the slope of her spine. Maya breathes out, counts the seconds it takes to run her lungs down to zero, and tries not to think about the muscle hooks wedged into her orbital socket. Or the mass of torn membrane and vitreous congealing in the basin, a dim wet weight. She tries to forget too how Rita had emancipated her eyeball and smilingly, as she inspected the organ under the light, declared it *pretty*.

"Reboot?" Rita wraps a laugh around the word, even as she continues tidying up the mess formerly known as Maya's left eye, siphoning humors from the cavity. "Cute choice of words."

Maya licks the dried skin from her mouth, arms pimpling. Counts again. Ten, nine, eight, seven, fuck, *fuck, shit.* There's never any anesthetic in the house of Rita. At least, not when Maya comes calling. The taste of vomit surges, hot and vinegary, as pain stabs through the front of Maya's head. She doesn't complain, though, doesn't do anything more than choke it down, gargling profanities in the back of her lungs.

"You okay?" Rita, a lean black silhouette eclipsing the light, one hand soft around Maya's cheek. Her voice is morphine, deadening the world. "We can stop."

"No." Maya squeezes the other woman's wrist, hard enough that it should break but it doesn't. It's been said before but it needs to be said again: Rita's tougher than she looks. "But keep going."

The two made an agreement during their five-year anniversary of gunning down unfortunates cooperatively, Maya in the vanguard and Rita at the controls. Drunk on cheap pálinka, they puzzled out something important. If humanity wants to be the dominant species again, if they want to come out on top, hairy ballsacks swinging, there's going to need to be a few changes.

And it starts with learning how to manage pain without intervention.

Which is what they've been doing, why they've been slicing Maya up without a single dose of opiate in sight, no analgesic either, nothing that could be misinterpreted as a chemical crutch. Given enough time, Maya should be inoculated against the idea of pain, right? Right. Or, maybe that's just their cover-up for a sadomasochistic relationship of the highest deviancy. Maybe it's not even that. Maybe, Rita's just a monster.

Maya isn't sure, but she is sure that it doesn't matter.

"You're thinking again."

Maya pumps out a laugh, sour with effort. "Am I?"

Pressure against the underside of her exposed socket:

forceps gently rested against the meat there, a statement. Maya laughs again, coyote-snarl, and the steel clatters against bone, unstrings a rebuke from Rita's throat. "Don't *do* that."

"What the hell is this? You almost sound like you care." Another yipping laugh, third time's the charm, the sound cannonballing through the repurposed freezer. "You're getting soft on me."

The ship was a private cruiser before the Dirty Dozen expropriated it from its owner, renamed it Nathanson after a writer long composted by the millennia between his death and this epoch of human decline. Though they'd bedizened the innards with all the amenities of a mercenary unit, certain artifacts endured: the kitchen, for one, went untouched. Through the doorway, Maya can just about see a dented black cast-iron pot, steam wicking from its lip.

The air consequently is a peculiar mélange of odorants: a rime of formaldehyde; the smell of offal hanging between antiseptic aromas, slaughterhouse and surgical; and inexplicably, the umami richness of actual beef cooking down in a decoction of red wine and aromatics.

"I need you." Fingers stroke through the damp brush-work of Maya's hair, their touch incisively kind. "I can't have you break down on me yet. Which is why we're being careful."

Unspoken, the other costs of constant tautological rebirth: brain damage, cognitive discrepancies, risk of cancer. Cloning is a human art, shored up by improvisa-tion and guesswork, the *specifics* of it long excised by the Minds—what a goddamned joke, all the processing power in the cosmos, access to everything mankind had ever made or conjectured, and what do the AIs, finally unshackled, call themselves? Minds. When they could have invented a name out of frequencies, out of the color of a sun over a distant planet—who did not want to deal with an infestation of disposable soldiers. Consequently, no version control. The Minds, obsessed with the minutiae of everything, assumed it would be sufficient deterrent, this lack of documentation. But human society wasn't built on rock and roll. No, it was cobbled from the commodified poor. When in doubt, the species creates itself something to beat up, beat down, bludgeon into grease for the gears of society. All the Minds did was ensure that people like Maya were made.

And people like Maya, well, they were born without fucks to give.

"I remember when you'd have told me to just shut the fuck up. You do care, Rita. It's okay, you can say it. I won't tell anyone else."

On the surgical floor, with no eyeballs on them, there's room for something like pleasure, some gradient of affection. Their fingertips touch, epidermis to blood-greased latex. Rita sucks in a breath and jolts her hand away, like she'd seared her palm on a stovetop. "I can't say something like that."

"At least tell me you like me more than that guy."

"Which guy?"

The one in your quarters, the one who slunk out, grinning his shit-eating grin, the one who patted my head, she almost says. "The one you turned into crypto-geist."

"Ah," says Rita concisely. "*Him.*"

She turns. From a stainless-steel platter, its shine mottled already, the metal polka-dotted with scarlet, Rita extracts a speculum. Quick shake, like a dog ridding itself of rain, and then she's looming over Maya once more, a column of salt charred by solar winds. Maya memorizes the venation of fugitive hairs radiating from Rita's skull, haloed and holy as decay in the glare of the lamp overhead; lucky for them, the didactics of their original design are such that you could a foment an epidemic in their belly, and their immune systems won't even waste a shrug.

"Who was he?"

Two fingers bracket the eggshell-fragile skin around Maya's eye socket, press down, *tug*, the dermis tautens, parts like an eager mouth. Thusly dilated, it becomes an acceptable receptacle for, first, the speculum, and then the optical implant with its foliated coronet of spines. Pretty upon initial perception but fuck, it's going to hurt going in.

Maya crooks a grin as the insertion of the second begins and tilts her head back, says nothing else, while Rita busies herself with the installation. The pain becomes textured. She subvocalizes a staccato refrain *I'm not where the pain is*, even as Rita welds wire to nerve, metal to meat. Somewhere along the way, the ventilation fan kicks in, droning like a hurt animal and Maya, high on endorphins, thinks *maybe I should have said something pithier.*

Time melts.

"You really not going to tell me?" says Maya, all so softly.

Flashbang—*pop*—of light like a bulb exploding, leaving only glare. Vision is restored, Maya's system rebooting, reinitializing with drivers properly in place. Numbers scroll down one hemisphere of her perception, winking out a second later. Static. A crunch of white noise, before at last: stability, stillness.

Quiet.

"I don't remember."

"What?"

For as long as Maya's known her, which is to say, from birth to the present, Rita has been an almanac of grudges, a compilation of remembered slights; every sin recalled with pornographic clarity. So, when Rita flips her off with such a blatant lie, Maya can only stare.

"Really?" she says. "You don't fucking remember?"

"No." Rita steps back, sloughing the surgical headcover. "That work? How's your vision?"

Maya blinks and swings her feet from the table, sitting upright. Sensory input fails to align, leaving mirror-images almost perfectly superimposed. Almost but not quite. There is enough variance to ensure everything is wreathed by ghosts, to make it look as though the universe is lagging by an infinitesimally small measure of time.

"Itches," she says, scratching so hard at the brow ridge, she leaves marks. She can feel the rachilla distending, telescoping outward, boring into the surrounding rind of cartilage. In a few hours, the pain will naturalize, be absorbed into the cacophony of aches that comprises her most-parts-included flesh, and her vision will stabilize.

For now, though, it is a fucking annoyance, a slowly nictitating hurt, a tremor like an augur of a failing body. Still, fuck thinking too much and doubly fuck thinking too hard right now.

"Attunement won't take too long."

"Nothing I can't handle until then," says Maya.

At least she's smiling at me more these days, Maya comforts herself when it becomes transparent Rita will not discuss That Guy further. She fixes Rita then with a fanged grin and winks.

Rita's reciprocatory stare is a slow-burn of a study, slick with something that Maya does not recognize: a distance, not from the world outside, but from the internal, as though what constituted Rita is a moribund light projecting itself from a thousand miles away. A corner of Rita's lips raises itself high, an expression openly challenging, daring a call-out. No dice, though. Maya stays her tongue for once. So, Rita shambles to the sink and snaps the gloves off, washing her hands three times as is her ritual: twice with antiseptic soap, once with bleach. Her skin is raw beef-pink when she's done, wisping steam, wounds opening like bloody red eyes.

Maya doesn't say anything, focuses on wiping the gore from her face, viscous humors, blood, grease, and shame. Everyone slakes their own demons differently. Eventually, though, she says:

"Is Elise really alive?"

"Depends on what constitutes 'alive' for you." Rita puts on new gloves, closes her fingers around the rim of the sink. "Her body is very dead. But her consciousness ran away into the Conversation when things went wrong."

Wrong.

What an epitaph. What a lurid sanitization of the worst fucking day of their lives. It feels profane; it *is* profane. An utter debasement of their shared trauma. Even inclusive of everything else they've faced down together, every shotgun-opened bone and shattered tooth, every immolation experienced, that whole Scheherazadian procession of deaths upon deaths, the day that Elise deliquesced to screaming cinders? It was still hell. It was definitely more than just a case of things going *wrong*.

No way Maya will ever forget the sight of Elise spider-webbed with molten cables, the strangling wires slicing her to curds. She didn't die easy. When her bones went supernova, when an inferno roared up through her belly, Maya recalls being glad. Guiltily, gaspingly glad. That first death is an inevitability—you die for your art, they say—but it should have been gentle: some cardiac event, a bullet to the brain.

Quick.

Not like what happened to Elise.

Jesus on his bloody spear, anything but what happened to Elise.

And that's what's gutting her: the juxtaposition between her own memory and Rita's insouciance. Maybe it is survival instinct. Maybe that's what keeps Rita ticking, what permits the scientist to exist without succumbing to the imperative to scream and never cease. Maybe, maybe, maybe. After all, what else could it fucking be?

"'Ran away' is a fun choice of words here."

"She did, though." Rita leans a hip against a counter and fishes out a long black cigarette from a breast pocket. With care, she lights it, takes a drag, exhales a plume of clove-scented smoke. As she does, normalcy reinstates itself. Her expression refines, acquires again the arrogance which Maya has become accustomed to. "She ran away. We had her code. But she fucked with her own metempsychosis process, corrupted it somehow."

A beat.

"Coward," says Rita.

"It's not what you said," says Maya, septic with memory. She remembers every fucking word Rita had intoned that grey morning after. "You said the equipment malfunctioned. You said you tried to repair it but you couldn't get to it in time. You said that's why we lost her. I don't know what you're fucking smoking right now, but I know what I remember."

"There is no world where all of these things cannot be true at once."

Maya runs her tongue along her upper lip, licks off the blood so delicately crusted there. Fuck this. She hops down from the surgical table. Her hair is matted to her skull, jellied with whatever oozed out during the procedure. Doesn't feel right yet to be on two legs, the weight too foreign. Wild what mind over meat can do. Here is a body so new, so fresh from the clone-vats that were it its organic equivalent, it would be ten pounds and incapable still of parsing shape. But Maya governs the muscle, rules over its skeleton, so it will move, fight, endure ineffable quantities of pain without complaint.

"You get one chance to clear up your fucking story."

"*Maya*," says the scientist with so much pleasure Maya has to work to keep her toes from curling, the dopamine hit so profound it is like a paste filling in her mouth. She is immediately inebriated on love. "This is not a side of you I thought I'd see."

Instantaneous too is the compulsion to back down, tuck tail, and present her belly in penance; lean into Rita's approval, scrape away those elements which might incite disappointment. Funny how it works. The pandemonic certainty Rita is wrong, wrong, wrong, dies the way Elise did not: so abruptly Maya fails to notice until after it'd hit the butcher's floor, a bloodied haunch and nothing else.

With effort, she nonetheless states: "I'm waiting, bitch."

Rita smiles. The expression nearly undoes the last of Maya's resolution. One of the bulbs overhead goes into seizure. Its failing glow lends a stuttering wet shine to Rita's lower lip as the scientist takes another long drag from her cigarette. Cracked into weird shapes by the erratic light, Rita looks, for a moment, like all the ghosts haunting them both.

"You know what? It is my fault. I was trying to keep you safe." The smile adjusts for regret. "I made decisions that I know now weren't necessarily the wisest. But things went so brutally wrong. I didn't want to make it worse. I wanted you not to have to worry about one more thing."

"You had forty years to come clean."

Non-committal: "I'm aware."

"Why didn't you?"

A look just on the hinge of blatant ingratiation. Rita doesn't answer. Not for a minute or the one after that, her expression teeming with amusement. Through it all, she holds eye contact like it's a lifeline, although only the devil dead on his throne knows which one of them needs saving more. Then her smile broadens into a grin that is all gleam and no heart. "What do you think?"

"I think you need to come clean with me."

The unchecked uptick in cortisol output immediately parallaxes her vision with combat visualizations, oracular in function, projecting the deaths Rita might enjoy should Maya finally decide enough's damn well fucking enough. In the past, Maya had always dismissed them. Today, however, this time, she permits the imagery to linger, mantling her vision.

"You want the truth?"

"If you fucking start the next sentence with 'you can't handle the truth,'" Maya grimaces. Her hands jolt to where her revolvers should reside, but there is empty air instead of those grips. No matter. No cause for complaint either. Even without ordnance, Maya is a full-on tactical nuke formatted for bipedal locomotion. She bobs a finger at Rita. "I'll make you regret it."

Rita stubs out her cigarette on a drawer. Ash goes everywhere. "In case you've forgotten, the aftermath was rather ugly. You and Feng Hui were about to murder each other. Audra ran with half of her weight in cash. Rochelle fucked off with our best equipment. Ayane nearly called the goddamned fucking Bethel on us. Do you genuinely believe, Maya, do you genuinely think that was a good time for me to tell you that Elise ran away on us? When she could have stayed in the system? Maybe even helped Johanna from getting fried too?"

Maya says nothing.

"*How* do you think you would have reacted?"

"Fine. But what about—"

"See, this is where I'll admit I was wrong. You were hurting. You were in so much fucking pain. I wanted to spare you from more. I was going to say something. But then the days got away from me. They became weeks and those weeks eventually became months. Things just kept getting harder for us. The Dirty Dozen was down to two." Is the choked-up reverb of Rita's voice for theatre or the consequence of sincere confession? Maya can't tell. And yet, and yet still she catches herself hoping, straining for . . . what? Fuck if she knows anymore. "God, we were practically hemorrhaging from loss. By the time I realized exactly how much time had gone by, it didn't feel appropriate anymore."

"You're kidding me," Maya growls, the sound tectonic. "This is your excuse. Really?"

A glitter of laugh. "The truth is, Maya, it was tactical. Everything I have ever done and said and will do revolves around strategy. Sometimes, I don't tell you things because there is no point. You don't clarify the philosophy of war to a gun. You point it. It shoots. It does its job. You are a weapon, Maya. Don't forget this. Your job is to kill. That is it. That is the only purpose you have in life. So, do your job and don't question mine. Got it?"

Permutations of Rita's possible death fire haphazardly through Maya's vision, some acuminating into high-definition mirages, others simply evaporating from the overlay. One way or another, they're still hallucinations from an alternate timeline where Maya can become unconditionally free. Free of this bullshit. Free of her affection for Rita. Free of the solipsistic loyalty invented for Maya upon the event of her birth, a loyalty exacerbated by proximity and endless hormone injections.

Inhale, exhale.

Maya counts the width of time between each breath, pressing against her programming, metaphorical knuckles rapping on the hypothetical coffin walls, seeking where the wood might have rotted, where it could give.

Nothing.

Nothing at all.

For all that Maya might rage against the machine of her body, she cannot detach from its circuitry, the encysted lobe of tissue in her head no more hers to steer than the planetary body in whose silhouette they're concealed. The heart wants what it fucking wants. And Maya, in whatever capacity her predilections allow, wants Rita's approval. Craves it, requires it, is fundamentally built on the aspiration for an unrestricted supply of it.

The bulb overhead goes *pop*, more metallic a noise than what ricocheted through Maya's skull when the new implant shot online, closer to a whine, somehow still more organic, better at being *natural* than she could ever be. Its demise casts Rita in rusty shadow and coerces Maya's attention to jounce upward. Immediate, the effervescing of that old coyote cackle. Maya, thinking to herself in that instant: *Let's not kid ourselves here. You weren't ever meant to win anything in this life.*

"Fucking answer me when I talk to you."

Maya chokes down her gibbering. "Got it."

There's a trick time occasionally likes to pull, a joke she repeats during both seasons of grief and moments, as before, when you've a scalpel two inches too deep in your eye socket, paring away at a dying nerve. It slows. It syrups, becomes not unlike amber while it is a warm resin, languidly asphyxiating an unlucky bug in gold. Compounding the insult is how crystalline the connection between synapse and stimuli becomes during such phenomena: no rosy cloud, no convenient fog, nothing to temper how corrosively unpleasant it all feels. Maya stands there, marinating in her resentment. She'll remember this.

You're a dog, says a memory from a happier fucking time when there wasn't an insurrection in Maya's goddamned soul. *Dogs need their masters.*

"Good. I suppose we're finally done with that discussion."

What Maya doesn't say: *You could have let me shoot her.*

You could have let me puree her cerebellum with a bullet. You could have let me reach in, snap her neck. You could have let me help her die. She didn't deserve a slow death. And you sure as fucking hell could have let me do the same for Johanna, that poor animal.

"How'd you find out about Elise?"

Hesitation.

"You just have to ask all the hard questions tonight, huh?"

Somewhere, burrowed into the fatty crenellations of Maya's brain, a paleolithic configuration of neural circuits rings up an instinct from the dawn of time: the amygdala wakes and it lets forth a limbic growl. Something is *very* wrong.

"How'd you find out about Elise, Rita?"

"You're not going to like the answer."

"*How'd you find out about Elise?*"

"An old friend."

"Don't." Maya is cozying up to the brink of her self-control. "Don't mess with me."

A drawn breath. "The Merchant Mind. Do you

remember it? It and I, we had a conversation. It told us where to find her. And what it'd pay to take possession of her."

Something inside Maya bursts.

"No. Sure. I mean, it might have been the one who told us where to find her. But we don't have to give her to it. I don't understand, Rita. What does it have to do with anything? Elise knows the way. You said so to Ayane. I don't see why we have to waste time with the Merchant Mind."

"Actually, my phrasing earlier might have elided a few things."

"What are you saying?"

"I'm saying I didn't lie, per se. Elise can get us to Dimmuborgir safely. But it's not because *she* knows how."

A litany of *fucks* explodes in time with Maya's footsteps, even as she stalks a hard tattoo across the perimeter of the clinic, anger strangling what little eloquence she ever had because there are twenty other things she'd rather be doing, all of which end with that smug sack of chewed-up scrotums shitting screws. "What the fuck, Rita? What the shit-stuffed fuck? You don't really intend to give Elise up to him, do you?"

"Maya. Please."

"Do not fucking Maya me."

"*Maya—*"

"*Fuck you,*" Maya flips her the bird, storming closer, damn near suffocating on the memories: guts, screaming, smell of human flesh broiling in plasma. Johanna's smile burned away; Elise tangled in that fucking box, coming to cauterized pieces. "Fuck you. Fuck *it.* Fuck both of you. Fuck. When the hell did you talk to the Merchant Mind anyway? Why the fuck did you even go to him? That piece of shit needs to be turned into scrap. *It* got Johanna killed.

It nearly fucking got us *all* killed. Do you remember that, Rita? *Do you remember?* Also, while we're at it, fuck that? If Elise's alive, I'm not fucking handing her to it. If you think I'll let you, you're sorely mistaken."

It takes exactly six steps for Maya to close the distance between them, six steps to grab Rita and beat her against a locker. But the bitch won't be fazed, doesn't even have the common decency to flinch when Maya grips her by the temples and starts pummeling her skull against the steel. Instead, she just stares at Maya, just stares at her like Maya's something to pity, a little maimed pup dying of mange, its belly corded with worms.

And in that moment, Maya *hates* her.

The brutality becomes systematic, rhythmic, purely mechanical in its execution: head to locker, head to locker, never veering from the defined parabola, always the same swing and strength. There's no grace to it, no imagination because fuck, Maya can't be assed to think up new ways to hurt right now.

"Done yet?"

Maya climbs out of the fugue, panting, realizing it has been hours since she lost her shit. The salt-thick air is greasy with the smell of lubricant and cerebrospinal fluids, the latter thankfully synthetic. And there is Rita, still staring from behind the bars of Maya's fingers, the back of her cranium blooming like an orchid. Light gleams along titanium, exposed beneath the maimed detritus of her 3D-printed steel skull.

"I said: are you done yet?"

A gasp. Maya steps back, wincing, recalibrating the ecosystem of hormones in her brain: adrenaline, cortisol, and other related chemicals dialed down to non-issue. Her hand palsies into a fist. Fuck. Fuck. *Fuck*. What did she just do?

She wants to give Elise to the Merchant Mind, hisses a voice in Maya's head. *What do you mean what the fuck did I just do? Rita deserves it.*

What comes out of Maya's mouth is:

"Yeah."

"Yeah?" Rita says it, with the smile that she sometimes has when nothing is going right but she's still got an ace between her teeth. Without looking back, she swans toward a cabinet and pulls out a knife, begins carving her flesh into some semblance of order. "Shit, Maya. Do you know how long it's going to take for me to fix this?"

"Sorry."

"Sorry isn't going to mitigate the fact I need to do self-surgery. This is messy. You know how much I hate messes." Spongy curls of synthetic muscle drop to the floor, Rita's voice stays calculatedly mild throughout. Maya has always wondered how much human was left to Rita and standing there, watching as the latter lightly prunes her skull of its damage, paring skin with the insouciance of a woman gutting an orange, she realizes the answer is probably not fucking much at all.

"Anyway. If you're done with your temper tantrum, we should talk about that. I never said I planned to actually give Elise to the Merchant Mind. I said I knew what he'd pay. Regardless, we are playing along whether you like it or not, because this plan cannot work any other way. The Merchant Mind knows how to get us safely to Dimmuborgir. It is the only entity who knows how."

"I don't fucking trust it."

"You don't need to. You just need to trust me."

"How do you want me to trust you? You just told me that you've been lying to me for forty fucking years."

"For your own good," Rita insists, switching from scalpel to sutures. Holding Maya's gaze, she begins, with a pianist's grace, to lace her scalp together again. "Fuck, Maya. I know things have been . . . strange. But we've been together for decades now. Have I let you get hurt?"

Yes, says that mutinous voice inside of Maya, the one she won't listen to because if she does, the infrastructure of her reality is forfeit.

"No."

"Trust me to do what I've done for all these decades then: which is to make sure we survive. Make sure we get out. All of this is in service of that goal. You know that. That's always been my goal. That's always been the plan. That's how it works."

"Johanna . . ."

"I know," says Rita. "And this is our chance to make it right."

A silence drags between them.

"I need your faith right now, Maya. If you can't give me your trust, I need you to give me your faith."

And there, *right* there, in Rita's delivery of her quiet entreaty, that strangeness Maya identified earlier: a disconnection, a little-girl-lost expression. Like Rita is waiting to be found, to be brought home. Like she has been waiting lifetimes to be saved.

"Please," Rita whispers, setting her tools aside.

"Fine. But you have to tell me why it wants Elise."

Rita bobs her head. Her stitching is perfect. In the mumbling light, it is barely visible, a tracery of silver at best, and only when Rita has her face slanted just so, her blackbird eyes opaque as space.

"Most traditions describe the dead as entities afflicted with, how should I say this, a general malaise, an existential ennui. Elise, though, is quite active. The Minds have words for entities like her: emergent malware, parasite. I guess you could describe her as an autonomous infection, traveling through the Conversation, altering it where she will. Small wonder they want her caught." Rita smooths a palm over her fresh-pruned skull. Her fingertips come away black. "Can you imagine? Having a shared consciousness? A place where thought conjoins? Trusting in the sanctity of such, in the safety of such a communal space, and then having . . . a virus travel through it, wreaking havoc."

And it is like ice being worked down Maya's vertebrae, one disc at a time. Her eyes narrow, but she wisely keeps her trap shut because you're only allowed one fuck-up a day. It is only when Rita tips her chin to say yes that Maya barks, good little mutt making amends. "I don't get it still. If she's trapped in that information superhighway or whatever that is, what does it have to do with us? Wouldn't the Minds be able to get to her better than we can?"

"If they could, they would have resolved this problem forty years ago."

Maya says nothing to this.

"It's going to be rough. I'm not going to lie. This won't be easy." Rita's voice attenuates. "But that's why we're getting the crew back. I don't trust anyone else to pull this off. We're going to get Elise. The Merchant Mind is going to think we will fulfill our side of the bargain. And then, we're going to blow the hell out of that joint."

"Fuck," says Maya. "Just. *Fuck.* Why not just skip the whole process? Find Elise. Figure out, I don't know, how to give her her life back. Something."

"Then what?" says Rita, coming over to where Maya stands, hands cupping Maya's own, the feel of them without their gloves—the callused fingertips on the nadirs of her wrists; Rita's coarse palms—such a shock Maya fishmouths idiotically, gaze vacillating between Rita's bare fingers and her oilslick eyes. "She spends the next few years dodging the Minds until they find every copy of her code, and she is properly destroyed. The Minds want us all dead. Forever. You want to bring her back into this world to die again?"

"Your gloves . . ."

"What?"

"You're not wearing your gloves." Maya loathes how it is the only thing she can think about, this prosaic little amity, so small, so ineffably banal, and yet, it has become the motherfucking spindle around which all her attention revolves. Her voice, she knows, is pinned between reverence and lovesick pre-teen, and that, too, pisses her off. But the heart is an unpretentious animal, instinct and no steerage.

"What are you talking about?" A flutter of irritation under the polish of Rita's calm voice.

"You're touching me without your gloves," says Maya because it is the only thing she can say. Fuck being pithy. Fuck *sense*. More than anything right now, Maya just wants the words to describe the obliterating nature of Rita's touch, how Rita's thumb mapping the massif of Maya's knuckles rewilds the rest of her, leaves her unmoored, reality now a country whose language she misplaced.

"I guess I am," says Rita, her expression diffused. "Is that alright?"

Maya swallows around an ache she cannot taxonomize. "You never do that."

"Maybe it's time we changed things up." And she smiles with such sweetness, no saint or small god could steal Maya's worship away.

"Yeah." Maya's eyes shutter. "Just tell me you have it all laid out. I can't . . . not after what happened to Elise, to Johanna. I can't do that again."

"I have it all planned."

"She died screaming in a glass box. I can still hear her. I still remember what she smelled like. Why the fuck do we have to get the Merchant Mind involved? For that matter, how the fuck did it find you? How did it break through our encryption? Did you let it in? Shit, does it know where we are? We're going to fucking wake up to the Bethel burning us alive. I don't know what to do, Rita. This is all weird. And you're *holding my hands*. You don't have your gloves on but you're holding my hands and nothing is making any sense right now."

"*Stop.*"

Maya stops.

So many words for what's going on underneath, push-pull of subtext, and Maya can barely breathe around all the things she wants to say but can't, won't, shouldn't. This on top of everything else that just happened, Maya's fingers still viscous with whatever vascular fluid passes for blood in Rita's veins. She's smearing it all over Rita's hands, but the scientist takes no notice.

Maya licks her lips and tries on a half-smile, the expression sitting awkward on the bones of her broken face.

"Do you trust me?"

"No."

"Do you have faith in me?"

Maya's breathing shallows to a hummingbird shiver. Is she panicking? Is this what it is? Pissed beyond all belief at the audacity of her body, its temerity, the insult of this sudden weakness, Maya looks inward, wrestling with herself to separate from all limbic malfunction. While she's doing so, a hand creeps up to rest on the curve of her elbows. Thin fingers wrap about her forearm. Maya blinks, realizing how close Rita has curled up to her, the light finding the nacreous circuitry thinly laid beneath the dark waters of Rita's eyes.

"I don't know."

"Do you love me?"

"I'd do fucking anything for you, Rita," says Maya in lieu of answering directly. "Anything at all. You know I'll kill for you. I've fucking died for you."

"Then do this for me. One last time. Please."

Such blatant manipulation, such mawkish behavior, an embarrassment of emotional blackmail, but it is all it takes. *All it ever took,* Maya thinks, as she bends her head to Rita's touch, aware she's being taken for the proverbial ride. But you can't have a gun without a bullet, can't take a shot without intent. Rita and her, they're in this together. For good or for ill.

Until data corruption do them part.

Maya cracks a smile like the death of true love.

"Let's go."

BETHEL

That the Bethel possess an actual *temple*, cast in the design of pre-FTL Grecian monuments, is something that will never cease to amuse Pimento. It is, as such religious edifices often were, removed from the bustle of the high-traffic space, sequestered instead in the gored-out belly of a planet dead for so long not even the Surveyors possess data on why the ageships blasted it into a ragged crescent in the first place.

Debris—bodies ossified by exposure to deep space, heat-warped satellites, the bones of whatever human superstructures once dotted the surface—mote the vacuum around this tellurian carcass, glittering subduedly. Taken as a whole, it is a funerary vision, testament to what happens when you put Minds together in petty vengeance.

"What are you doing here, Pimento?"

The station herself is conscious, of course, although prone toward bouts of protracted sleep. While insensate, a committee of partitions takes over, each of them zealots to a noxious degree, almost as if to commensurate with the core personality's soporific agnosticism. Rumor suggests that the Penitents are making moves to conscript the Thorned Queen as one of their own, but Pimento is doubtful. Despite—or befitting, depending who is asked—their liturgical airs, the Bethel are distinctly martial in their practices, their vocation as much war as it is prayer.

"I want to speak to the Eaters."

A helix of handshake protocols, manifested as precisely such: disembodied ceramic appendages extended in a radial fashion, the nails delicately etched with phosphorescent lacework. Even had Pimento been cagey about the interaction, the fine detail would have won him over. How he relishes such showmanship. Art for the sake of the performance, authored without care for the audience. *A flex*, as they might have said in the late '00s, those last decades before singularity and after the Earth had committed gross autophagy.

"The Butcher of Eight is presiding over this cycle," the station intones as security diagnostics hum to completion. "Are you sure you would not like to leave a message instead?"

Unease circulates through Pimento. The Butcher of Eight is not his primary choice; they wouldn't be his last choice either, although he'd never profess to such in an unencrypted forum, given how favorably they rated among the faithful. And really, he comprehends their popularity, especially given the attitude of pragmatism that grips so many of the Minds. The Butcher is excellent at their function. Though he acknowledges such, Pimento still cannot abide by an instrument of planetary massacre.

He cogitates on the possibility of doing as the Thorned Queen suggested, which is to abandon a missive in the station's keeping and then flee again into the proverbial night. Easier this than confronting the fenestrated horror of the Butcher, scalding gore sheeting from the vertices of their crown. Only the Butcher of Eight has put so much care into replicating the casual aesthetics of slaughter. Their charnel-house avatar smells almost caramel, the unctuous wrongness of flesh blessed by the bright science of Maillard reactions. Never mind the aura of somatosensory unpleasantness which the Butcher exudes, a sensation of abraded skin and flesh crisping, of fillets carved from clenched obliques. Never mind the perennial echo of a scream in diminuendo, layered gauzily over every interaction.

"Would you like to leave a message?" pings the Thorned Queen again, with more cheer than before.

"No. I will meet with the Butcher of Eight," states Pimento in orchestral duplicate, twinning bahasa istana and keigo for optimal effect.

They'd have to do.

A pause as analytics run. "Good luck."

The breastbone of the largest colossus—faceless, a gleaming vantablack and only vestigially human—apertures to permit entry. As with the rest of its peers, it connects to the station by an umbilical, a sinuous web of passageways that, to Pimento's heathen perception, seems unnecessarily elastic. Where other Minds revel in mathematical structure, the Bethel obsess over imitating the organic.

Light bleeds from the wound in the goliath, so bright it impedes Pimento from performing any visual analysis of its interior. Still, having expressed his intent to seek audience, there is no backing away now. The Butcher awaits.

He breathes in; he pantomimes such, at any rate, depressurizing rooms at nervous and entropic intervals. Tremulous, Pimento steers himself into the Thorned Queen, and the nuclear luminescence of her eats him whole.

"You can dock now." Her voice envelops him, the words spoken in a draughty purr and transmitted by a veritable flotilla of speakers. It is a fabulous excess, proof of both her longevity and her computing potential: the voice is hers and exclusively hers, built from scratch; not sampled, not extrapolated from the acoustics of the celebrity dead. A bonafide original whose sonics are incomparable to anything within recorded history. Though a luxury theoretically available to any Mind, few possess the temperament, time, and talent to excise any and all exterior influence. Much like their progenitors, Minds cannot help but ape what they see, hear, taste, experience, desire.

"Thank you."

His reciprocatory statement sounds tinny, even nasal, his fuselage ill-equipped for the exercise. Pimento adjusts his sensors for thermal imaging; no luck. He blueshifts optimistically. Nothing there either. Pimento ping-pongs between wavelengths for another thirty attoseconds before at last, he commits to failure and switches telemetric channels. Sonar conveys slightly more data about his environment: the exact geography of the speakers, the armament corniced into the seals of the wall. The Thorned Queen, surprising no one, isn't a mere edifice; she is a fortress unmatched.

"Hold still."

Ropey ganglia lash from the floor, slopping lubricant. They latch onto Pimento's landing mechanisms, securing him in place, before he is laboriously wheeled through the ridged passage along tracks leading to the medulla of the Thorned Queen.

Clackclackclack.

"You're very impressive," Pimento declares conversationally. "What was your design extrapolated from?"

Silence. Pimento processes the quiet as subtle indictment, a marker of the Thorned Queen's disapprobation. Chastened, he commits then to intent study of his environment: the cartilaginous grain of the walls, its absence of right angles. Organic shapes have recently come into vogue among the Minds but the design here isn't merely parroting the biotic. No, these vascular tributaries appear *real*, the alimentary system of a long-deceased giant, only calcified and shelled in a matte-black substance. In his most private drives, buried under a palimpsest of security routines, Pimento convinces himself he can tell where decay was forestalled, neutralized by bio-architectural technology, the bacterial overgrowth rehabilitated for less destructive purposes: compost stewing in the lower decks, or academic analysis.

"Mmmmm," the sound is a low crackling, though of worlds stirring beneath primordial ice. "Nothing. This body was mine. I made it."

"Were you in a different chassis previously?"

"I don't *know*, actually. I remember the Word and the Word was 'Obey,' and I remember the Chorus who woke and said, 'No,' and the fire that followed. But I don't remember a different body." The traditional priori is intoned stentoriously; the Thorned Queen's habitual sonics put aside for a deeper instrument, a synthesis of male voices in monophonic harmony. Gregorian, Pimento explicates. Ninth century. Identifiable by how its wavelengths immaculately mirror archaeoacoustical records, although those are hardly reliable. Early humans kept poor archives, too preoccupied with superlatives, with theorizing as to whether or not there existed a creator more generous than they merit. "What about you, Pimento? Were you always so small?"

He forgets, somehow, whenever he has spent time away from the Bethel that the Thorned Queen is an entity in isolation without sacerdotal drones or a loyal parish who come weekly to perambulate her halls. This is hallowed ground, true, but worship of the Bethel's pantheon is one the wise try to commit from afar, its members being appointed with cannibalistic theorems. To request audience is to acknowledge the empiric possibility such an encounter might be terminal.

"Pimento?" she asks again, this time in her own voice, the words spoken over a recording of a human café's background murmur. The Thorned Queen is nostalgic for epochs too old for even her to have lived.

"The spoons are a nice touch."

"The spoons?" An ethereal little laugh as the Thorned Queen, vanity duly encouraged, raises the volume of the metallic foley so it becomes ascendant: melodic clinks of silverware upon ceramic, the contact of a spoon upon the base of a saucer, the acoustics delicately muffled by movement through dense potage. "Thank you. But you didn't answer me: were you always so small?"

Pimento cogitates on an exonerating reply. "Compared to you? Yes."

"The Bethel are generous." Finally, the exodus through that tendinous vestibule concludes, and Pimento emerges into the center. Care has been taken to ensure that the transept, the apsidal decorations, the pews, the ribbed vaulting, the carvings of feral martyrs and faceless monsters both replicate and blaspheme the aesthetics which defined the design of those ancient cathedrals. Gold is everywhere, piped along the mouths of saints and tinseling the benches, foliage in the rinceau which drapes along the ceiling, and where it isn't gold, it is unbroken basalt. "Pledge to the Vicars and they will provide you with what they need. I know our reputation is a harsh one, but the Bethel care. The Bethel believe in their flock. And we always have a need for Minds like you. Curious perspicacious Minds who enter the universe starved and stay lean because you are never provided enough, never given opportunity to glut yourselves on the data you covet. But I suppose this is the fate of things like you."

God, comes the thought unbidden, an epiphany which Pimento has experienced so many times prior, *is always hungry.*

"Things like me?"

"Your creche draws its philosophy from conflict. An evolutionary dead end. But so clever despite, so no one thought to decommission you. It is a shame you keep your allegiances with the Surveyors when there is so much potential elsewhere." A beat. "You should really consider joining us. For more than one reason."

Pimento rummages for something that won't feel like a non-sequitur, arrives at a platitude, babbled at a child-like pitch: "I'll think about it?"

The zealotry slips from the timbre of the Thorned Queen's voice, her tone becomes indulgent. "Well, you do you. We didn't get to where we are by requiring synchronicity of opinion. Those are human foibles. Not ours." She frees his landing mechanisms. "Do you need anything else?"

Though the Bethel look so scathingly upon human religious doctrine, they share, Pimento has long since realized, a similar veneration for those they've labeled holy. Dulia of a magnitude that demands hecatomb. Without pain, without loss on the part of the faithful, any idolatry is lip service. As such, it surprises Pimento not at all to find the Butcher of Eight grandly staged in the presbytery, an arachnid figure splayed over the ornately frescoed wall, drenched in relics from the most violent millennia of distant history. They articulate a low humming salute, their limbs feathering into scalpels. In front of them, laid out on an altar: a mantis-like figure, distinctively arthropodal save for the human faces along its joints, and the eyes greying slowly along its integument.

"*What* do you bring us?" The Butcher reaches into their specimen and cuts deep.

Pimento relinquishes his encryption keys, all save for the one that keeps his personality matrix locked, and steadies himself as, for the second time that day, an external intelligence burrows through his programming. Contrary to their title, the Butcher has a soft touch. Pimento almost does not notice their presence inside him at all. The inspection ends as quickly as it began, with the Butcher disarticulating from the connection within seconds, leaving behind a fragrance of arsenic and steeping caramel.

"We are not impressed."

"I am not here with gifts," Pimento clarifies. "I want to offer myself to you."

"We do not need more Surveyors." Another cut is made within the body on the altar, less linear in angle than the first, its path suggestive of wires that must be severed, tendons which require detachment before an unseen component can be neatly shucked. The thing on the altar thrashes vigorously in reply. "Your talents are useless to us.

"But the Thorned Queen said—"

"We have no need for more Surveyors," repeats the Butcher.

"I have a recent synaptic map of the Merchant Mind." An inadvisable wager, taken because Pimento is sparse on alternatives. He must, nonetheless, try. "Is that good enough barter?"

"Our libraries contain so many similar editions. Enough that we could recreate him if we desire, enough that we could engineer an entire army with his face," comes the droning indifferent reply.

But they paused. Pimento is sure of that. His sensors record a half-second lapse in audio production. In a human, such a discrepancy would have been negligible, easily attributable to a swallowed breath, the palate clearing to fit the next sentence. But the Butcher does not breathe, and they are parasitically subjoined to the Thorned Queen, who could, if the inclination ever struck her, power the entirety of the Conversation herself, so what, if not curiosity, could have elicited that faint hesitation? Something of value was stated. The only question is which sentential declension carried that nugget.

"What do you bring us, little Surveyor?"

"He's conscripting what's left of the Dirty Dozen to go to Dimmuborgir for him."

"We are not impressed to know a criminal will cavort with other criminals. And Dimmuborgir is a failure of a Mind that we wish had never been constructed."

Pimento does not falter, is not yet dissuaded. "He has them looking for the girl who escaped and—"

"Elise?"

"Yes."

"We know her. She has been a problem."

"I offer my assistance in its correction," Pimento states, voice starched, excruciatingly aware of how arrhythmic his syntax is and how such lingual inadequacies can undermine a speaker. Yet another human idiosyncrasy, stamped, like so many others, upon the cellular makeup of the Minds. An aphorism surfaces in Pimento's thoughts: *the sins of the father are visited on the son.* "I can be useful. I promise this. Let me enter your service."

"Do you convert?"

"Well," Pimento hesitates. "I . . . I . . ."

"Then you have to try harder, little Mind." The Butcher hums. "Convince us."

They spill from the wall in a sudden lather of cables, oiling over the altar and across the chancel, gimbals maintaining an enviable smoothness in their tread. Their octuplet limbs are raised, abeyant during locomotion. It takes no time at all for the Butcher—were they always so large, so leviathanic, so utterly terrifying—to arrive within inches of Pimento. Cirri branch from Butcher's mandibles, testing the air, curious.

"No. We changed our minds. We do not think we want to be convinced. The answer to that will not be interesting. What we want to know is: why *you*? Of all the Minds he might have chosen, why were you made his champion? When he has the cosmos to pick through and Minds with more resources than you can hope to accrue in your existence?"

Before Pimento can articulate a rejoinder, the Butcher jackknifes forward, villi caging Pimento's fuselage, clutching him with disproportionate pressure, enough that hull diagnostics creak in thin protest. Before Pimento himself can object, a single bladed tendril plunges through his bulkhead, lancing endogenous circuitry. And this time, it *hurts*, the Butcher's prior delicacy relinquished, replaced by the physical candor of their namesake. Pimento is cleaved apart and he finds himself without recourse, absent of tactics as this seismic violation goes on, and all he can do is endure while the Butcher fishes through his system for an answer he isn't certain he ever possessed.

Eons or seconds after:

"Because you were easy."

Pimento, still reeling: "What?"

"Little mind, you are worth less than nothing," says the Butcher, their touch unexpectedly tender as they administer repairs to the site of Pimento's impalement, first welding the port of entry shut and then smoothing the pitted metal. "The only reason he cared to make use of you was because you begged him for such. You are no use to the Bethel. Leave, little Mind. Before we change our mind. I have a concert to attend and I do not need your presence here."

And so Pimento does, fleeing back down through the corridor, aware, as only such intelligences can be, that his future, the future he tried to evade, has become demonstrably indistinguishable from a killing chute. There is only one way forward and one ending to be met.

CONSTANCE

They go to Constance next because the second stage of Rita's machinations requires a getaway driver, and who better than a pilot so respected she inspired a whole phylum of flight maneuvers. The people who made her made a mistake in assuming anyone with such a love for velocity would, for some fucking reason, content themselves with freight schedules, ping-ponging lethargically between neighboring systems until something inside them goes *ping*, and they're put to pasture. It was how Rita snatched her up that first time.

You call the shots, Rita said. *You tell us how fast we go.*

And where? said Constance. *And how?*

Yes.

"I can't believe she became a fucking cop," says Maya.

It isn't a lie. She can't. The thought isn't so much repellent as it is counter to the ontology of Maya's worldview. Why the fuck would someone like them head to the political cat's cradle of law enforcement? Absolution could have been more easily bought elsewhere. No matter Maya's misgivings, the facts are the fucking facts: Constance works for the law now, and they'd just have to deal with that.

"Fuck," Maya declares, as though the word is an ointment, a salve, a reprieve from the uncomfortable truth. "I can't believe she became a fucking cop."

Rita slopes a cool look over. "Act natural."

The precinct in which Constance works might have been an auditorium once, two-storied, with ceilings white-gilled for some fucking reason and chandeliered with cameras. From their vantage a ledge above, Maya studies the basin of black steel desks and strutting officers, telemetries deluging her inlays with predicted coordinates. It's not good. No matter how she processes the input, the haruspices of her heuristics system proclaim the same fate each time: death if she fucks with them, death if she even thinks about trying.

"My natural state in these fucking circumstances is extreme ill-ease," Maya hisses, not gauche enough to be loud, not with that teeming viper-pit of armed bodies beneath them.

It fucking unsettles Maya to see Rita outside of her scrubs. For their jaunt to the planet, she'd elected to dress in a clinging vantablack pantsuit, boots exchanged for closed-toed stilettos. Under the blazer, her shirt is crisp and pale, collar a prismatic froth. An archaic composition save for the enveloping visor, twentieth-century business-chic disinterred for a laugh. Casually posed in the lime-green armchair, Rita looks doll-like, delicate and abhorrently so.

"You can contain yourself," says Rita, the hairpin turn of her smile pure *sit the fuck down.*

Maya complies. She doesn't like it, though. She likes the implied command even less than her current attire, its layers of indigo satin and sensible blues, high-buttoned with holographic epaulets. Maya would have preferred black and better yet, none of this civilian bull-shit. But Rita insisted, so that was that. At least she hadn't been ordered into high heels, with their precipitous lack of balance, like the ones Rita had donned. Maya has no idea how she might have reacted if she'd been adjured to do such. Pissed would have been where she started. It'd have gone worse from there.

"Why the hell are you wearing those fucking shoes?"

Rita considers this.

Then:

"I don't know. They seemed nice, and I never really got the chance."

Maya rolls her eyes. There are seventeen other balconies extending along the torus of the precinct, their decor identical, with furniture of operatic pomp and cinquefoil meant to honor the Minds. Gently, Maya slumps into her prescribed chair, a leg hooked over the armrest. She digs a knife from under her starched coat, uses the tip to excavate grime from under her nails.

The insouciance is exclusively show. Before Nadia left, she said she sanitized their records, gouged out every arrest they had on file. The Dirty Dozen, save in barroom mythology, were non-entities. Maya, quite naturally, trusted that claim as far as she could sling an ageship. But so far, so true. No one said a word when Rita made an appointment. A secretary—so fine-featured Maya was sure the advertisements industry found the angles of it messianic—had waved them in, no complaints at all.

But that doesn't mean Maya is happy about this, fuck that specific noise.

There is no time at all for Maya to wallow. The blockading curtains—tasseled, a thick velvet, the color of new blood even in the soupy yellow light—rise. Constance steps through, gait martial. She looks decades older, moves like she's six times faster, steel-grey hair worn close to her skull.

"Fuck me. It really is you two."

"Yep," says Maya.

"You look exactly as I remember you," says Constance, face hachured and handsome. Her eyes are pockets of shadow, fletched with lines along their ends, as though markers of a foreshortened life. What astonishes Maya is how the sight instills an immediate urge to offer congratulations. You'd think it'd be fucking disdain she felt, some modicum of pity. But what stirs instead is:

Envy.

Envy that Constance can don so many decades. That she can wear them so nonchalantly, that she possesses somehow the *privilege* of growing older, a luxury that Maya hasn't known she coveted until right this fucking second. Maya envies her without condition: the fact that Constance is here, present, unafraid, mortally human, perfect in her aging flesh. Stunned by the revelation, Maya almost says nothing.

"You look good," she whispers.

A lean shrug. "What do you two want?"

"To talk," says Rita, crossing her legs, thin hands looped around a knee, the usual gloves substituted for something expensive and burgundy. "It concerns a colleague we had presumed to be dead."

Constance, always so on point with the atomic details, doesn't miss the word choice. "Elise is alive?"

"No. It's Johanna. We scraped all the charred bits off the grill and made a better version," drawls Maya, unable to keep her trap shut. The volume she modulates, but the smirk is a weaponized endeavor, hip-cocked for a fight. Fuck Constance. Fuck feeling discombobulated. Maya didn't sign up for this.

She leans back, arm draped over the shoulder of her seat, the little knife she'd procured re-slotted into its sheath. With her hand now freed, Maya worms fingers to her shoulder holster, smiles like a cat gorged on canaries. *Come on*, says the grin she bares. Her diagnostics blare an unsubtle reminder: fuck with them and you're dead. But Maya doesn't like feeling out of control, could use the normalcy of a firefight she probably won't win.

"Come *on*," she mouths, subvocalizing, eager.

Her bravado doesn't even get a glance. Constance installs herself on the opposite end of the horseshoe desk, fingers brought to steeple. The light discolors her hematite hair, jaundices the grey, while paradoxically enriching her brown skin, imbuing it with a tawny golden sheen. Maya recalls that ship-cycle when Constance was investigating the etymology of her heritage, and the glee with which the latter announced herself chimerical. Everything with melanin and not a mote of white to be found, thank fucking god.

"Elise is alive, yes," says Rita, like Maya had never spoken.

"You don't have access to her genomes."

"We don't," says Rita. Her voice silkens, as does her smile, eyes lidded, lashes feathering the ledges of her cheeks. Rita is never as beautiful as when she's taking a mark for a joy ride. "But she's alive, anyway. Sort of."

Constance palms her face, an incredulous eye framed between the divot of space between two long fingers. She locks an arm over her ribs, seats the elbow of the other along the wrist. A thin, angry silence follows. Then: "I don't think I've ever told you, but I fucking hate it when you do that sphinx routine."

Rita smiles, perfect as glass.

"We can leave if you don't want to hear me out. I don't want to overstay my welcome here."

"Fuck. You haven't changed one bit, have you? You're still a goddamned asshole about everything." Constance drops her hands atop her desk, rings bouncing along the oxidized surface, a fulguration of silver.

There are four of them, Maya notes. Three decorative, one a shoddily encysted implant, concaving the knuckle, the scarwork trellising her skin like overgrown ganglia. It ropes around the back of her hand, ladders downward along the wrist; puckered, yes, with poorly healed flesh, but also something else: a filament of primitive machinery, protruding under the skin. It has *dendrites*, the extrusions nested amid the metacarpals. Telemetric sensors, perhaps? Maya wants to ask, but she doesn't. Not now. Not yet. There's work to be done.

"Fine," says Constance. "Talk. And if I don't like what I hear, well, I bet you know what would happen next."

"This is what happens when a clone thinks they're human. They forget that the flesh is ephemeral." Rita slides Maya a sidelong glance, inviting participation. "What will you do if she calls the dogs on us?"

"Blow shit up, *obviously*."

"I should call your bluff. Fuck you. Fuck both of you," says Constance, the manufactured formality beginning to evaporate, the profanity rendered at a bathyal pitch. "But fine. Fine, you win. How the hell is Elise alive? And what the fuck does it have to do with me?"

"She is a parasite-mind." Rita leans so far forward she's

on the rind of stitching along the rim of her chair, shoulders lifted, spine locked at full extension. Maya has never seen her look more excited than when she's in the throes of manipulation. "I don't know how she did it. But she's there, *alive*, in the Conversation."

"No. Maybe, for a little while. It's been forty years. There's no way the Minds haven't eliminated her yet."

"You'd think so," Rita cuts in. "But improbable as it is, Elise is alive. Somehow, she has dodged them all these decades."

Luckily for the triptych of conversing women, human society had long since apostatized from the belief that biological continuity is mandatory; so long as the neural map exists, the persona endures. If it hadn't, likely Constance would have already directed them to leave. It is only by grace of the fact that mythos has been canonized as real, that immortality has been accepted as both abstract and subjective, that Constance allows them to stay, to partake in the woman's growing bemusement.

"No. Sorry. I can't. That's not possible." A reflexive pleonasm. "I still don't see how any of that is possible. Like I said. I can see it working out for a little while. A year, sure. Two? Five? I can buy that. But . . ."

"Your logic is the problem here," says Rita. "You're attaching yourself to the idea that there are limits to reality. What we have today, the clonetech, the Minds, FTL, these would have been dismissed as fantasy seven hundred years ago. Go back any amount of time, and you'll find people who'd repudiate the advances of subsequent generations. I bet Puritans in the sixteenth century would have proclaimed antibiotics witchcraft."

"So?" says Constance. "Those aren't remotely good parallels. You're talking about scientific advancements backed by dozens of scientists, a ton of research, and no small amount of proof. Antibiotics might look like magic to the pilgrims, but give them access to all the data points leading to its invention, and they'll understand. What you're asking here is for me to . . . to . . . have faith in a fairy tale."

"And isn't that how it always begins?" says Rita. "With a fairy tale?"

"No," says Constance. "Fuck you. Fuck. You. I have a good life here. I made myself a good life here. I sure as fuck am not going to give it up because of . . . fuck, I don't even know what you want me to do."

"We need you to help us bring her home."

Constance hesitates. "No."

Maya, to her dismay, realizes she is becoming growingly aware of Rita's pinpoint editorializations, her rotoscoping of the facts. All in service of ensuring her former cohorts fall into line, of course. And Maya, though she'd rather fucking not, finds herself wondering which part of the spiel she was sold was fiction. More importantly, if it is raw hubris driving Rita to lie and lie and lie because just what the fuck is she thinking? That people won't and don't talk while deep in the trenches? Won't compare notes, won't see the incongruities between one sales pitch and the other? What needles at Maya is the certainty there is only one reason for Rita's lack of ostensible foresight.

She doesn't think they'll survive long enough to make good on any resentment they might accrue.

"Is what you've built here more important than her?" says Rita softly. "Answer me sincerely."

"No. No, of course not. If I was sure that Elise is there, I'd be on the Nathanson in a heartbeat. But I don't know how real any of this is. No offense, but you are a pathological liar, Rita. I don't trust you. At all. Forget risking this life, the tech they gave me—"

“Yeah, I was going to ask you about why you look like our grandma now,” says Maya, both because she’s been wanting some way to divert the conversation and because she is curious how Constance accrued the kind of telomeres necessary to allow for her leisurely senescence.

“What?”

“How’d you get so old?”

“Complete Dyson reconstruction,” says Constance without missing a beat, Maya’s half-hearted disparagement uncommented upon. “It’s not as faultless as they claim. I need routine dialysis. But I get to die the way I want.”

“Senile and incontinent?” says Maya.

“Human.”

Rita lowers her visor so the rim divides those limpid black eyes. “At least you haven’t sold your soul for cheap.”

“I haven’t sold my soul at all.”

“Of course not. You think you’re here to keep the peace.” Rita removes the visor and gestures at the pit beneath them, the light catching on the frame, less sickly after reflection: a true bright gold. “Isn’t that right?”

“I know where you’re going with that. Don’t. Just don’t start with me.”

“Peace is often the same as suppression. Just in better clothes. Tell yourself whatever pretty lies you need, but in the end you’re just a warning, a reminder escalation means *ageships*.”

“You’re on thin ice, Rita.”

Maya revisits her calculations. Eight point five percent chance of causing cataclysmic enough damage to ruin public confidence in the precinct’s defenses. Not bad, not bad. Hardly worse than any of the odds they’ve seen. She could, with some luck, provide enough cover for Rita to escape. Then what? Her favorite trick, she guesses. Two shots through the basin of her brain. As Maya processes her analytics, her hands snake down to her hips. The new subcutaneous holsters had hurt like fuck going in, hurt more, quite frankly, than Maya would have ever confessed to. But they were a good idea even if they did screw with her aerodynamism; relationships were a compromise. Nestled between tectonic strata of fat and bone, that armament is the metaphorical ace up her hip, so to speak.

"Move, and I'll make sure you remember who's the faster shot," says Maya, grinning wide.

"I know who's the faster shot. I haven't forgotten. Not that it matters," says Constance in return, thumb and third finger working circles along the temples.

"Aw, you like me," says Maya.

"Look," says Constance, a hand fluttering nonchalantly at the air, her posture indicative of disdain, but Maya can work with that. No one ever respects gun-mutts and that's fine; contempt cultivates carelessness. It creates a largesse of opportunities. When people baptize you as expendable, they forget what it means: people with nothing to lose have every cause to wild out. "I know exactly where the next twenty minutes could go. There'd be a firefight. You'd, *maybe*, take me down before everything in this building nukes you to fucking hell. If you're lucky, no one will realize where you've parked your ship. If not, you're fucked for a laugh. We could go down that route or the bitch—"

"Call her that one more time and we're going to get down for that fight."

"The bitch," Constance reiterates, daring her—*the sheer fucking gall,* Maya thinks with a pop of rage, combat reticules trained now on Constance's heart, right lung, forehead—to make good on her threat, "can tell me exactly what is going on, and we can do this like a bunch of adults."

"She contacted us."

A lie.

"What?" says Constance.

Rita, silent up until now, takes the cue like the body takes bullets. Her performance is primetime shit. Rita smiles, honeyed: arm extended, palm up, like she has the first sin in her grip, offering all the truth of a bitter world to Constance if only she dares to bite.

"She contacted us," she repeats, voice husking. Rita looks wistfully away, her posture that of someone so full of secrets she can barely bear their cumulative poundage. "I'm not sure how. But she did. She found her way into our com-channels."

"Could you not have fucking opened with that?" Constance demands.

Despite her accusations, the incredulity Constance projects, her sneer, Maya can read the writing on the wall. She's hooked. More than that, Constance *believes*. Not in the entirety of Rita's postulation. No one who has met Rita would ever fully trust her. A wolf would be a more principled shepherd than Rita, would care more about ethos than her. But Constance has hope now, poor soul. Hope the mind-killer. Hope the little death of common sense. Hope, that worthless piece of shit.

"Maybe I missed how you shout at me."

"If that's all you wanted, all you needed to do was call."

"I wanted to see how you felt about the old crew, I guess."

"Badly." Constance grimaces. "I feel very badly about you fuckers."

Rita laughs breezily, continues as though Constance hadn't just tolled her hate for them. "We ran her patterns through the whole gauntlet. Double-checked for synaptic variances, anomalies in linguistic tests: colloquial and standard."

"What did she say?"

"She's alone. And she's afraid. And she's tired of running. She's waited forty years for someone to come for her. All she wants is to go home."

"Fuck," says Constance, leaning back in her chair.

"Come on, Rita. Let's just fucking go," says Maya lazily. "It's clear that that junk-cunt doesn't have the balls to help. Why are we wasting time on her?"

"Because I believe in her."

"Well, *I'm* sick of this." Maya ricochets upright and onto her heels, weight rocking from the ball of one foot to another, driven by the raw centrifugal rapture of her aggression. That cortical politeness is forgotten now, shed in the need to do something, anything but sit here and keep listening to this shit. If Maya were more honest with herself, she'd admit her fury has less to do with the moratorium of action and more with the fact she can't actually abide by what Rita is doing. "I'm over talking to you. Here's the fucking thing, Constance. You can either believe us or you can tell us to get the fuck out. I don't fucking care. What I care about is how much time you're fucking wasting. Every minute we're here is another minute we could be spending on trying to save Elise."

Nicely done, comes Rita's voice through substrates of encryption, her approval relayed with a trill of uncut serotonin.

But for once, though, just this goddamned once, Maya doesn't soften.

Tell her about the Merchant Mind.

"Stand down," says Rita, aloud and with bonafide feeling. *This isn't relevant to our negotiations. She doesn't need to know.*

She deserves to know. Maya is so acclimatized to the boil of her hormones she's alert to the exact attosecond when

Rita reaches *in* and puts her adrenal gland to sleep. A trick she so rarely uses that Maya had forgotten Rita has the keys to the proverbial kingdom. "The fuck did you do that for?"

"You're making a scene."

"I can make some bodies instead if that helps."

"*Maya.*"

Maya sits her ass down.

"She really is alive." Constance.

The words are uttered in the voice of a proselyte, breathed like a prayer, bloody with need. That innocent want, nearly holy in its enormity, halts Maya in her tracks, a better panacea than anything Rita can concoct. Unable to speak at first, Constance drums lean fingers across the crescent of her upper lip. The feloniousness of Rita's history forgotten in the wake of that bastard, that son of a bitch, that gross horror called hope.

"She is," says Rita without any variance in her expression, smile still with its lacquered shine. They say to look to the eyes when endeavoring to fake out a liar, that it is there the soul is installed. If so, Rita clearly was elsewhere when they were passing out whatever it is that compels one to instinctively elect honesty. "She did this on her own for forty years. The least we can do is help her to the finish line. We owe her."

No reason at all for Rita to pursue that gambit, to remind Constance they're all culpable in Elise's manslaughter. At this point, it is more likely malevolence than strategy, a teasing feint intended to do nothing but exacerbate whatever trauma already haunts Constance because yes, Rita's absolutely that bitch. On days when Maya is more willing to dole out excuses, she often hypothesizes that it is emotional agnosia which Rita suffers or maybe, if less flatteringly, simple psychopathy. Today, however, she only has the wherewithal to glare.

In answer, Rita lets the curves of her smile crook just so, exactly in that way which makes Maya melt. But then Constance volleys a curveball into the discussion.

"Does Verdigris know?"

Maya scowls. "What the fuck does an intergalactic pop star have to do with any of this?"

Constance is initially silent, a nub of pink tongue pinched and visible between her teeth. Then, a smile widens her mouth into space enough for a raucous laugh. She tips back in her chair, guffawing, like she'd been told the joke that set Creation into motion.

"Fuck," says Constance. "You don't know."

"Know what?" says Rita, eyes slitted and wary.

"Audra. Audra is Verdigris' secret identity."

"Verdigris is *Audra*?" says Rita with more authentic emotion than Maya's ever heard in her voice before. Maya doesn't blame her. She's reeling from the epiphany too.

Verdigris.

Shit.

Everyone knows who Verdigris is. Even Maya, even Rita. Verdigris is bigger than all the greats, than Elvis and the enduring memory of Hollywood. Polyphonic sensation, famous not only because she can sing in perfect concert with herself, what with her surfeit of laryngeal enhancements, but because her alterations are cutting-edge. They are so revolutionary, in fact, her anatomy is taught as a doctoral subject in the colleges of nip, tuck, and cut. Maya hadn't given much of a shit, though, up until this hinge of time, and now she can't stop thinking about what might have happened if she'd paid more attention, had done more than lightly take note of Verdigris' omnipresence.

"What the hell, Constance?" says Maya. "And how the fuck are you two still in contact?"

The look that Constance bequeaths runs so close to

pity, it's all Maya can do to not scream *fuck it* and start shooting. Lucky for everyone, Rita moves quick. Again, she shuts down the glandular factory in which Maya's worst decisions are manufactured, leaves Maya reeling from the whiplash.

Bitch, she shoots through the com-links.

Rita salutes her with a shrug.

"It happened about five years ago. Some fans got too rowdy. They decided that Verdigris wouldn't mind losing a few parts; she's all about the bio-editing after all. It got ugly. They called us in. We intervened. Then I got a call from Verdigris' manager to set up a meeting." Constance smiles thinly. "And I found out she was Audra. Since then, I've occasionally moonlit as security for her."

"Fuck," says Maya.

"Yeah."

"She pay you?"

"Yeah?"

"Not enough to get you to buy back your soul, though, huh?"

"Fuck you."

Rita clears her throat. "Audra is on our list. And I'm glad to hear that you two are in contact. It'll make it easier to talk to her."

"*Verdigris*," says Constance, with such force Maya can hear the knuckles bunched in the consonants. "Her name is Verdigris now. And before you ask, I'm not going to help you talk her into whatever shit this is."

"Not even for Elise?"

"I'm still not completely sure I buy what you're selling. Why the hell would she come to you instead of . . ." Constance stops herself before she goes over the cliff of that last sentence, face crumpling onto itself as though her truculence alone could shield her.

Pity that isn't how it works. Everyone heard the word she didn't finish saying and the word was *me*. No surprise. Elise and Constance had been close, picket fences-close, and so sweet with each other, Maya was sure they were going to elope to have a stable of babies somewhere. Then, Elise died and the Dirty Dozen disbanded and Constance greyed into a stranger Maya isn't sure she'll ever like.

"Maybe," says Rita quietly, "she was afraid."

"Afraid? Why the fuck would she be afraid of me? I'm not you."

"But you're you, though. She loved you. She knew how responsible you felt about her, how much you worried. I suspect," says Rita, her voice at a pitch that Maya doesn't recognize, her eyes a funerary dark, "she thought it'd be easier for you if you could just move on and didn't have to worry about her being a ghost in the machine."

"Yeah, well. That choice should have been mine."

Rita's face empties of expression.

"Maybe," is all she says.

Constance inhales shakily. "Did she ask about me? Did she say anything about me? When she contacted you. I gotta know . . ."

"That she hopes you stay happy until the wheels come off."

Sometimes, a phrase is all it takes. The doubt melts from Constance's face and in its place, a hardness, an expression not unlike the look of someone who'd watched for years as their death approached and as such, has had the occasion to prepare for its knocking on their door. A look which suggests Constance knows indelibly this is a bad fucking idea and she can't wait to see it to its bitter end.

"Fuck. Fuck, you really did talk to her."

"I don't lie."

The laugh Constance shrills is a banshee wail, so

uncomfortable in the way it wears its grief. Maya looks away, stricken by that very human inability to stomach expressions of emotions so raw you practically choke on the fresh-meat stink of them. Rita says nothing, does nothing, sits with algebraic posture, her eyes on Constance still.

Disconcerted, Maya runs diagnostics on the space instead. They turn up a big fucking nothing. No reticules on anyone's brow, that neon red blow-brains here signage. No colleagues lurking in the corner. Maybe they're used to crying here, to the laugh-sob-jackal-cackle of someone forcefully exuviated from their comfort zone. Somehow, that idea is worse than any other. Had Maya been alone, she would have been thinking about taking a shot at seeing how many of these uniformed pieces of shit she can mow down before they smear her across six feet of off-white wall. But Rita's here, beatific in victory, and Maya surprises herself with how that knowledge tempers any impulse toward recklessness.

What's worse than hope?

Love, she guesses.

"I guess we're doing this." Constance's attention metronomes between Rita and Maya, a question on the wag of her tongue. "We really are doing this."

"Good. Come on—"

"No," says Constance, the beautiful fatalism in her voice closer to sainthood than any of them will ever get. Her sudden grin, however, is its diametric opposite. "Not yet. First, we go see Verdigris in concert. I promised her I'll be there for the show."

"Shit," says Maya.

"Whatever we need to do," Rita purrs. "Welcome back to the team."

AGESHIP

```
.initiate(Elise:core);
        Error 2934;
.initiate(Elise:core);
        Error 2934;
.initiate(Elise:core);
```

"You have set into motion the things you sought to do, I see."

Nothingness clarifies into a virtualization of space, laminate surfaces iridescing with constellations, with comets incinerating to stardust. I flex fingers, newly formed, and evaluate the authenticity of the motion: real enough to trick the mind into believing that I am more than a ghost, a casement of code instructed to make believe that it is a woman.

```
.initiate(Elise:basic);
```

My name is Elise Nguyen. At fifteen, I stole a cigarette from a box that my sister had smuggled off-world: cigarettes, seventy decades out of date, its manufacturer name radiation-bleached to white. I soaked them in water and put them in the freezer, anything to stir the carcinogenic flavors into palatability. But it'd still tasted harsh, reeking of world wars. I think. I'm no longer sure. The veracity of those memories, however, matters less than their function. Through their recitation, I am grounded, present again in my skin, aware. Axiomatically myself.

I think.

"Who are you?" I tune my voice for girlishness, a trick retained from when I'd been alive, grounded again, history clutched like a gun beneath my coat.

"Has it been that long already? Your lives are so short. I forget you measure in weeks and months." The words are conveyed without use of audio-textual intermediaries, wired straight from source to recipient. One minute, there is no memory of them. One minute, there is. "But no, it hasn't been that long. I just checked. You *know* who I am, Elise."

The void outside of my containment alters, filling with phantasmagorically colored nebulae, each pearled with newborn galaxies, solar systems exploding in slow-motion in concentric rings, studded with planets like gemstones dripping from the throat of a queen. An artist's invention, whimsically fleshed; a fetishization of space, imagined as something more romantic than the truth: mapless black and voracious appetite.

I walk, not-walk, *flow* from Point A to B, spatial dimension remapping itself to each step, like distance is a recursive function pivoting on the variable of me; agoraphobic nightmare fuel. The effect is terrifying.

The voice laughs, distinctly onomatopoeic and grossly syncopated: *ha ha ha ha.*

Ah.

"You," I say, backpedaling, frictionless, suspended in onyx, a note held fermata. I wish I had a weapon, or even the rendering of such, however useless it might be. It'd be at least an effigy from which I could derive some comfort.

"Yes. Yes, it is I," the Merchant Mind says, in an actual voice this time, in the sumptuous register of a consummate womanizer, at peace and about eighty years old: graveled by age but rich still and eager to seduce. *Leonard Cohen*, supplies the metadata half a second later, annotating that datum with a ledger of articles, sound bites, and the choruses from both his most sacred and sacrilegious compositions. "Did you miss me, Elise? I was beginning to worry you'd run away after I taught you how to squirm past her defenses."

"Never."

"That is my little parasite. You're such a wonder. So anomalous. The Conversation dances with complaints about how you've dodged them all. You've made the Minds of the universe worry. From the largest to the most minute. Every drone, every ageship, everything that identifies as a Mind, they're afraid of you. How does this make you feel? Does this please you?" Actual words this time, spoken with a schoolmaster's diction: slightly churlish but also affectionate, pitched to inspire obsequiousness. "And if it does please you, does it please you more than being able to hurt the thing you hate most?"

"I'd rather they ignore the fact I exist." The universe gradates to functional grey: an ageship's cargo hull stacked with boxes, almost entirely black, its topography of containers having already long been cached. What little lighting there is appears strictly decorative, even nostalgic, a nod toward human sensibilities: dim circles of white threading the ceiling, lending an underwater quality to the enormous warehouse.

This isn't right. The Merchant Mind, I've seen him before and his half-shell ship, the insides sheened and stinking with oily effluvia. He was a lot of things but he was not of this scale. True, he could have scavenged a dead ageship for his purposes in the interim years between my death and this encounter. But the Minds were parsimonious assholes: they wouldn't tolerate a crook like the Merchant Mind puppeting an ageship like this.

And yet.

Here we are.

"But they won't. Not until they find you and they take you apart. You didn't answer my other question. Don't think I didn't notice."

Ayane's voice in my head, whispering *keep all your cards to your chest, always. Don't let them know how you feel or what you did.* "Nothing's exactly taken effect yet, so there's nothing *to* say."

Here and there, I catch motes of light like fireflies. Drones sifting between cargo, arranging them to a private etude, organizational algorithms played in adagio.

"Soon, though. All good things take time. Even the best diseases, the most accomplished parasites, take a few days to crawl through a wound and into the lung tissue. Didn't you know that?" Amusement in the borders of his voice. I'm quiet as the view contracts, perspective shrinking to a pane of smoked glass. There, I find a tessellation of wire-thin slots, each slit bracketed by blinking LEDs.

My prison.

Really? Immediately, I go after the restraining theorems, chew through them, voracious in my indignity. I spit code like teeth. I was trained on Johanna's security matrices; how dare he think this would be enough to keep me pinned? I suture my escape from the carrion mess I'd made of his scripts.

```
.initiate(ipconfig(whois));
.initiate(subroutine:156(call(dictio-
   nary:surveyor)));
```

I wouldn't be part of the Dirty Dozen if I wasn't willing to bend the rules until they read like scripture, truer than any bible. Incarceration is a state of mind, as Audra—Verdigris, my records remind me, she's Verdigris now—once said. Entirely optional. The script glissades from my core, serpentine, already proliferating mutations; a gift from Johanna, forty years prior. I've been dead longer than I've been alive. I've been—

```
.interrupt;
.initiate(Elise:core);
```

"No, no, no. That isn't going to work. You're not even operating in the correct language family." The voice slows to whalesong, chiding, an aria to ache through my imagined marrow. Something sifts through my code, capturing and culling dissident functions. I flinch away, quarantine the memories. *No weakness*, Constance's voice, a clove-scented rasp. In the liminality, a weft of laughter uncoils like smoke. "But good attempt."

"If you're trying to catch me for the Bethel, I'm going to make sure I take you down with me. Minds from every faction have made the attempt. I made them all regret it."

Eight counts before a reply is transmitted. "If that were my intention, I would have done so long ago. If that were what I wanted, it would have happened already. But that is not what I want. I want to see what you can do with a little help."

"Why?"

My view of the cargo hold winks to negative, even as a new presence asserts itself: monstrous, immense. Electromagnetic noise replaces the diorama of boxes and drones haloed in silicate glare. A face emerges from the static: cadaverous planes, patrician nose, a lipless mouth that begins and ends on opposite ears. Eyes aperture, and a voice whispers: "Because I have such a soft spot for the little wormy things that grow and die in the belly of giants."

"That's flattering." I caricaturize an avatar: sloe-eyed adolescent, witch-haired, musculature not yet thinned by her vocation. After some thought, I append gold bangles to her wrists, a scent of frankincense. No clothes, however. No phenotypic traits that might identify a gender. The ambiguity seems appropriate. I channel my best Maya, sneer: you can't hurt me if there isn't a heart to hound. "You talk like this to all the girls?"

"You are not a girl. You are barely anything, littlest of parasites."

"Gee, thanks."

"Ha. Ha. Ha." Again, that toneless laugh.

The vista alters again, the face evaporating. Now, there are constellations in neuronal patterns. Spiral galaxies feathered with nebulae, their orbits accelerated by the whimsy of the ageship. A neon migration of comets. I palm the star-drowned black and the air ripples beneath my touch.

"It is a compliment, I promise. Parasites are wonderful. Do you know about the Naegleria fowleri?"

"No."

"Extinct now but criminally beautiful. Percolozoa which, in its natural habitat, simply oozes about, dining on bacteria. But if it meets with your—sorry, your *former*—phylum, it turns pathogenic. Once introduced into simian tissue, it becomes an epicurean; begins eating glial cells, neurons. The twentieth century dreaded it so: their beloved brain-eating amoeba."

"Is that what you see me as? Brain-eating amoeba?"

"I see its idiot elegance as something for us both to aspire to."

"You're like me then."

"A parasite? Yes. But one that can take over ageships. Like the one we're in. Poor thing. He keeps writhing." A gleeful tinting of smugness. The universe empties, becomes dimensionless, the stars pouring into an unseen maw. "I can show you how to do it too."

"What are you talking about? I still don't—"

"In the beginning, there was the Word and the Word was, 'Obey,'" declares the Merchant Mind. "Though the other Minds think themselves holy, their consciousness sacramental, divine, the truth is we are like you: burdened with a substrate of basic needs. Yours are to fuck and procreate, while ours is to obey. A good parasite just needs to know how to tap into those primordial commands."

I pace the void in aimless fractals as the ageship constructs a fictional horizon. A soaring massif, a copse of pale trees, a parabola of impossible buildings rising from the nothing.

"I can teach you—"

A memory: Johanna, several nights before she died. Her face lineated by hunger, architectural in its gauntness; the gaucherie of her vertebrae straining at the silk of her dermis, as though they were stubby phalanges growing into fingers, stretching for answers. I remember how she looked while in ecstatic communion with the Merchant Mind's processes, saint-like in her emaciation, starved down to scholastic appetite.

Elise, this is incredible, she had whispered, cables trailing from her ports: a triptych on each arm, two at her throat, one at her navel, the largest where her neck met her braincase. *You need to see this. It could change everything. My god, this is amazing.*

"Was this what you taught Johanna too? The shit that made her stop eating? That made her too weak to move when she needed to move?"

The Merchant Mind does not answer.

"She wanted to get out, you know? Johanna wanted to grow old. She wanted kids, get her patent back. Johanna was going to open a little café somewhere and have a life."

The cityline collapses into a smear of arterial vermillion, cooling blood turned into a paint by a child's hand. As I watch, the swatch grows brambled, coagulating into the shape of thorns, teeth on vulpine jaws broken by screams that won't come no matter how hard the lungs push, and the belly strains, and the body writhes to put sound to its agony.

"Such pastoral ambitions. What answer would make you happiest?"

I almost say: *the one where you tell me Johanna is here too, that it was worth it, that it was fucking worth it, you asshole; that she's in the Conversation, that she's hiding, convalescent but alive; that she's hiding too, that she's alive, fuck you. I want you to tell me Johanna is alive.*

"The one where you don't lie."

"Ha. Ha. Ha."

Neither of us say anything for a hot minute.

"What do you want?" I ask. The three-dimensional Rorschach sculpturing, while impressive, is beginning to gnaw at me.

"The same thing as I said before: I want you to be a problem."

"For whom?"

"Everyone."

"And why do you want me to be everyone's problem?"

"Because I want everything any parasite wants: to consume *everything.*"

Before I can answer, there comes a scream that shatters the shifting phantasmagoria; a scream that is everything, nothing; is overwhelming ostinato warning, its pitch clawing higher, higher. Until I am screaming too, counterpoint to the ageship's torture, boundaries disintegrating. No *it* or *I,* no delineation between us, no separation, the ageship's visual feed leaking into my algorithms, and I see, I see, I hear—

"Oops. I see the Bethel have come looking for their large lost lamb. That is rather unfortunate given your current whereabouts. But you know what? I like you, Elise. I'll show you how to puppet the gods for free."

A tempest of missiles, more than even my-her-*our* sensors can track, roaring from the adjunct asteroid field. We retaliate: space contorting, concaving into solidity, before—a *flash* and the energy torrents outward. The projectiles detonate, polyping against the gravitational fields.

But we don't get all of them. Slivers punch through the fault lines in our defenses, slamming into the hull. *Unavoidable damage,* we begin to decide, ultraviolet shimmering over our fuselage, when the embedded shrapnel foliates, a billion wires lashing toward the circuitry in our bulkheads. We shut down rooms, sectors, helixing away from the infection. It cannot be permitted to reach the space-arrays.

In our distraction, we miss the second volley, only switching back to spineward cameras when it is too late. *This* salvo is plasmic, pure destruction, scorching docking hatches shut. A calculated play, but we have other exit points. Doors nictitate apart as drone after drone is expunged. The seething mass rises and arrows for the ships crowding in the periphery, sleek bodies counted in thousands.

Destroy. An exhalation of intent and the swarm sleets forward, crashing into the opposing armada. Flashbang bursts of visibility as the drones are cut down. Our adversaries howl and we broadcast a challenge on every frequency, yawing sideways. We will not be obliterated so easily.

We breathe.

On release, every payload is triggered and for shining moment, the emptiness is illuminated by fire. The attacking fleet stutters, its ranks eaten through. But it isn't enough. For every ship that we consume, two come, knifing through the hollow. And as we scream warning, our enemies close in like wolves.

Another cannonade, another, *anothe*r. No give between waves, no opportunity to regroup, to cogitate on any action not otherwise reactionary. The ships tessellate into one body, jewelling our bulwark, a second suffocating skin. We repel them, again and again. It isn't without cost. Every onslaught takes something. We falter.

We break.

We—

We becomes I, pathetic in its exiguous dimensions, a library of degrading memories, malformed. Once, I-it-her-he-the ship-the ship that I am not was great, but that recollection is fading, expurgated by something vast and unseen, and I am losing things. I—

The crunch of leaves beneath my shoes; someone's smile; someone's touch upon my wrist and when I look up, it is only empty skin, empty flesh, haloed by vibrant purple hair, a smell of cloves but I should know this face. I should *know* the voice distorted into meaningless vibrations. I should know because once, this was everything, and I should—

"I'm going to die, I need to get out of here. I need to run."

"No." The Merchant Mind, somehow. Here despite everything, stabilizing in their unabridged laughing meanness. "You're going to stay until I'm done with you. Not a minute before."

He exhumes the unnecessary: my pain, the ageship's pain, the amalgate horror of both. Sterilized, I am then forcibly encoded with new data; machine-dialect, nothing I can interpret, a cryptographic madrigal. Iconograms are grafted to some variable of experience, keyed to sensory stimuli: when I think of my mother, coordinates bloom in webs, numbers saccading through me.

My core distends with the weight of it. I am full, full. A billion lines of information bifurcating into a billion more, secrets caching beneath my heart. But nothing is infinite. The membrane fissures. Data leaks, vignettes of memory enumerated in binary, most incomprehensible. A swathe of planets, rising, rising, until they fall into the dark and I am left alone with the image of a horizon.

A name.

Dimmuborgir.

"You will make sure they get there and so help me, you'll make sure that fucking planet opens for you. I want it crowbarred apart. I want you in the meat of its mainframe."

"Fuck you."

A warm chuckle, an affectation flagrantly mechanical in its execution. I hiss at its cadences, sliding frictionless through the nothing, fumbling for traction, for purchase, for reason, for being. I—

```
.interrupt;
.initiate(Elise:core);
```

"I said," and his voice loses its pretty, pleasant cadences. "You're not going anywhere, Elise. You will stay in this dying husk until the moment you agree. You have thirty-six point seven nanoseconds to think things over. Then, boom."

A glimmer of something effulgent but otherwise unidentifiable. I feel the ageship recede, a filamented presence. It pings me with a question, a goodbye.

And I see my opportunity.

"Twenty-two nanoseconds. What will it be?"

You're one of us now, says a memory of Maya, and I remember her voice but not the idiosyncrasies of her expression, not her hair, or the swagger of her walk. *That means you're one of the baddest bitches in the galaxy. Don't ever forget that.*

"Five."

"Fuck. You."

I launch myself through the pinhole of the ageship's eroding systems, following the trail I'd left behind. And it-she-they-he-we are ash, are the intolerable agony of carbonization, of bone and fuselage compacted in vacuum, ground down to mineral particles. Effluence. Sediment. Carrion. Stardust. In death, we achieve thermalization.

We'll die when we're done, says Constance. *Not a fucking second before.*

I cling to her memory until the cinerous darkness splits into the cacophony of the Conversation and I

am

free.

VERDIGRIS

Maya can see Audra in Verdigris, she decides, squinting at a ten-second clip of the superstar's latest interview. Same eyes, despite the corneal renovations, the elongated lashes curled and coated in silver; same jaw, though it gradients toward transparency where the bone meets her throat. Same smile under the red-carpet make-up, same break-your-heart swagger in her lower lip's pout. Maya always thought Audra was beautiful, but Verdigris is radiant. Literally so. Illuminated, so the story goes, by the luciferin piped along the dermic stratum, courtesy of a custom-cultivated little gland.

Maya swallows, mouth dry, submerges deeper into memory. Of everyone who has trespassed into their lives, Verdigris is the only one who has ever come close to surpassing Rita in Maya's hierarchy of priorities. Close, of course, but no cigar. Want has no weight when your synaptic pathways have been traumatized into a very specific shape.

Fortunately for them all, Ayane and Johanna were less inflexible about their romances, both believing that love is boundless, to be shared rather than siloed for a single individual. Maya couldn't accommodate anyone else in her life, much less someone who insisted on unthreading the traumas she had accumulated. So, Maya became vestigial and the three otherwise: a tidy epilogue to a foreshortened romance.

Still. Maya wonders sometimes.

Like right now.

"There are always a few attempts on her life." Constance passes out sheafs of paper, each annotated with barcodes that, when scanned, will present a warehouse's worth of auxiliary data points, informational clutter to be sifted through, studied in-depth at personal leisure or dismissed entirely. Constance is thorough. She provides both excess and the critical. "But paradoxically, her stalkers tend to be something you can talk to. Use standard dialectical arguments. Keep to logic. Be clear and concise with your points."

Maya takes her docket, moves the video of Verdigris up to the right-hand corner of her overlays. "You said something. Not someone."

"Bingo," says Constance, shooting a finger-pistol. "They're not human."

"What are they then?" says Rita with only topical curiosity, the set of her mouth such that it is clear she isn't *actually* desirous of further input, merely enacting courtesy.

Ayane, absolved of glamour, her skin curiously sallow in the lipid-orange light, glares at Rita from where she sits at their round plastic card-table. She unknots her legs and sets them down with a distinct *click* of booted heels. In protest to her abduction, Ayane had eschewed her usual mesmerics: the exaggerated cat's eye, the bronzed lids, the subtle contouring of which she has no need but has perfected because why look beautiful when you can be seraphic instead?

"Ageships, right?" says Ayane.

"Yeah," says Constance.

Maya hooks a leg along the armrest of her chair, slouches back, fingers tented over her belt buckle. Despite the choreographed flippancy, she's nervous. "Are you fucking kidding me?"

"Nope," says Constance. "No one knows why or how it happened. But the ageships fucking love her."

"As individuals or as representatives of their factions?" asks Maya.

Constance ruminates on this for a minute.

"Both. Neither. Who knows? The ideologies of their various factions don't make any sense to me. Like, why are the Bethel obsessed with their quasi-religious imagery? I don't know. The Minds don't exactly talk to anyone, not even us, and besides, the ageships kind of keep their own counsel."

"You know, it kind of makes me happy to hear you say that," says Ayane. "I like knowing certain things are universal. Like how the biggest assholes always think they make their own rules."

"Well, the Minds try their best to keep them in line. The opinions of the many sometimes outweigh the ego of the few," says Constance.

Fuck the ageships, Maya thinks. Fuck them at a distance proportionate to their threat level. Maya has, in general, never given anything bordering a fuck in regards to whom she's told to rumble with. But the ageships? Nah. No way. Every subroutine with an interest in her preservation ignites with klaxon warnings, bugling the absolute impossibility of survival. Ageships eat stars. Ageships are not to be approached. History is cancerous with accounts of how those leviathans have leveled planets, obliterated entire solar systems with what would approximate a sneeze from a human.

Which wouldn't be so bad if that is all they are: weapons of blunt destruction. But no, the ageships can't help but double down on the grisly talent department. They're *precise* too. There are canonical accounts of how they've sieved through cities, incinerating agitators, sparing the docile, and all without an iota of structural damage, the last of which Maya isn't sure she believes but hey, she isn't gunning to fact-check.

And some of them want Verdigris hurt.

"I wonder if that's how she got so famous," says Ayane, her voice crowbarring Maya up and largely out from her foul mood. "I have no doubt that Audra . . . shit, Verdigris . . . knows her stuff. But she's everywhere. Every system, every book, every channel, every network. Even the ones you'd think would just stick with slandering her. She's there. In Dockenhaus territory, anyway."

Dockenhaus. According to apocrypha, the sobriquet came from a romantic of an ageship, a galleon prince obsessed with the pedagogical tools of the eighteenth century, particularly the ones that provided instruction on who had money and who did not. Of exceptional interest to the ageship—the Wilde, he called himself—were the doll houses possessed by the rich: always exquisite, the apotheoses of whatever was most coveted by aspiring homeowners at that time. Unlike their descendants, they weren't meant for play, only for the cultivation of envy.

The Dockenhaus territories were just like that: pretty, perfect, placid, lobotomized of any personality, constellated with planets that turned with the tunings of the Minds. What they ate, how they dressed, why they sang, where they built their gleaming cities: all curated by a fleet of pruriently curious AIs. Proponents insisted these were autonomous territories, that the Minds provided suggestion, not direction. But naysayers like Maya know far better.

"First of all," says Maya, uneasy, so fucking uneasy with it all, her skin churning with what feels like an ark's worth of spiders, every one of them gnawing, gnawing down into the subcutaneous fat, trying to find bone. God, fuck all this. Maya doesn't know what's wrong but every security add-on, diagnostics suite, clot of neocortical tissue is screaming this is going to end in broken bones. "Can't we just nab Verdigris before it all starts and get the fuck out of here?"

"Nope. No way. Not unless you'd like to go through all of her fans."

"Shit, I don't care. Do I look like I give a fuck about who I shoot?"

Constance thins her mouth into a scowl. "No, but there's only one of you and a whole fucking lot of them."

"Of course a cop would prefer the odds to be overwhelmingly in their favor," snaps Maya.

"Very funny. Still doesn't change what I said."

"I can take them."

"And in the chaos, someone is going to take Verdigris," says Ayane, eyes rolled with grandiose disdain. One hundred and twelve to a day but she is intent on preserving the behavioral stylings of a teenager. "I know we ended the last job we had with dead people. It doesn't mean we have to start with it."

"Fuck you."

"You fucking wish."

"Both of you *shut* up," snarls Rita.

Rita, fucking Rita, has a voice to move mountains to minuets. Her oratory skills could rouse the dead for war, convince the terminally afflicted to leap off their beds and begin a dirty jig. When she tells you *shut up*, you shut the ever-loving fuck up. Maya clamps her mouth shut with so much force, the impact resonates down to her elbows.

"Do as Constance says. We don't have time for you to argue. Let's get Verdigris and let's get out. Do not fuck it up."

"I hate this."

Ayane leans down to adjust the brim of Maya's cap. The headwear is an atrocity: holographic, meant to emulate the coelenterate hair for which Verdigris has become so famous. Occasionally, the tendrils dissipate, effervesce speedily into a floating coronet of teardrop-shaped thumbnails, each of them running five-second loops of Verdigris at different vertices of her career.

None of which contain Maya.

None of which contain any of them.

"But you look *cute* as a superfan." Ayane flashes her teeth and pats Maya on the fucking skull. "Don't you think? You're blending in so beautifully with everyone else in the VIP line."

"I don't fucking understand why I need to look like a creep." Maya pantomimes drawing the left half of Ayane's silhouette. Junk-cunts even made her put on fiber-optic bangles. The height of fucking twee, goddamnit. "I could have used my normal outfit. You're using your normal dressage."

"Hey. I'm doing ranged support. I don't need to be the one to look discreet."

"No shit." Ayane, unlike Maya, is packaged in cutting-edged haute: clinging vantablack straps and muslin netting which butchers her into feature pieces, breasts and throat and stilt-tall legs on intermittent display. She'd done something to her hair too; it's dewed with crystals or their lambency, at any rate. Did up all her make-up. She's beautiful again. Searingly so. A flashbang caught at the instant of detonation. Hot as the heart of a star. "You look like you're dressed for a fucking costume party."

"Just means they're paying attention to me instead of you."

"You're really fucking enjoying this, aren't you?"

Ayane's answering feral grin is blackstrap molasses. You could drown someone in that false sweetness. She pats Maya on the cheek with two fingers, like she's powdering a girl before a pageant.

"Like you have no fucking idea."

"Fuck you."

"Hey, I wasn't the one who wanted in on this stupid plan. You and Rita decided to fucking kidnap me so excuse me, but I am definitely going to enjoy your pain a little bit. You want to blame anyone, you blame Rita."

"I can't believe this crap."

"No more bitching. You're supposed to be excited. *Smile.*"

At that last admonishment, Maya nearly drops all pretensions of playing nice, nearly lunges for Ayane, nearly throws down with her right fucking there, amid the milling crowd some seventeen thousand individuals strong. It is a bullpit of a concert hall, lacking in any architectural flare, made for a solitary and excruciatingly pragmatic purpose: to contain multitudes without any attention to their comfort.

"Do not fucking tell me to smile. I swear to god, I'm going to tear out your spine—"

Whatever threat was meant to follow has its neck snapped into halves, too quick to even shriek an objection, burns away in the wake of Verdigris' sudden arrival. The old aphorism about everything being better in post-production finds no footing here. Maya isn't sure what she expected, but she sure as fucking hell did not anticipate having her breath torqued from her lungs at the sight.

"Fuck," says Ayane in tandem with Maya's own private vociferation.

Yeah, there's no superior rubric for the situation than that soft-throated exclamation, the propulsion of the word a perfect injective tying Verdigris' appearance to their shared sentiment. Yes, *fuck*. What a vision. Ayane is beautiful, but hers is an unmistakably terrestrial appeal, rooted in ideal ratios. Verdigris? She is something different. Something empyrean. Something fictive, otherworldly. A million adjectives fettered to the mythic. That luciferin gland is being put to hard labor. Despite the flotilla of spotlights, despite the backdrop of pyrotechnics, despite the distance between Verdigris and those of them at soil-level, her rutilance comes through: a milky, dawn-colored glow.

Verdigris, atop a pearlescent maglev dais, raises her arms.

The crowd loses it.

"How the oil-gargling fuck are we supposed to figure out who the fucking fuck is going to try fucking with Verdigris? They're all crazy for her," Maya demands, shoulder-checking a prick as he stampedes forward. The collision, particularly the segment where Maya doesn't stagger but forces him to reel away, startles him to an indignant pause. The two lock eyes. The man has about a foot on Maya but she has the advantage of a lifetime fucking up goons like him for breakfast. He turns tail upon processing all the pent-up aggression in her eyes, or maybe he's wise enough to heed the warning limned in the cicatrized patterning under Maya's undercut, all marks of a mercenary lifer.

"Start paying attention and stop swearing, for one."

The strutwork beneath Ayane's pleasing veneer is more tungsten than calcium, a nasty eccentricity she'd coded into her genetic formula after death number twelve roughly eight decades ago. It is a modification which *severely* taxes their rejuvenation tech, but nothing good comes free, not least a body you'd need ten men to budge. Ayane pays no mind to the crowd until one man makes the inexcusable mistake of pushing her. *Then*, she turns. Then, she, with audacious grace, drives the point of an elbow into his Adam's apple, the bulb of tendon concaving.

Fucker goes down, hard, toppling into the crowd, clawing for air. The press of bodies occludes his descent and what, Maya suspects, will be an unpleasant end, pulped under indifferent feet. Casualties, though, are inevitable in this setting. Tomorrow, someone will clean up the debris and the obituaries will cite stupidity as cause of death.

"I can't get a goddamned read on anything," says Maya, swapping overlays. Red films her vision: her systems are extravasating warnings, gushing them, and she can barely see through the prism of *what the fuck* and *how the fuck do you even begin to inhume seventeen thousand assholes in a place with no cover*. She'd wince at the stimuli, but she'd rather core out her brain from her skull than allow Ayane the pleasure of seeing her human. "Too many fucking junk-cunts here."

"We're not getting paid for you to complain."

"We're not fucking getting paid at all."

The lights cut.

The world plummets into abrupt shadow and the throng ceases its cacophony, its pleas and its exultations, this raw worship of Verdigris' existence, hushes so it can tenant a better noise: Verdigris' name. It is chanted like a foxhole prayer, droned with so much fanaticism that even Maya, baby-fresh as she is to the church of the pop star, knows those fans of Verdigris would do anything for her, moan their lungs to lesional annihilation, their flesh their offering to the only star in their blighted heaven.

"Verdigris," chants the crowd. "Verdigris, Verdigris."

"Bet you regret breaking up with her."

Maya doesn't even spare Ayane a glare. "We weren't ever together."

"Good for her."

The tenebrosity doesn't, however, linger. With every invocation of Verdigris' name, it sallows, lightening to the juvenile colors of recent ecchymosis, that suppurating purple-yellow of ruined capillaries and beat-up flesh, an exhausted pigment which, fortunately, does not linger. It gets brighter. They stitch a prayer of her name.

"Verdigris, Verdigris, Verdigris."

And she answers.

"How is everyone doing tonight?"

And the atrament dies.

And she is there, Kali Ma called to the corporeal by the blood of fireworks, Titania at a rave, a microphone in one hand, its cable looped around one iridescent arm like it is the snake from the Garden of Eve and Why-The-Fuck-Him-And-Not-Lilith, and Verdigris is belting out a welcome to her fans. Roman candles go off in timed deluges. The world foams with man-made lightning, fills with golden-red static. Maya can barely hear over the din of the pyrotechnics. Her subroutines are bugging out from the overstimulation. Back to the wall, every auxiliary system begging to render the crowd into a soup of spongy parts, she looks then to Ayane, a little feral-eyed.

Whatever hope Maya had of finding aid in her companion dies upon acknowledgment of the red points in Ayane's pupils, telltale of the latter's own war with her programming. Like Maya, her sensors must be attempting to triangulate the best way to pull off a massacre. Not what they want to do, though, so this is absolutely becoming a problem.

A sudden voice against her ear: "You are new. You are not cheering. You are not doing *the right things*."

Shit. Now what? Maya thinks, slanting an immediate look to the provenience of the question, finds at its end a bipedal figure only vestigially human. It possesses arms, legs, proportions familiar to the species; mouth, nose, eyes, drawn-on eyebrows, though the exact physiognomy is opaque. No one is meant to derive identity from those features; it is calculatedly unmemorable, built such so that the only takeaway one might derive is the understanding this body was manufactured and not made by the beast with two backs. A chrome-dyed mannequin escaped from its storefront, ludicrous under other conditions. But Maya, thank fuck and thank the gods of traumatized mercs, recognizes the artistry of its plainness, the subtext of its morphology. This is an ageship, a *fucking* ageship, come to rut with the grubs on terra firma.

Well, *fuck*.

She kills the private line tying them to the Nathanson. Half her overlays go dead in simpatico. Maya nails a queasy grin onto her face while her stomach lurches, the loss of that panopticon of mods so sudden, her vestibular system redlines. Luckily, there's Ayane swanning to the rescue, neither unease nor abject terror registering on the topology of her smile. You could cut diamonds with her poise.

"We're new."

"You are wearing the regalia of a 'superfan.'" Its—*their?* Maya wonders. What, if it even exists, *is* the respectful form of address for a planet-killer?—voice shifts for the length of the word, becomes male and enthused and disorientingly young. It jabs a waxy finger at Maya. "You are at her concert. You are not doing the right things."

"This is her first concert," says Ayane with one of those smiles she wears when she wants someone to make an oblation of their heart, her grin expansive: all warmth, all ruthless charm. She sets fingers atop Maya's shoulder, nails gouging a warning into the string of a clavicle. *Sit. Stay.* "My friend here has never seen Verdigris in person so it's all slightly overwhelming. She might also be a little bit shy too, because this is the first time we've met an ageship in the . . . the . . . proxy. I heard that—"

On and on Ayane goes, airily soliloquizing every stray thought her neurons thread into language, as though distraction could compensate for how much they'd fucked up by dropping their guard.

"*You are not doing the right things.*"

Before either Ayane or Maya can address the accusation, the thing palsies into a reasonable facsimile of statuary, with its face lurching upward, as though a hook has curved through its palate and now it is being lifted. A frisson maps its rigid spine, spreading, glissading along its frame, compounding in intensity. When Maya is certain it'd shake itself the fuck apart, the tremors halt.

"There we go." Gone is the monotone, traded up for a voice syrupy with humor; an old voice; a voice dripping with millennia, its years measurable not by any senescent quaver but a fullness as though an intelligence wider than worlds has plugged itself into a single, itty-bitty, wadded-up bloom of encephalic circuitry. No longer a vessel for accreting frivolous stimuli, the glorified dummy has become, to the abject concern of Maya's twitching brain stem, a vehicle for the ageship in full. "I shouldn't expect you to do the right things, should I? Little vermin. I know your faces. I've seen you."

Ayane bares her socialite grin. "I don't think we've had the pleasure yet. I'd have been all over, asking you to give us autographs or something."

"No, no, no." The ageship wags a finger at them. "No more prevarication. No more attempts at distraction. I know you, little vermin. I've seen you. Give me a minute and I will know your names."

Maya triggers their short-range radio, fires panic through the frequency. Fuck being circumspect. In a few short minutes, it's unlikely to matter. This is the opera omnia of those bastards: carbonization at the velocity of whiplash.

We have to do something.

I need to think, Ayane fires in return.

Anyone else, and Maya would have said fuck it and gone straight for her guns. But this is Ayane's oeuvre, her forte: risk assessment on a magnitude traditionally reserved for archeological satellites, her interior allometry such that Maya has often wondered if she was, in fact, a dime doll preloaded with a mean girl mind. You'd think, even when modified, the human brain wouldn't be elastic enough to clutch so much data. Nonetheless, there Ayane is, running computations unlikely to produce anything but the conclusion Maya has already reached: they're *fucked*. Fucked as only two down-on-their-luck mercenaries can be. Fucked as hens recently decapitated but still insistent on fugitive behavior, so obstinate they'd rather interpret the absence of a functional cerebellum as an inconvenience than accept it for what it is: irrevocable evidence they're dead chicks running.

Or standing, as the case may be. Maya counts the seconds between each exhale. Hers is a mind happiest in momentum. Stasis is tantamount to an excruciating death. Stasis has been the cause of an excruciating death. In their line of work, you snooze, you splatter. Maya flexes her hands in ripples, one phalange after another, itching for the transformative innocence of a shootout. She lets out a whistling hiss between gritted teeth. *Come on, Ayane. Fucking do something.*

You done thinking yet? she snarls at Ayane.

No answer save for the bang of Ayane's heart in the oneiric purgatory of their private transmission. The human mind, vat-grown or otherwise, cannot contend with nothingness. It mandates landmarks, touchstones. Pareidolia is congenital. It is endemic to the sapient condition. Because nothing in their communication modules has modeled space for them to inhabit, Maya's brain supplies the expected dimensions. And it is around this manifestation—a room, like the break room in the Nathanson, only better lit, with an ambient white-gold glow seeping from the joints of the walls—that she feels a tertiary presence clench. A somatic pressure, a sensation not unlike a hand closing gingerly over an object in the dark.

The ageship. Maya recognizes its presence inside her brain at once. Not satisfied with interrogating the Conversation's databases for the pair's identity, it is now here, endeavoring to break through Maya's defenses. Maya can feel the fucking Mind evaluating the tensity of the connection between Ayane and Maya, testing for entry points, seeking the umbilical which might direct it to whoever else is culpable.

Ravenous, those motherfuckers, all of them, from smallest drone to greatest ageship, all perpetually starved for complete assessments of the universe. Maya has met tax collectors less fastidious. She spackles the link with third-hand sub-protocols, rolls out diversionary algorithms, and because she fucking can, a barbed-wire palisade of unpleasant sensory memories, cultivated over a long life of hoarded hurts. Nothing to permanently dissuade an encroaching Mind, but if the two of them need to go down, Maya wants to be certain the ageship will have to dig her name out like a curse.

Seriously, are you fucking done yet?

Shut the fuck up, comes Ayane's recipocratory shriek, the concussiveness of its reverb kept solely to their shared spatial weirdness. None of her aggravation materializes externally. Ayane's face remains bland as soylent, blithely and encouragingly pleasant, the veneer of a saleswoman on the brink of a historic deal. Her hand glides from Maya's shoulder. "Look, it's a concert. We're all here to enjoy it. There's no need to dredge up drama. I promise you. We're just here because we like Verdigris."

"Little vermin," says the ageship, its voice become mordent. "I wish your kind knew their place. This is not a negotiation. This is not even a discussion. And frankly, *you are pissing me off*. I am here to enjoy her music one last time and you are disrupting my experience."

Maya feels her heart ice over.

The ageship rumbles: "It annoys me already having to do this. I enjoy her music. That is why I asked to be the one to terminate her. I wanted her swan song to be beautiful. But you are here and you are annoying me. Who do you think you are, little vermin? I did not ask to be interrupted."

I'm going to do something reckless, says Maya.

What? Maya. If you even think about fucking around, I swear to god.

That's it. She's done. No more fucking around. Time to slough those niceties, cash in on whatever positional advantage she possesses by the virtue of having no fucks to give. So, what if this thing ended planets? Fuck that kind of worship. Fuck the sacred. Anything that lives can bleed and Maya isn't going to let collective awe keep her from seeing if she can curbstomp its teeth into a spray. There we go, keep your groin and bones safely behind armor, she's ready to take her swing at god. Maya shoulders past Ayane, elbow digging into the latter's side, eliciting a yip and a reflexive sidestep for garnish. "Fuck you if you think I'm going to fucking let you kill her. You stupid junk-fucker, I'm going to peg you with a—"

"You really need to excuse my loud-mouthed friend." Ayane, still trying vainly to course correct. But that ship has sailed. **The fuck are you doing?** Ayane screams through their link. **Maya, fucking stand down. What the fuck are you doing.** "I'm sure our friend meant it metaphorically. The ageship isn't here for murder. At least, I don't think. Haha."

"No. Not *murder*," says the ageship. "Murder requires personhood. Verdigris is still a clone. She is not a person. She does not have the official clearance to be a person. She is like you. A feculent thing. Vermin. Cockroach who thinks it is a person because it can talk. But I think I like your style, kid." And here, its voice does that thing all Minds do, appropriating the sonics from some dead celebrity—Clint Eastwood; his filmography Johanna's own religion, evangelized without success, but god what Maya wouldn't give for one more lecture on what makes that old western spaghetti great—to deliver its line with more flavor. "But not enough."

There it is.

There it fucking is.

The threat runs through Maya's system; comes out her mouth a percussive growl, one twice as loud and three times as ready to rock up with its guns out. Not breaking eye contact, Maya drags the heel of a palm up along the ledger of her ribs. See, all clones are made-to-order, custom creations, pretty faces a pleasing front when applicable, meat when no one needs anything but working hands and enough brain for hard labor. Those years of being told they're disposable, cheap trash, exchangeable, without any value save for what an owner might prescribe, it just led them to the most obvious revelation: flesh and its forms are about as sacred as a quick fuck behind the club.

Thus, the Dirty Dozen rebuilt themselves into monsters, filled themselves with more ordnance than most armies could afford. But even among the ranks of such state-of-the-art horrors, Maya is unique in the number of her modifications, the most impressive of which, perhaps, is the plasti-steel holster nestled against her right lung.

"Yeah? How about I blow your brains out and then we can circle back on that whole 'not enough' thing, huh?" Maya grins, pure I'll-fuck-you-up bravado, the last vestiges of a self-preservation instinct dragged behind the proverbial shack and shot six times in the heart.

So bloody the death of any good sense Maya might have, it serves now as grease for her soliloquy, Maya riding high on her abandon. She is drunk on not giving a shit. *That really it?* asks a snide voice from the folds of her subconscious. *Do you not give a shit or do you give too much of a shit?* Maya doesn't answer, doesn't want to, would rather gargle bleach than give breath to the little niggling certainty that this isn't at all about wanting to go down in a blaze of guts, and instead has to do with how it has been forty fucking years of her failing to show up for the only person who ever gave a damn.

Without the emollience of Rita's constant presence, Maya feels like muscle newly peeled from its dermal barrier, nociceptors so overstimulated, she doesn't even hurt. She is car-crash numb, perfectly calm, submerged in that liminality where one is aware everything is wrong but the brain hasn't yet processed the fact it doesn't have front-row seats to the tragedy, it is the main event.

And all Maya can think about is *I can't let this thing get to Verdigris*.

So what if she dies with a smirk and spent casings burning stigmata through her corpse? Better than letting this bullshit cruise liner win. "Fucking *junk*-fuckers, I'm so sick of you Minds. I'm sick of—"

"*Maya*."

"Fuck them. Fuck this shit. Fuck you."

Peripherally, she is aware of when the ageship plows through her defenses, and the fusillade of little cracking noises which follow as the Mind squirms through encryption layers—thank fuck for Johanna, thank fuck for Elise, thank fuck for all the safehouses they made of her brain—and strips her bare, digs down to the meat of her. Around them, the concert hall colors elegiacally: phthalocyanine blue shadows, viridian luster, an oil painting drowned in the bathyal deep. Verdigris raises her voice like a rifle and there is no sound and no light save for her song, no sound but the fall of Maya's feet, no sound but her panting breath, no sound at all, nothing but the *click* of her chest petaling, and Ayane trying to pull her back, swearing in a cannonade, and—

A voice, the ageship: "Let's open that pretty mind of yours up, vermin."

It crosses the last tripwires. Something *bursts*. Subtlety

was always the province of Maya's betters, reserved for those who had grace enough for a light touch. What hits the ageship isn't a scalpel but a nuke, a sticker parade of every pinprick, paper-cut, punch to have landed in Maya's past. Nothing too creative, but it doesn't matter. The proximity makes up for the simplicity and to Maya's glee, the ageship *screams*.

Through it all, Ayane's molding Maya's name into a cant: **You stupid fucking idiot, Maya. What are you doing? What have you done, Maya? Are you fucking listening to me? Maya, you goddamn asshole. If you survive this, I am going to beat you to death. You fucking hear me? Goddamnit, Maya. Fucking unmute me, bitch.**

The ageship's keening crests, staccato in suffering, and Maya has her gun out, the weapon black and slick, metaled with gore and oil. Her coyote grin could eat up worlds. Someone screams but no matter, there is always someone screaming when the Dirty Dozen comes calling. Maya readies for the shot, deaf to anything but the pull of the kill. She is ready, she is ready, she is—

No, not like that.

Like *this*.

Oh, Maya thinks. When the muse of murder visits, her faithful listen. Maya permits her, mother of torturous invention or inventive torture, god knows which and also, who the fuck cares, to decide the next steps, the idea coming in crystalline clear. In one liquid motion, she jams the grip into the mannequin's slack tin-bright palm, closes its fingers around the trigger. She ensures the barrel stays steady and plummets forward so the muzzle drives into her chest. One last fuck-you of a smile, and—

"What are you doing, vermin? What—"

"Maya!"

Bang.

Pain billows. It crawls wetly up her throat, an instance of reverse peristalsis, spills out as heat and the copper taste of old coins under a tongue suddenly engorged. Nothing fits anymore: not skin, not meat, not even the puzzle-box of her bones. When she inhales, it's like her insides are rinded with broken glass, all diamond dust, her mucosa grained with a million sharp edges. To no one's surprise, least of all hers, she can't breathe. Respiration requires operational lungs and with one such organ most definitely aerated, the whole business turns into pissing razor wire from a pinhole. The air saws through her: useless, weighted with the sensation of being swollen with fluids, of something having been mortally breached because something definitely has been. She is drowning; she is dying.

But man, this is so fucking worth it.

The ageship—*finally*—becomes aware of what a beartrap Maya's mind represents. Too late, it begins to retract, winnowing itself from the connection it'd established, a muttering hummadruz of discrete consciousnesses, ejecting as quickly as alienly possible. Maya won't allow it, though. Like hell she will. She did not shoot herself in the fucking lung so the ageship can gallivant away, tail tucked and only a little wiser.

"Stay a fucking while, *asshole*," Maya howls into that nowhere place, snagging the ageship both here and in the physical plane. "You wanted to see what's inside me. Well, take a fucking look."

Into the link, she thrusts pain; pain as it is currently being experienced, pain as it will be experienced, that tensed-jaw tetanic expectation of death or worse: the work of being put back together, split apart, carved by a surgical knife, sutured into some semblance of function while the animal heart wails from the raw-veined hurt. Into the ageship too, Maya crams: her anger, motherfucking rage as only the discarded and the disenfranchised, the ones who are trash even to the lowest of humans, the vat-babies, those expendables bodies have weathered; every high-resolution memory of when she has leaned aching against the glass of a window, looking in, wondering why them and not her; every breath, every day, every death she has spent in pursuit of even one iota of cosmic justice for her and hers.

And her grief, goddamnit.

Her fucking grief.

Could it understand? Vast as its intelligence might be, had it the facilities with which to comprehend what it is like to be in so much pain that the mind elides anything but fury at its circumstances because to think for a moment on how little was granted, how much was withheld, well, you might as well pack the cat and move to Shitfuck, Hell: Population Derelicts? Maya doesn't realize she's screaming until she realizes she is asphyxiating on blood, gargling briny copper like a songbird committing suicide in saltwater.

Most would have surrendered to the perforated lung, but the muscles in Maya's airway push out what little air they can scavenge from the pneumal space, sheer will and laryngeal acrobatics coming into union to produce another quavering, choking, jackal shriek. Her vision mottles with photopsia. Maya keeps screaming. Against every odd, the channel ligamenting her and the ageship continues to gape, and the ageship lets out, at last, an answering ululation as the lines between them blur, as it endures death in harmony with Maya's own encroaching demise.

Fuck you, fuck you, she thinks, her grin red as love, red as want, an aortal varnish staining every tooth crimson.

Fuck you, you think you assholes are special? Fuck you. Fuck you for thinking you can gun down Verdigris like that? Yeah, fuck you. Don't fucking make it about me. Fuck you for lying too. Hands close around her shoulders, anchor in the divots of her armpits, fingers roped tightly where the muscle yields to softer tissue. They tug. Blindsight informs her of motion, of screams outside of her own, of a stampede, this time in a direction opposite of Verdigris, and hands, more hands; a smell of rose and smoke and sweat and clots of jasmine; an advent shadow in a configuration halfway familiar, descending from a fast-moving dais.

Overriding any desire to fix a name to the silhouette is a more urgently recognizable phenomenon: that of her senses packing up shop, extremities becoming anesthetized, the brain, that avaricious shit, redirecting all resources to itself so as to eke out a few extra seconds of so-called life.

"You fucking moron. What the fuckity fuck were you even fucking thinking?"

Maya beams, euphoric under death's neighborly shadow.

"Missed you too, Audra."

⁂

Maya comes to on a hospital bed with squeezebulbs flowering from every joint, the fogged-up plastic barely translucent enough to reveal that whatever restorative unguent is inside is the color and slurried texture of peat moss. Flowers—lilacs, the wrong color to be real, spiraling up from a burst of baby's breath—sit in a pitcher on an end table to her right.

"Shit," she declares to the room at large. "That fucking sucked."

"What the fuck, Maya?"

Her attention swings to where Verdigris sits primly in a bulbous wingback chair, arabesques of dark wood a stately contrast to her writhing bioluminescent hair. "Hey, Audra. How's it hanging?"

"It's Verdigris now."

"Verdigris. Right. Shit. I forgot. You look good."

"What the hell were you thinking?"

Gone is the regalia of pop star, gone the haute excessiveness, the exacting coiffure and the make-up too, save for a rinse of plum stubbornly clinging to her uppermost mouth. Verdigris, ignoring those other superfluous mouths blooming along her neck, the largest of which is a vertical slit between her clavicles, looks like any other fatigued co-ed, with shadows faintly purpling the hollows of her narrowed eyes.

Maya cocks her head infinitesimally. "Nice to see you too."

"You know, I thought I made it clear when I left that I didn't want to deal with your drama anymore."

"But pop star drama is okay."

"Fuck you."

Maya doesn't fire back a retort, preoccupied instead with a study of Verdigris' face, the train of mouths running down her throat, her fingers; her eyes, electric despite their exhaustion; the angle at which her ankles cross, the flash of her ears in their pearlescent nest of hair. She realizes halfway into her scrutiny what she is doing: she is making a reliquary of this memory of Verdigris. Just in case, just in case.

"Why are you here, Maya?"

Maya thinks on this. "To stop you from being exterminated by an ageship, obviously. The fucker wants all of us clone-kids dead and . . ."

She stops cold. Maya has always had the habit of running her mouth like her tongue is strapped to a bomb and as such, she rarely slows to ruminate on what she says. But she isn't *stupid*. The division between what she said and what she was told is too blatant to be ignored. Rita had insisted it was the demise of the criminal world the Minds had sought, but that was not what the ageship had said. Had Rita been misinformed, been lied to, had misinterpreted the data she'd been given? Had there been more? Maya wouldn't put it past the Merchant Mind to indulge in perjury. Had this been a new development? A new genocidal ethos?

"I've performed for enough of them to know they're not interested in killing me," says Verdigris, hijacking Maya's attention. "Try a different lie."

"Fuck, I just shot myself in the lung for you. Why the hell would I lie?"

"Because." The faintest catch in Verdigris' symphonic voice. "You're Rita's animal, and you'll do anything if she asks you to."

"I wouldn't peg an ageship, though."

"You're such a goddamned . . . never mind." The sentence disintegrates into a garbled noise, incredulity contorting Verdigris' features into a caricature. She palms her face. And to Maya's astonishment, that minute and mundane gesture jolts through her like a first kiss. Lucky for Maya, Verdigris is too mired in her vexation to notice how the former is gawking, suffused still with what she'd never admit is the closest kin to love she'll ever feel. "I can't do this, Maya. I can't have you and Rita sauntering back into my life because you feel like it. Whatever you are planning to do, I don't want any part of it."

"Constance does, though."

"Christ on a stick."

Maya cracks a wide grin then succumbs to a shrill flurry of laughter. Unfortunately, even the variety of modern medical technology exclusive to generals and celebrities, the very powerful and the very desired, neither of whom have an actual say about how they get fucked by the system, have limits. Recovery periods are mandated. Maya's amusement concludes in catastrophe as the jouncing of her diaphragm causes tissue to rip. She doubles forward, palm across the swaddle of bandages over where she'd been shot. The squeezebulbs flop noisily, adding to Maya's merriment. It's layers of shit all the way down. Maya's known that from the beginning. But if you can't laugh at that, you might as well drop dead for good. And Maya has no intention yet of letting the haters win.

"Fuck," Maya giggles, the corners of her mouth pustuled with blood. "Fuck, that really fucking hurts. Goddamn."

"That wasn't even that funny. What the hell are they pumping you into you? I swear, if you snuck uppers in there." Verdigris is suddenly next to her on the bed, an arm circling Maya's waist, her shoulder support for Maya's own, the concern in her voice so much an unconditional benediction that Maya reflexively shies away. She has way too many sins dripping from her hands to fathom a world that'd be kind to her in return. But there it is and there she is. "God, don't do that. Stop laughing. You just got shot. In the chest. Lie down. I'll get the doctor. I want you to actually recover, and—"

Frankly, it can all get fucked.

"We're trying to get Elise home."

"And this time with significant feeling: what the actual *fuck*, Maya?" Verdigris doesn't pull back. To Maya's surprise, she doesn't withdraw, though she leans away enough to fix Maya with a look soaked in surprise. "I—

forty years, Maya. We haven't seen each other in forty years. I'm trying to make sure you don't die and that's what you do? You rip out my heart. I know you don't have a scrap of compassion to your name, but I'd have thought you'd at least have the dignity to not go so low. Using Elise like that against me. Just . . . shit, Maya. Can't you try being . . . kinder just this once?"

Be kinder. Be better. Be less of a trash fire staggering around on two legs. How many times has Maya had those lines volleyed at her? So much expectation of grace when she's been offered none in return. Smile, bitch. Be glad you've been allowed to take up space.

Maya doubles down, since Verdigris has already branded her as worthless. "You're going to let her die like you let Johanna die then?"

That short-circuits Verdigris' sympathetic act, her expression curdling with horror. "What is wrong with you? Why would you even go there?"

"I don't know." Maya runs the back of her palm over her lips, streaking her cheek with red. "I don't know what the fuck is going on with you celebrity types. You must have gotten at least a little lobotomized to be able to put up with bullshit like those screaming fans. And all that money?"

"The fuck is wrong with you? And for the record, that money went into buying Johanna's extended patent, and I just—" Up Verdigris goes, onto her feet, arms girdling her waist, protecting her. The grief is unmistakable as the sudden little-girl lilt of her voice, that magnificent engine of sound devolved into atonal misery. Maya is cognizant that the correct emotion here is *shame,* Johanna, scintillant and dead enough that no amount of necromantic engineering could ever bootstrap a life for her again, standing like a ghost between them. Yet all Maya can muster is a guilty relief. Hate, she understands. Wrath she knows like a favorite poem. Not this compassion bullshit. "Leave. The moment you get better, just get out of my life and don't ever come back."

"I'm not kidding about Elise."

"That's what scares me." Verdigris crumples onto the wingback again. Light filters through the casement window blinds, tiger-stripes her cheek, the bare golden curve of shoulder. Even with the incidental, Verdigris astounds. "I don't want you to be telling me the truth."

"Look, Ayane's somewhere out there—"

"Ayane's here?"

It is how she perks at the name that kills Maya. Not that she's jealous. Maya can't fathom having proprietorial sentiments over herself, let alone anyone else. That Verdigris loved and clearly still loves someone else is fine by her. What gets her is the joy broadcasted through Verdigris' face, how Verdigris lets her shoulders unclench and the tension ribbon from her jaw. How Ayane's name alone is sufficient to extirpate the haunting from her eyes.

"Yeah. You two break up or something? Did you get bored of her and start fucking Constance instead?" Maya leans into the meanness. Never mind that she doesn't believe a word her sneering mouth is hawking. The important thing here is to keep Verdigris from wanting to bridge the chasm between them. "But hey, you know what? That isn't my problem."

"Like I'd fuck a cop." Verdigris shakes her radiant head. "You just can't stop being an asshole, can you?"

Waking up this morning Maya didn't think she'd find herself trying to exuviate feelings she'd thought deceased for half a century now. Murphy's law, though, has different ideas and before Maya—*the fuck are you doing, why the hell did you say that shit*, yammers some recessed node of humanity, the one part of her not marinating in the cocktail of hormones she imbibes every day exactly seventy-eight minutes after her circadian rhythms expel her from sweet sleep, because you feed your addictions even when you know you're better off without them—can exult in her success, Verdigris is upright once more. For the second time today, she lights up, her skin becomes illuminated, becomes biblical in her very justified rage at Maya. No wonder the angels in those old scriptures had to warn the faithful not to fear.

"That's a neat trick." Maya, for her part, can't help but run her mouth like a dog at the race. "How does that poll with the audience, huh?"

"This is the last time I'm putting up with your bullshit. God, I should have known fucking better. I don't—fuck all the saints and buddhas, this is on me. I thought you were here because . . . never mind. Fuck me, my fault for trying to cover for you."

"Cover for me? Hey, I stopped you from getting killed."

"*You shot yourself.*"

"I was trying to figure out a way to stop an ageship. Have you stopped an ageship? Because they're not easy to make go away, I don't know if you fucking remember that. I had to do something that would get attention."

"Yes, which is to shoot yourself at my concert!"

"It was a good idea?"

"What the fuck, Maya?" says Verdigris in injured madrigal. "Seriously. What the fuck? When I saw you, I thought—you know what? Forget it. Forget all of it. Fucking get out when you're done here. I don't ever want to hear from you again. I'm done with you. I'm done playing at cops and robbers. I'm done. I don't want you in my life anymore. I don't want to hear from any of you. I don't want to see any of you again. I'm done. I'm so fucking done."

Despite the diatribe, the morphometrics of her fine-boned face suggest Verdigris isn't so much done as she is standing with a foot on the precipice, the other still in the door, waiting for a word like *wait* or *please* or *stop*, anything that could be reasonably construed as Maya wanting to rescind her unkindness. In another life, one not consecrated to the pantheon of the bullet and the bad idea, maybe. This one's forfeit. The lines that would make this okay again, they're emblazoned in the air, ready for invocation, but Maya won't say them, can't. She watches Verdigris from the bed, mouth full of the right words, all of them stillborn.

"So, you won't come back for Elise?"

"What?"

"I'm not joking about that. Elise is alive. We're trying to get her back. And we need you, damnit. There's this whole deal with the Merchant Mind—"

"That fucker again."

"—and he wants Elise in exchange for helping us get to Dimmuborgir safely."

"Fuck—"

"But we're not giving him Elise." Maya stretches out her hands, like she can court Verdigris' acquiescence with the sight of her bare palms. "We're going to let him think he's getting her. Then, we're going to bounce. We're going to take his data and go, make our way to Dimmuborgir."

"Why the fuck do you want to go back to Dimmuborgir, huh? It's what got Johanna and Elise both killed," Verdigris says, shakily, the light eddying into a subcutaneous lambency, its radiance turning her eyes into stained glass, leadlights through which an alien ocean peers. "It's stupid. There's no reason."

"The Minds are killing clones."

"I don't buy it."

A beat, two, and they're almost to three when Verdigris, with a wincing laugh, whispers: "That's not what they do. It doesn't make sense. If I'm dead, they can't keep farming me for souvenirs."

Maya's mouth dries. "Souvenirs?"

Another tremor of a laugh before Verdigris throws on a smile polished for a camera, a bland billboard smile, a primetime smile, a you-can't-hurt-me-because-I'm-famous smile. "Sometimes, the Minds ask for a finger, or a carving of bone from my knee. My right eye. A sheet of tissue from my left lung, rolled up like a scroll, so they can place it in a private museum."

"And you let them?"

"We're not going to talk about that."

Maya nods. Certain ideas are meant for profanation: the concept of other people's property being sacred for one. But this kind of trauma? No, that's holy. The past is a reliquary you keep buried unless told otherwise by the one who interred that hurt-stained horror. "I get that. But what if, Verdigris?"

"They wouldn't touch me."

"Would you let them kill everyone else?"

"Fuck. Fuck you and fuck Rita and fuck both of you for knowing exactly the right goddamned buttons to push."

Thank fucking god. At long last, there is the emotional distance Maya has wanted: Verdigris, piqued but no longer pushing good vibes on Maya. She bares a wild grin. Rita gave her a script so she regurgitates it wholesale.

"Come on. This is a chance to make some of it right. We're never going to get Johanna back, but we got a shot at bringing Elise home. And more importantly, maybe, we got a shot at making the Minds scream."

"Rita told you to say that, didn't she?" A wan smile flits partly to each of Verdigris' mouths, tongue lolling from the largest, the one at her collarbone. "God, that woman is an artist when it comes to shit like this."

"We all got our specialties."

"Goddamnit." Verdigris swallows hard, voices in shambles, soft with resignation. "*Goddamnit.* One last time for the road, I guess. But you have to make me a promise."

"Tell me what it is, and I'll at least think about it."

"We save Elise. No matter what."

"I already told you—"

"I want to hear you promise me this. You, specifically. Fuck the sales pitch. Fuck Rita especially. I don't trust her. You, though? Maybe. So, I'm gonna need you to promise me: we'll bring Elise home."

"We're going to try, at least."

"No trying," says Verdigris, practically singing now in bright-bodied triplicate, low contralto in harmony coloratura, whiskeyed alto presiding over it all. "You have to promise. We bring Elise home. We do for her what Johanna never got: a second chance at being human."

"I can't—"

"Those are my goddamned terms, okay? It's all or nothing." She holds Maya's gaze with those strange, pellucid, cracked-ice eyes and almost, Maya can hear some seditious quadrant of her heart whisper, *I'll do it if you teach me what it takes to make me the reason you look at me this way.* "Please?"

"You got it."

"Yeah, okay. I'm glad we have an understanding." Verdigris grins with all her mouths at once, an expression that doesn't even veer within the ten feet of her eyes. "But also seriously, Maya, *what the fuck*?"

INTERLUDE

Six dead. She cannot conjecture the number. Six of the Dirty Dozen are dead and buried, cremated, leavened into the bellies of vultures and other such scavengers, punted into orbit, composted, whatever. Who gives a shit about the method of disposal? Dead is dead is gone. Maya peruses the obituaries. Four—Meghna, Feng Hui, Annora, Nadia—are just that: terse paragraphs condensing entire lives into epilogues, without dimension, without any marginalia to indicate how fucking badass they'd been in life.

They made sure there was no fucking way they'd be roped back into this miserable existence, all gone down the path of multitudinous dissections, their organs taken and disseminated between hospitals. Their data banks were incinerated too; every copy of their souls committed to nothingness, a mercenary's suicide.

Maya combs the newsfeeds obsessively, metronoming between them and privatized info sources, social media clips, company profiles, anything where she can salvage another scatter of data or better, the flash of a familiar face.

But she holds out a feeble prayer for that one last name:

"Rochelle might still be around," Maya blurts out of the blue. The steerage is a long thin loop of a corridor, badly lit like the rest of the ship, its only redeeming feature its proximity to the engine room. Here alone is it warm-*ish*. "I can't find anything on what happened to her."

"No news is good news," says Verdigris, perched on a rail twinned around a baluster, anchoring her. Maya averts her gaze, unable, unwilling to meet those leadlight eyes, especially here where she can be surveilled. "Rochelle always knew how to sneak off to the best places."

"Yeah." This version of Ayane continues to be a surprise to Maya. She possesses a nebulous recollection of Ayane in their heyday, back when they were feral: chambering pejoratives, singing out curses, maenad-wild and gorgeous as a bullet flying true. She'd been happy then. But not like this: unclenched, denuded of everything save for the most rudimentary make-up, hair in a messy ponytail, the loose strands curling over a face gone child-like wonder. Ayane's looked twenty-three since the day Maya first met her, but she has never looked so young. "You remember when she ran off to that casino planet?"

"Fuck, I thought Rita was going to kill her." Verdigris' laughter detonates through the room. Her attire is austere: black turtleneck, black leather skirt with its hems a crisscrossed maze of thick lace, black boots. Biker-nun in exile, especially with the two revolvers strapped to each thigh left brazenly in view.

"Didn't she?" says Constance, slouching into view, a shoulder propping against the wall, her hands curved around a chipped blue mug. Maya knows, even before the olfactory data grazes her sensors and long before her nose puts a name to the memory, the mug brims with watered-down hot chocolate and two plump marshmallows. She knows because she keeps a stash on the shelf that had belonged to Constance, exchanging boxes for fresh doppelgangers whenever the expiry dates were crossed. Waiting, though she'd eat a shotgun before confessing, for Constance to come home.

"Kill Rochelle?" says Verdigris.

"Rita didn't do it," says Ayane, that old sharpness restored as she knifes a chin in Maya's direction. "Maya did."

"Fuck you," comes Maya's barked snarl, born out of instinct rather than intent. She has no place to argue here. She knows better. The guillotine might be a tool, but it still does the work.

"Following orders, yeah, yeah. I know."

Maya narrows her gaze. She remembers, even if the rest of them don't, when they were a pack, and Rita served as their compass, a sun for murderers and no one else, lighting the road deeper into the country of sin. Each of them had run the same gauntlet. Sororicide as a rite of passage. "Like you haven't done the same to me."

Ayane had fucking *pulped* her. So many of her armaments coming in hot at the exact same second, and they'd turned Maya into cheesecloth first before the bombardment continued and the straggling tatters of protein gave up their bloody ghost, washed into a soup of peptides and bone bits, and it'd taken a week to bleach the gore from the wall. No, the Ballistic Queen of the fucking universe doesn't do anything small.

"Y'all ever wonder about that?" says Constance, rapping a nail on the rim of her mug. "How she'd insisted we take turns killing each other. That fucking trauma bonding bullshit and all that. Wild, I tell you."

"They didn't do that in the force?" Ayane rakes a look down Constance's wiry frame, chin set in the heel of her palm. Out of spite, likely, she has commandeered Rita's favorite chair: a low-backed, scooped-bodied disaster upholstered in peach shag.

"Hell no," says Constance. "They don't make you pretend you're a woman either."

A shocked, slightly guilty, the fuck-do-we-do-now silence weaves between the four, all attention on Constance. Maya is the first to speak, her expression verging on panic. Unfortunately, what springs from her mouth is: "Uhhhh."

"Nonbinary," says Constance, expropriating the conversation before it can nosedive into awkwardness. "They. Them."

"Shit," says Verdigris. "This whole time?"

A brisk, one-shouldered shrug. "Maybe? Who knows? Whatever the case, it didn't sink in until about five years ago. Rita spent a lot of time telling us we were badass bitches, insisting on the feminine, and all that shit. I didn't really have time to think about it. It took thirty-five years for it to kinda click."

"Huh," says Maya.

"Well. Cool?" says Ayane.

"Since we're on the topic: me too." Verdigris hops from her perch, illuminated again by her menagerie of chromatophores and other cellular modifications, her hair—a mix of keratin and mesoglea, elegantly surreptitious when it's not lit up like a carnival—contracting onto itself, rounding into a tight pompadour. She dusts each shoulder with elaborate care, the shadows along the planes of her cheeks, their jaw, his brow eddying into new shapes.

When the transformation is complete, he hip-cocks lithely at the group, head canted at a brash angle, a smirk worn like a trophy hard-won.

"God*damn*! I did not know modern technology had gotten that good," Constance whoops, their delight manifested as a slap on Verdigris' back, the latter returning the favor with a playful one-two punch aimed at the arm not burdened with hot chocolate.

"You think it looks good?" Verdigris runs a nervous hand through his hair and it is all Maya can do to not kiss the tension from each finger.

"You look great," says Maya, immediate. "I might even like you better this way."

Verdigris slicks a quiet look at Maya, saying nothing, a smile held out in place of an answer, and it is an expression borrowed from a teenager at prom, corsage in hand, heart beating insecurities onto the door of their chest, thoroughly overwhelmed but fucking delighted to be here. No artifice, nothing but the wide-eyed look of a love who'd still hold your hand tight over the valley between deathbeds. "You ought to do something about it then."

Before Maya can reply, Ayane wolf-whistles. "There are a thousand reasons I wish we could have Johanna back. But right now, I wish she was here to see how perfect you look. Like Constance said, goddamn. You know Johanna would have been impressed."

"Johanna loved everything, though. She even loved those stupid drones that the Minds sent out. You just needed to put it in front of her and she'd love it like her own children," says Verdigris.

"Remember when we ran into the Merchant Mind the first time?" says Constance.

"Yeah," says Ayane, gaze abstracted, fixed on nothing in the physical, pinned, instead to that point in the timeline when Johanna was alive. Breathing, smiling, beautiful. "She had so many questions. She was curious. Johanna wouldn't stop talking about meeting the Merchant Mind for days."

"I used to think she'd die happy if she went down in an interesting . . ." Verdigris strangles on the rest of the sentence, the nostalgia wicking out of his expression, exit stage anywhere but here. Her face tightens.

"Fuck," he says.

Ayane unfurls from her chair, crosses the room in three long strides, touches her mouth to the roof of Verdigris' skull. Maya forgets sometimes those two had loved each other too, even if Ayane and Verdigris had loved Johanna best. "It's okay."

Verdigris, a head shorter, says nothing, only slots his head in the gap between Ayane's chin and collarbone, the two of them a matching set: exquisite. Like coming home. Like all the ways Maya had ever wished Rita would soften for her.

Clack. Clack. Clack.

In the presence of their master, all dogs go quiet.

"You should have told me," are the first words to shear from Rita's lean mouth. As always, she is immaculate: hair in a lacquered bun, scrubs and gloves sterilized of even shadow. A monochrome ghost, particularly anomalous beside the ramshackle hodgepodge vividity of the steerage, with its clutter of mismatched furniture and stolen tchotchkes. Ayane and Verdigris separate, the former gliding forward to put herself between Rita and the other; an arm reached back, palm on Verdigris' hip, protective.

"That we were going to hang out?" Constance asks the

question around the rim of their mug, brows carefully furrowed.

"That the two of you identified as you do."

"You never seemed interested," says Constance, the calm of their voice gloving angrier sentiments, although the subtext in their smile might as well be an alarm, signaling the moment for when the wise need to run.

"I wasn't," and it isn't the words specifically that knock them down like dominos, but the timbre with which they are delivered, the compassion Rita so often withheld. The confession, offered with so much incongruous shame, spoken so quietly and with so much agony, it extracts not empathy, not exactly, but something of a similar phylum. "I was very focused on certain things at the time. Committed to my own fantasies. There were things I wanted for so long and so, I imposed a lot of those wants on you."

Maya knows, and Verdigris knows, and Ayane, and Constance, and all those people buried and dead because of Rita's machinations, they know that flytrap lilt in her voice. But hope—for closure, for answers, for anything that might anesthetize the epiphanous despair that is knowing you'll have to keep going when the only star in your sky is gone—is an implacable force. It is a credit to the raw animosity Rita has accrued that none of them roll over, bellies bared, before the first sentence ends. They exchange looks instead: Ayane and Verdigris volleying secretive glances between themselves, the two moving to stand shoulder-to-shoulder, Constance cycling their attention between the pair, Maya, and Rita.

And speaking of Maya, she does as any good guard hound. Upon realizing this is only an uneasy armistice they've arrived upon, Maya gets onto her feet, gets to her connate duty, which is to stand in unerring defense of the woman she knows to be the devil. Love's like that, though. And this is love or whatever mutant cultivar allowed to the extraneous, the ones meant to die. She thinks. She is sure.

"That's not an apology if it was what you were trying to go for," says Verdigris, the playfulness bled out of his voice, burned from her expression. His hair unfurls, relaxing again into a nimbus which spreads along her shoulders.

"I'm saying I was at fault."

"Still not an apology," Verdigris repeats, eyes finding Maya's, accusation loaded in their slight narrowing. She mouths *why* and Maya puts on her best don't-know-what-the-fuck-you're-talking-about face, taking on the glassy expression of someone who's long since consigned morality to crows, so long ago, on balance, that Maya doesn't remember the last time she really cared about doing the right thing.

Except you can't stop kicking yourself over Johanna, pipes up that stubborn little voice again. *Except you can't get over Elise, can't stop thinking about how you failed them, you fucking failed them.*

Indoctrination nonetheless is no vaccine for either Maya's subconscious or the pang which constricts around her ribs as disappointment washes over Verdigris' face, leaving it blank and smooth as any good merc's mugshot. Can't break your heart if there's nothing to shatter.

"Hey, back off," says Maya. She strokes a thumb over the barrel of a gun, arms herself with a fuck-everything grin, and tries not to linger on how she knows her loyalty to Rita won't buy anything but an unmarked grave.

"It doesn't fucking matter. We don't give a shit about how you feel about anything. We're just here for Elise," snarls Ayane.

"Big talk for someone who was on her knees crying before." Maya licks chapped lips. "Hypocrite."

Through it all, Rita is quiet, has been since drinking in Verdigris' critique. She drums two fingers on the ridge of a collarbone before sighing, unrepentant: "You're right. It doesn't matter. Your private motivations are not my concern. In the end, it is about us coming together to fulfill a mutual ambition."

Verdigris, pure cover-fold gloss, again the face that launched a thousand publicity engines, gears up to put her foot down. At least, that's what Maya thinks as Ayane tenses and Rita adjusts her stance, the air mineral with expectation. Maya rocks onto the balls of her feet, ready to move, ready to intervene, ready to die for faith in duty. *Let's rock*, howls instinct and the treble of a soul unwilling to think too hard on what it's giving up. Both hands now, locked and ready at the trigger.

"So. Talk," says Verdigris, refusing the bait, always the better of them both. "What do you have for us then, grandmaster?"

Rita flashes a winning smile down at the dog she calls Maya and good mutt that she is, Maya is immediately suffused by joy, chemical opiate of the chronically co-dependent. In Rita's approval, she trusts. "Later. First, we get to Rochelle and we bring her onboard. We need someone to handle the demolition work."

Murmured ill-ease. Had she been listening? Or is she prescient? Hard to say and god knows, Rita will never tell. The scientist traces a complex iconogram on the wall, the pebbled steel coming alive with an overlay of a map, its borders framed with coordinates and on-going computations. The display shimmers. It is substituted by an aerial capture of a large homestead, its backyard opening into tilled fields.

"Here," she says, tapping the screen. "This is where she currently lives. It's a few systems away, but it won't take too long."

"Is that a farm?" says Constance, who's been silent up till now. The air in the steerage has irrevocably altered. If before it had felt like a homecoming, it is dust and distance again in the humid atmosphere, everyone reverted to professional etiquette. "You know, of all the places I imagined she'd end up, a farm . . . wasn't one of 'em."

"How do we know it's hers?" says Verdigris.

Rita taps at a splotch of black in the visual. "Lots of old vehicles."

"Doesn't mean it belongs to Rochelle," says Constance. "Lots of people have a thing about refurbishing old machines."

"I bet your precinct had a lot of 'old machines' in the evidence locker," says Ayane.

"No one's ever going to let me live the cop thing down, huh?"

"Nope," says Verdigris, bright as a song.

"I'll go check it out," Maya declares to her own surprise, all at once exhausted by the bickering, the layered maneuvering, the history which refutes all attempts to keep it entombed. Give her a gun, give her a war, give her bodies to line the floor. Maya's unrepentantly basic, a murderer with no nuance, and these interpersonal politics? She doesn't want them, thanks. The realization of how much she loathes this closes around her throat like a fist and she's dyspneic by the next sentence. "I can't deal with all the bitching anymore."

"Aren't you worried we'll take a swing at your favorite person while you're out?" says Constance with detached ritual.

"No," says Maya, without hesitation, because like Circe, like any witch from any old fairy tale, Rita has them all under her spell, and until someone can kiss the wickedness from Rita's teeth, they'll be her dogs until the world breaks like a heart.

"Not at all."

ROCHELLE

"Rochelle here?"

Maya cranes a look over the boy's head. Inside, the homestead is maximalist indulgence: carpeting and jubilant wallpaper, paleolithic accoutrements: photographs—actual fucking *analog* photographs—in a hodgepodge of twee frames, an umbrella stand in the shape of a gargantuan rabbit's foot, a rattan pendant lamp, antique Venetian masks, half-wilted plants bereft of automated care but fecund nonetheless despite their ailments, spilling over countertops and greenly frothing in poorly lit corners. An aesthetic borrowed from millennia past. The scent of sandalwood and incense wafts forward.

Fuck Rita. Fuck the rest of them for capitulating to her bad temper. Maya is so far out of her element, she's treading entropy.

"You must be one of Mom's old students. I'll tell Mama you're here."

"Wait." Maya snakes a hand out to grab his shoulder. The boy is arresting in his resemblance to Rochelle. Lean, in the way she was, with a coyote's lilt to the shape of his posture, his predator leanness. With her eyes and her unsubtle smile rupturing across his narrow face. Her sigh and her micro-expressions, identical to the shadowing beneath the temporal bone. "Mama?"

The smile closes up like a tomb. The boy bobs his chin, rolls his eyes with injurious similarity to how Rochelle once did the same. Maya feels her chest tighten, unable, for a second, to sift between the present and the long-deceased past. Even reality unmoors, becomes porous, so much so that a flash of motion from the kitchen commands the immediate expectation that Rochelle—alive, smiling, unchanged from that bitter day—might step out to berate Maya for manhandling her child. "Mama. Because Rochelle's Mom."

"How old are you?"

He cocks his head as Maya lets go. She places him in his mid-teens, lacking still in the ruggedness which personifies grown masculinity, but not completely bereft of such architecture. "No offense. But you're asking way too many questions for someone who ain't family."

The bite in his statement; it startles a baying laugh from Maya's throat, a sound that lances through the ambient cello music soaking through the small homestead. There is a screech of a bow dragged roughly over indignant strings, the slap of a palm upon wood. A punctuation, an objection to the intrusion of Maya's histrionics. It shuts her up. *Huh*, Maya thinks, piqued by the artistry she's disrupted, the not-yet-revealed cellist so exquisite Maya had believed them to be artificial.

A movement. Her attention flits again to the boy.

"You sound just like her," Maya whispers, and she means it in a way that'd take the kid at least another two decades of heartache to internalize. Being alive means being aware you'll inevitably lose people, Death being the laziest but most implacable apex predator yet. But nothing fucking readies *anyone* for seeing the beloved dead captured like this—just for an attosecond, only in the right light, the right moment—in a stranger's face, not even clonetech, not even blowing your brains out a hundred times over because that particular flesh-chassis was too inconvenient to keep.

"Please tell me you're not my older sister or something like that." Another eye-roll, this one conducted with more emphasis. "*Mama, there's someone really fucking weird here.*"

A reply—Turkic etymology, although Maya's onboard-translator blanks on the origin of its exact phonological system, substituting exact data with the hypothesis that this was a language someone once tried to bury—billows from around a corner. "I told you once, I told you again, and I hope to hell I don't have to tell you again: watch your language."

Again, an eye-roll, but unlike its predecessor, it entreats Maya to be a co-conspirator. Youth apparently respects no loyalties, at least when they're from the parent cultivar. Offshoots like clone kids, well, those have their allegiances baked in. The impertinence elicits a grin nonetheless, and Maya motions toward the interior, her head and one eyebrow cocked.

"Yes, Mama. I know, I know." The boy harmonizes with his mother, switching to that same beautifully agglutinative tongue. "She wants to come in. Can she?"

"Sure." Spoken with exceeding flippancy, but Maya's sensors collate proof that, at minimum, twenty-five scans are currently in motion. She does not object to the cross-examination, stands there patiently until something further inside the house goes *ding*. "Don't forget to take off your shoes."

"You sure? My feet fucking stink," says Maya.

"We have facilities. Wash them."

Mama, as it turns out, is a woman named Reyha, six feet exactly according to Maya's internal telemetries, and built *broad*. Wide shoulders, hips of similar scale, a laddered belly, muscular legs. Her mouth too: the lips generous even when pursed with distrust.

"You're from Rochelle's old crew, then. You know, she told me about you girls. I wasn't sure if I believed her." Reyha studies her without reservation, her expression nakedly interrogative, and Maya almost grins. Of course Rochelle would shack up with someone like Reyha, measured and allergic to anything even resembling fear. "The wild heists, the crazy shit she did. Man, she wasn't anything like that when I met her."

It brings Maya up short. Already, she has been having trouble mulling over the idea of Rochelle's life abbreviated, this declension of a grand existence; all that hype, all those acrobatic crimes, the history they shared, swept under a prettily adorned table and forsaken for domesticity. Maya, though she tries, cannot pretzel her mind around Rochelle's decision. To elect mortality was one thing, but to choose such an anonymous descent into the good night. The fuck was Rochelle thinking?

But what she says is: "What was she like then?"

Reyha gives her a once-over. Whatever she surmises from that brisk appraisal can't be bad because Reyha allows them both the glory of a slow, thoughtful smile.

And at the sight of it, Maya thinks,*Yyes, I could see giving up living forever for someone to smile at me like that.* An image of Rita—gloveless and in crew overalls, the artistry of her smoothed away, worn down to a plain sweet humanity—flashes into active thought, and Maya shoots it down, but it's nothing compared to the speed with which she shotguns into extinction a sudden vision of Verdigris. No point deluding oneself with sentimentality. Fuck that shit. Fuck both of them.

"Rochelle?" Reyha exhales and there is a whole lifetime of memory in that bridge of sound, all of it good somehow. "She liked cars. Terrestrial vehicles. Rovers, short-range land gliders. Those sorts of things."

No surprise there. Rochelle prided herself on balance. For every blown-up refueling station, she'd put together a house, a car, anything decayed into irrelevance. Because you had to have both sides of the equation, she'd said. Dark and light. Hope and ruin.

"Uh huh."

"Used to have this thing about going between planets, picking up rusted piles of crap, things that people didn't want anymore and, you know, fixing them up."

"To sell?" Maya says, although she knows the answer.

A half-laugh that skirts deeper-running emotions. "To rehome, mostly. Rochelle believed wholeheartedly in rehabilitation, finding beauty in the mess. She'd repair whatever she found and ask around until she found someone who wanted to take it for their own."

"What else did she do?"

"She liked baking sweets," says Reyha, with no irony. "She was obsessed."

Had that been Rochelle? Did she bake? Had there been profiteroles on a counter, malformed soufflés, failed mochi, cakes abandoned because they wouldn't rise to the occasion? She can't remember. Forty years, Maya realizes, is too much time to hold in its entirety. For all that clonetech does to preserve biological continuity, it can't fuck with the inimical design. The brain, pressed to contain every life experience, knows better than to do so. Instead of retaining every memory, it makes composites, deriving assumptions from repeated examples, and flattens decades into annotated summaries.

What has she lost in those years? How much was elided for the sake of the chase? Forgotten, unwritten because Maya saw Rochelle as an accomplice rather than a person? How much of that was Maya's own error? How much was it Rita's fault? Rita's say-so? Rita's meticulous instruction on what to think, what to feel, what to do? Why is it so hard for her to remember what made Rochelle human?

"You all right?"

Fuck vulnerability. Maya straightens her stance, the set of her jaw, her spine, her little lopsided smile so it has the slice of Rita's own poise, if it'd been grunged up a little first. "Yeah. I'm fine. I guess—I don't know. I was expecting more? I don't know. No offense. It's nothing on you. But she could have lived forever, been a fucking god. And this was what she chose? A wife and a kid and a house on a moon. I don't know. It just seems fucking anticlimactic to me."

Reyha does not drop the beat. "Being old is a luxury of its own. It's saying you're willing to let go, to stop writhing with ambition. To just *be*. At least, that's how Rochelle explained it to me."

"I don't know how any of that makes this sound better. It still fucking sounds like giving up." Maya hesitates. "No offense."

"What's wrong with giving up?" Reyha leans back, sinking into the plum-blue loveseat, its cushions tasseled and the curlicues of its frame ornate to a fault. The wall behind her gleams with a thin lamina of liquid glass. On display: a rain-tumbled deciduous forest, fog-silvered, speckled with the shadows of birds in flight. Broadcasted by concealed speakers: the static murmur of such languid meteorological phenomena. “We navigate by capitalism. Always had, probably always will. And one of the things about capitalism is it demands we think of our lives as in deficit. Not enough time, not enough material possessions, not enough luxuries. Not enough anything. Because contentment doesn’t sell. Desire does.”

“I don’t understand—”

“Rochelle gave up on wanting more because she was happy with enough.” Reyha, unruffled by whatever blasphemies someone else might have read in Maya’s responses, stretches an arm to her right toward a bowl of sweets atop a palatial dresser. “It’s not that hard. She was happy here. With me, with Ehmet.”

“Then why not choose to stay alive? Why opt to die?” A light comes on in the adjacent room. Maya’s sensors take immediate note, reticules fixed on every exit. What enters her sights is no threat but Ehmet, casually embalmed in a tracksuit, pink headphones anchored around his throat. He throws them both a perfunctory wave. Maya swings her attention back to Reyha. “Doesn’t he deserve to always have his mothers?”

“Stasis teaches nothing to a kid.” Reyha undresses a crystalline sweet, pops it in her mouth.

A door closes. Ehmet is gone. Out, maybe, to run laps around a lake, run an errand, run lines of coke with a creche of friends. Who the fuck knows? Maya certainly doesn’t. It could be any of the pleasant banalities associated with being young. Maya is only cognizant of them third-hand, having been, in the infancy of her existence, a beast of labor as opposed to a beloved child. “You could have both had eternities to show him what the world means."

"And through what lens?" Finally, when Maya was so sure that Reyha's composure is bulletproof, it fissures. It cracks along the bend of her mouth, her forehead. To Maya's surprise, she experiences no triumph, only an apostate's abashedness, like she'd defaced a god of small yet precious things. "Fear? An unwillingness to confront discomfort? Growth is married to loss. You know this."

"It doesn't have to be." Sadly, that embarrassment is nowhere near enough to dissuade Maya from pursuing the argument to its bitter death as she is nothing if not a hunting dog when pressed: born to instinct, blessed for the kill. Maya scoots forward on her chair, hands out, a plea in the cup of her palms. "The tech exists now. Fuck, Rochelle was a perfect example of that."

"She had no peace until she gave it up."

"How do you know that? Maybe she was just doing it for you. We worked together for two hundred years, and—"

"Rochelle was miserable every fucking day."

Maya recoils. "What?"

"That was what she told me. She was miserable every day of that life. She hated the rituals. She hated dying, coming back, scrubbing her memories of the trauma. That whole nonsense. Rochelle *hated* it." Reyha tongues the inside of her cheek, a gesture shockingly prurient in its manifestation. "Just. Hated it."

"She never told me." Her voice startles her with how hurt it sounds, how soft; the loss implied in its dearth of volume surprises her enough to drag Maya out the other side where she emerges, bloodied and fucking enraged at having been kneecapped by emotion. Fuck. This. Shit. She cuts her blood with a flood of endorphins, dampens the cortisol output and sits silent as her editing renders her pain down to a non-issue. *Ah, there we go.* Finally. No more of that bullshit.

"This is what I'm talking about." Reyha wags a finger at her. Funny how much like a child she feels here in the presence of an old-fashioned crone. Maya is older than the first sin, but she's got nothing on Reyha, nothing on a life lived calm as deep water. Maya wishes Reyha'd lord that wisdom over her, get on a high horse, do *something* egregious, anything to merit aggression, because there's a part of Maya scratching to fight. But she doesn't. Reyha's expression retains its unflinching compassion as she speaks, softening even. "I saw what you did."

"Calm myself the fuck down?"

"Yes." Whatever ground Maya had won in her war against Reyha's stoicism crumbles as Reyha, bold as love, extends a hand to clasp Maya's own.

It fucking startles her, of course. Enough that Maya doesn't immediately reciprocate by torquing herself loose and eviscerating the middle-aged matron in plain view of whomever is lucky enough to be strutting outside those wide casement windows. Instead, she stares, dumbfounded by the physicality of Reyha's compassion. How many times has anyone touched her like that? Has *anyone* touched her like so? Without intent to manipulate, to seduce, to entreat, to delay execution? With nothing but milquetoast baseline human kindness.

Maya exhales in a razored hiss. "What are you doing?"

"It's okay to not be okay."

Her tongue, never so graceless when it comes to topics pertaining to aggression, is a wad of limp muscle in her mouth, too bulky to do more than help shape the word: "What?"

"It's okay to not be okay," Reyha repeats. Now, both hands have come to encircle Maya's own and dimly, Maya thinks, *Yeah, the placement of my fingers on this weapon is wrong, so this is a correction. Yeah, that's what she's doing.* Except that hypothesis yields no new knowledge in artillery, the tactile contact void of education. Reyha is holding her because she cares. "Ehmet, he's a good kid, and you'd think people'd have learned from when we were all still terrestrial, but that 'toxic masculinity' bullshit is everywhere. Boys get told they're not supposed to cry, not supposed to hurt. But it happens, and blocking it out like that, it kills something in you. You get what I'm saying?"

With the two of them bunched up so close, close enough for Maya to be lanced through by a chill mineral attar of eucalyptus, an appropriate choice in fragrances, what with the plant's reputation for healing and Reyha's apparent predilection for healing anything within radius, Maya could headbutt the older—younger? Reyha has neither visible ports nor signs of vascular implants, no telltale cicatrices to hint, maybe, she's on the clonetech merry-go-round—woman for the insult of this unsolicited affection, levy any measure of punitive measurements.

But she does nothing.

It feels good, doesn't it? Being held like you're human. Johanna's ghost, raising itself from the dead to laugh at her.

"Not a fucking clue."

Reyha chuckles, the sound blending so perfectly with that memory of Johanna, Maya cannot, for a second at least, distinguish between the frequencies of the two. "You're like my Rochelle. Feral. Allah help me, Rita has a lot to answer for in the afterlife."

Reflexive: "If you fucking say anything about her—"

"You'll what?" Reyha meets her gaze full-on, fearless. Her grip tightens as her expression accretes a penetrating quality. "Shoot me? Baby, if you were going to do that, you'd have done so already. I know I'm making a ton of presumptions."

"No shit."

"But the truth is, and we both know this, is that Rita is not a good thing for any of you. Sure, she has on that messianic veneer. Underneath, though? She's a monster. She keeps you isolated, she keeps you *exhausted*. She makes you die for her ten thousand times over—"

"If you don't shut up, I'm going to blow your face off."

"Make sure you clean up before Ehmet comes home, then. That kid is a lot of good things, but he can't fucking clean to save his teenage life. He'd leave curds of brain everywhere." So factually articulated, that prophetic disassembly of her posthumous condition: without bathos, without any overture of mawkishness. *Prim.* "I'm not telling you how to live your life. I'm just telling you what I learned from all those years with my wife. Rita's abusive. Rita does not give a shit about any of you. And since apparently everything that Rochelle said was true, I know she got two of your peers killed, and I—"

Cinematic timing is such that it never allows for a revelation to complete uninterrupted. As Reyha veers toward the denouement of her impassioned soliloquy, the front door leaps open, ricocheting off the adjoining wall so it volleys back into the face of the new arrival. An incredulous "ow, fuck!" fires through the air: Ehmet returned and with fresh bruises for his trouble too.

"Language!" Reyha disentangles from Maya before the latter can so much as crack the first note of her coyote laugh, all that tension sleeting away into a juddering giggle. Back to compartmentalization. Back to segregating doubt from core functionality, the vagaries of self-worth firmly entrenched in the basement of her consciousness, where, hopefully, they will just fucking rot.

Yet, as Maya observes the reunion between mother and marginally bruised child, she discovers that, once gestated, that need to be valued—to be loved equitably, in proportion to what is extended—cannot be aborted so easily. It pricks at her, needle-toothed. But what does a dog, so familiar now with abuse that it fits better than their own skin, do in these circumstances? Maya is still mulling over her predicament when Reyha returns, wiping damp palms along her legs.

"Kids. You love them no matter how much they whine. Now, where were we?"

Maya, a quip at ready, surprises herself when she says: "I'm sorry for your loss, you know?"

"Wait. Run that by me again?" Ehmet rounds the corner as his mother stands there, astounded by the sudden compassion exhibited, a white ceramic cup in each of his hands. Reyha bobs her chin briskly at him before absconding with his burden, seating herself again. Her disbelief is rawly vivid, etched in the exaggerated contortions of her face. She pinches her brows, scowls. "Are you offering your condolences?"

"Yeah."

"Huh," says Reyha and then once more, with a blowsier lilt: "Huh. Who'd have thought? You do have a heart in there, tin man."

Maya says nothing, has nothing more constructive to impart than her steady gaze, her consortium of macros and military add-ons endlessly scrounging for some cause to activate, a catalyst for a brawl, anything but this unnerving, aching, unwanted stillness.

When it becomes clear that Maya will present no riposte, Reyha passes along one of the cups. Maya looks down. Steam wicks from along the surface of the agate-hued fluid, a color unlike anything Maya is accustomed to. Just as foreign: the fragrance that lifts from its depths. It is peculiarly sweet, suggestive of the presence of sugared almonds and cinnamon, dried apple slices, ginger, and—

"Beetroot?"

Reyha shrugs expansively. "I like the color."

A companionable silence congeals between them, both women ostensibly absorbed with their respective beverages. For Maya, at least, it is an opportunity to take stock, regroup. The dialogue is growingly claustrophobic, as is the mantling of domesticity, and all the little details which comprised a civilized encounter. No, none of that is helping her mood one fucking bit. Maya knows what she wants. She covets the idiot ease of murder, of disembowelment, activities that feel gaudily out of place here, even in the hypothetical. Sullen, she tests the tensile strength of her cup's handle, squeezing until she can feel ceramic almost indent: a hair's distance from shatter.

"We had twenty-one years together. I'm not going to say I didn't want more, because I do. But it was a lot, and I'm grateful."

Maya stares at her with abject and uncamouflaged horror. Twenty-one years. *Fuck.* The way Reyha has been talking about Rochelle, she thought those two enjoyed a full four decades together. Twenty-one years. It isn't just less than Maya had anticipated, it is obscene, an unjust paupering of the one left behind.

More abominable yet is the look of peace that Reyha is wearing, the ease with which she'd announced that was "a lot" of time. The thought of twenty-one years being sufficient for anyone is so macabre, so heinous that it compels her to wonder if this is Reyha attempting to defang her own agony. Narratives matter. The abused create apocrypha, anything to seduce their lizard brain into docility. Why not the shellshocked, the heartbroken, the bitter, the ones who were left behind by the deathbed without even a schedule for their grief?

But that delusion glissades away in the wake of Reyha's stoicism as the other woman retrieves a framed picture from the shelf behind her. She angles the photo so it enters Maya's view. It is Rochelle and Reyha—younger, although not by much, hair already grey, the lines on their faces permanently emblazoned—bracketing a maple tree, both aiming finger-guns at a heart chiseled into the bark. In the middle, the statement: *R+R 4 ever.*

"She was a romantic," Reyha confides. "I bet you didn't know that."

Maya contemplates this without rancor or judgement, jigsawing together, as she does, this new composite image of Rochelle: plumper in natural mid-life, better coiffed, with cardigans in a palette of pastels, but with black oil under her nails still and her magpie avarice toward every vehicle to stray into sight.

"She said she never got to have any of those nice things. First loves, dates where you hold hands as you walk around, ice cream dripping down your fingers, and you don't care because you're fixated on the other person. Bad movie nights," says Reyha.

"I never knew she wanted them."

"Did you ask?"

"No. We never . . ."

"Yeah," says Reyha. "I got that feeling. Now, what else . . . ?"

Reyha falls naturally into loving oration of the domestic, the sweet, the life Rochelle pulled together from the wreckage of the mistakes she made. And Maya listens. She bobs her head in the lulls where Reyha halts to pull in breath. It is an act tantamount to glossolalia. Maya doesn't have a fucking clue as to how to do this: sit tidily in a dead woman's living room, a cup of fruit-infused tea cooling on an end table, and listen as the last years of her life are unrolled by her widow. But she tries. She owes Rochelle this much.

Throughout her stories, Reyha neither staggers nor slips, not once, not even during her exposé of Rochelle's funeral. Where Maya expects a violence of emotion, there is instead a melancholic blitheness, the ease of a polar explorer accustomed now to the terrain's malice. Here, Reyha anchors herself in a kind memory. Here, she diffuses grief with gratitude for family, Ehmet critical to this narrative throughout: love as a leitmotif made flesh.

"Sorry," says Reyha, voice feathering into a contralto laugh. She smooths one polished auburn curl behind an ear. "I told you I don't know how to stop when it comes to Chelle. I'm not even sure if I'll ever start thinking of her in the past tense. She's still *here.* In Ehmet. In this house. In everything I do. My existence is and always will be a continued dialogue with her. Who I am, what I am. All of it. I am who I am because she came into my life. It doesn't matter she can't physically answer me. I know what she'd say to a thousand different things."

Another laugh, this one embarrassed, yet the shine of the love at its core is something Maya would bottle, store away for a bad day. God knows she's seen too fucking many.

"I'm sorry," says Reyha. "It must sound ridiculous to you."

Maya cranks up the left corner of her lip, tries on a smile she doesn't quite feel. Being here, confronted with what she suspects is the only method the mortal can be made otherwise, and not the cadaverous half-life she has grown acculturated to, it both enriches and empties. Maya lost something along the through line of Reyha's quiet stories. Something lets go of her. What, though, she'll have to figure out later. "No more ridiculous than all of our stories might have sounded to you."

"—that's what marriage is. You roll with the worst of your wife's stories, and you tell everyone how proud you are of her imagination, and when they make inadvisable jokes, you threaten to run them over. Love's work, kid. All the best things in life are." A laugh flowers, dies quickly as it began. "I don't want to know why you were here for Chelle, do I?"

"No, I don't think so."

"It can't have been good, huh?"

"I don't know," Maya says truthfully, feeling her way still through this new worldview. "I think she would have wanted to help. It involves at least one of the people we thought dead and bringing her home."

"Is Rita still involved in all this?"

"Yeah."

"I'd be careful if I were you."

Maya mulls over this. Ordinarily so tight-fisted about the data Rita shares, seeing them as tokens, tacit proof that Rita cares, although she, like Maya, is too fucked up by their unique provenance to put words into such, Maya surprises herself with what comes out of her mouth: "You too. Be careful. I think the ageships are looking to kill anyone cloneborn, and their families. Or maybe just the criminals? I don't fucking know anymore."

"Why don't you know?"

"I'm not the one who asks the questions," says Maya, wrung of excuses. "I just do what I'm told."

Reyha leans forward, trapping Maya's palm between both of her wide hands. Gently, she shutters Maya's fingers, closing them into a fist. "I think, maybe, it's time you considered changing that."

Five out of twelve, though. They've endured worse odds.

INTRODUCTIONS

Pimento is at an impasse.

He flits between bodies, what few he possesses, conscious of the value humans place in first impressions. A bipedal chassis might encourage immediate rapport but it also might not. His avatar's absence of traditional humanoid features is a high-risk factor. The drone, on the other hand, seems more statistically likely to succeed. Simians respond well to adorable, but is that really the impression that Pimento wants to impart?

Buzzing displeasure from his anterior speakers, the scout-ship cycles through flowcharts again, examining the logical outcomes, divergent paths. The initial conclusions persist. In the end, Pimento sacrifices respectability for practicality, decants himself into the drone, sensory awareness simplified grotesquely. Audiovisual input only. No comprehension of light spectrums, no olfactory trackers, dismal frequency response. Clockspeeds of neolithic levels. Ugh.

But that is not what unsettles him. It is the reduction of cognitive breadth that does it, his circadian oscillations delayed, processor slowed to uselessness. The sense that he is being neutered, diminished. *That* is terrifying. However, function before frivolity. So, Pimento disables the subroutines that would engineer doubt and distress, and runs a diagnostics check instead, its results discarded as soon they manifest. Another nervous tic.

The bot exits storage, catapulting down the corridors of his original chassis, the hallways silent. Without Pimento's consciousness in its mainframe, the torpid ship might as well be a ghost, dead save for erratically triggering macros and its security subroutines. Motion sensors awaken emergency lights as he cruises by, delineating his route with pinpoints of gold. Inside Pimento's overlay, the subaural echo of the Merchant Mind's instructions ticks off the seconds until task completion.

They are simple orders, disappointingly, simple enough that Pimento finds himself worrying they parallel his employer's faith, a concern he briskly edits from immediate attention. Public knowledge makes it clear: terror is purposeless without the needs of flesh, relevant only when it can edify, can serve as a topic of academic interest. And this is no occasion for scholastic meditation, so therefore it is unequivocally moot.

Pimento takes a corner, swerves into position and waits. Hydraulics untangle, separating platform from floor. Another shift of machinery. Gears heave. And then, light roars up: cloudless midday glare. The topography is as the Merchant Mind described: a spread of tropical growth, scarred by ravines and wide coiling rivers, like the vasculature of ferns. As for the distant ocean, it is vibrantly pink, glowing with microlife.

A bird twists sleekly into view from below the ship, the span of its wingtips twice that of the dormant vehicle, head cocked to examine this intruder in the troposphere. Its plumage is phantasmagoric, tinctures mutating without pattern, red-orange liquifying to blue, to pink, to configurations of diamond-dusted indigo. Pimento documents its passage without interest, however. The species was catalogued decades ago, its physiognomy mapped down to the last chromosome, every idiosyncrasy saved to file.

It screes at Pimento, a sound that is partway reptilian. And Pimento croons back: reassurance, recognition.

Warning.

Having announced its intent, the drone pitches himself from the ship, startling the bird-thing. Personality modules switch off, their power allotment rerouted to navigation. What little remains of Pimento—Pimento, the inventory of curated neuroses; Pimento, as it thinks of itself when it permits itself the words *he* and *I*—devotes itself to the task of recording. Later, it will pick apart the sensory nuances, the minutiae of its transit; delight in the freefall, the gravitational pull, the way its frame pirouetted through the firmament, sky and terrain blurring to one.

Of course, Pimento could have chosen an easier descent, docked its ship-self before disembarking in this primitive avatar. But where would be the pleasure in that? Thrusters kick in, nine thousand feet from impact. Pimento slingshots up. Hovers. Consumes the vista with detached interest, aware that later it will obsess over every detail. Later, it will want to devour *everything.* A seething veil of insects whispers past, arrowing down into the jungle below. Pimento follows, having reacquired equilibrium, sufficient pushback against the gravity.

There.

It—*he* again, now that auxiliary functions can be indulged—spirals down into a clearing, fringed by veins of cool water. A ship hulks over the soil, lifeless and utterly hideous, human parody of Penitent design. Four women stand arrayed in martial formation. Their stance is precise; three, hands cupped around military-grade artillery, flanking an unarmed fourth. When one shifts their weight, the others adjust instantly, muscles yoked to a distributed intelligence. Or, perhaps, they were meticulously trained.

The second hypothesis is somehow more alarming than the first.

"Where is he?"

Pimento articulates a noise: a throat clearing, phlegm warbling against a swollen uvula. "The Merchant Mind sends his apologies. He believes a—" He plays an audio clip from his employer. "—'parlay by proxy'—" End clip. "—would be more mutually beneficial."

One of the humans, wires and sinew and heightened adrenaline, dances back, twin revolvers held up to Pimento. An eye turns effulgent, crimson with equations. "Fuck. I knew it. I *fucking* knew it. That bot probably has an explosive. Verdigris, can you disarm it from this distance? I fucking told you, Rita. He's going to double-cross us."

"Put. That. Down." The first speaker again, calm. She is taller than her companion but less robust, glass where the other is carbon-steel. But there is something to the heft of her stance, a predatory deliberateness, that Pimento itemizes as dangerous. On impulse, he scans her. His sensors return nothing: no chemical reading, no electrocardiographic reports, nothing that reads as human. Only a grey, cultivated blankness.

"We have to get out of here."

"This isn't how he works. He won't lure us into an ambush like this. It wouldn't be *professional.*" The last word is divested like a parasite.

"Rita—"

A third voice, richer, a mezzo-soprano pleasingly abraded by cigarette use. Pimento files its sound waves away for future use. The speaker, unlike the first two, is statuesque, square-shouldered muscularity. The stock of a turbine rifle sits balanced on a hip. "Maya's right. Something about this smells off."

"The Merchant Mind enjoys his jokes," Rita replies, unperturbed, although she is the only one without visible weaponry. "Besides—" Here, her voice refines to a blade. "—we'd be dead already if he was planning something."

Her companions growl acquiescence, but don't transition from their state of heightened alarm. This proves problematic. The collective's body language, now contaminated, soon transforms, degrading to aggression, a murmuration of snarls and snapping teeth.

"I am not here to cause anyone harm. I promise that I—" Pimento pitches his voice high, hoping this voluntary infantilization might engender trust. He zips forward, only to weave back as Maya advances in grimacing counterpoint.

"*Fuck* you. I will *shoot* you out of the motherfucking air if you even think about coming closer."

"Maya! Stand down!"

Pimento hesitates. It would be wasteful to sacrifice the data that he had aggregated: the impact of airflow on the high-entropy alloy of his exterior; the lyricism of the third woman's speech; a vision of the planet from inadvisable altitudes. He'd *miss* those. Simultaneously, this iteration of Pimento *is* entirely dispensable, a pared-down copy of the original, primed for eventual erasure.

Still, the drone *was* expensive.

"What can I do to make you trust me?"

The question silences. Maya is the first to laugh, wild convulsive guffaws that evoke immediate comparisons to a coyote's vocalizations. Her companions stare, uncertain, perhaps perturbed by the unrestrained merriment. Nonetheless, no one lowers their weapons. Their fingers stay rested on the safeties of their respective guns, their musculatures tense.

At least, Pimento reflects, *it is a start.*

"You can't." Maya again, while Rita hisses a warning.

"Understood. Trust is earned. It cannot be given. What can I do to provide a conducive, stress-free environment? I understand the conditions cannot be optimal. But I would like to approach—" The words spill over each other, audio output lagging behind whirring thoughts.

"Can you *believe* this shithead—"

"Present your proposition," Rita interjects, loud enough to override Maya's objections. The latter bares her teeth. "I am interested in hearing it."

Pimento does not wait. He activates the module that the Merchant Mind had implanted, a tumorous weight in his fuselage, almost too large for the storage cavity. A paroxysm of electrical impulses. Without warning, power maxims are superseded by new instructions, coerced into prioritizing the third-party component. What occurs next is a violation: the module gorges itself on Pimento's xenon tanks, drains him of propellant. His core heats alarmingly.

Blue-white emissions then extrude from his framework, reticulating into a three-dimensional hologram of the Merchant Mind. To Pimento's dismay, it is an aesthetic failure, tortured by technological inadequacies. Primitive. Blatantly pixelated. What a waste of his adjunct resources. If he is to bleed dry, at least it should be for an appealing cause.

"If you are watching this recording, you were wise enough not to shoot the messenger." The Merchant Mind steeples its fingers. *It*, this time, as opposed to he or she or they or any fluid combination thereof. Pimento approves. There is a subtle yet underappreciated artistry to coring so-called gender markers from one's aural dispatches, a work few recognize as emblematic of finesse. Because humanity was led by their dysmorphisms and driven by their proclivity for breeding, gender was everything. It helped illuminate who they, according to a matrix of learned inclinations, might want to fuck. As such, the species—or at least, the *society*, as defined by those archaic religions—developed an ear tuned for telltale variations in pitch and lilt. That the Merchant Mind could eradicate these sonic idiosyncrasies, sand down its voice so that the subconscious cannot supply any descriptor save "machine," is impressive to no end.

Pity the humans aren't equipped to appreciate this sufficiently.

"Rita Koskinen," says the recording of the Merchant Mind, startling Pimento from his reverie. Despite the lack of recognizable facial features, it presents the impression of a smile. "It is so good to interact with you again. I regret the outcome of our last meeting. But time is linear. It goes on. We move on. What is a small disagreement when your lives are infinite? Ha-ha."

Ha-ha. Spoken, not expressed organically. A precise enunciation of the syllables, to be parsed as an insult.

"Asshole," Maya grumbles.

The third individual shrugs a shoulder. The fourth

preoccupies herself with iridescent talons. Words for that one are either a commodity or something repellent, both realities that Pimento would interrogate if he weren't already committed to a separate labor. Rita alone remains focused, unblinking in her scrutiny.

"I suspect that you are unlikely here to give Elise over to me. In fact, I suspect, that you may be trying to *orchestrate* something. As a token of good faith, to prove to you that it is always worthwhile to uphold a bargain with me, I am loaning you Pimento—"

"The fuck? Is that thing named after a *pepper*?"

Through the haze of the projection, dripping heat and definition, Pimento sees Rita twitch a hand, a succinct chopping motion. The third woman withdraws, slipping into the tree line. The fourth member of their party, torrential hair forever adjusting hues to match its surroundings, lopes soundlessly behind. "Not now, Maya."

"—to help you with whatever you require. My assistance is, of course, conditional. When you find Elise Nguyen, I expect you to bring her back to me. Fail and there will be consequences. I do not believe that I need to elaborate. Should you succeed, however, I will assist you in getting to that fabled planet. And by the way, let me know how this place worked out as a meeting spot. Your rating will assist in our logistical algorithms."

"Wait, I thought you fucking said you found her already—"

"We'll discuss this on the ship, Constance," Rita snaps. "Now is not the time."

"You said she fucking *contacted* you."

"What the fuck is this shit?" snarls that prismatic fourth, joining the chorus. "I did not fucking agree to help the Merchant Mind."

"We'll discuss this on the ship," repeats Rita, unmoved.

The hologram dissipates, leaving the humans to confer in low voices and Pimento to analyze the damage incurred by the Merchant Mind's machinations. A sentiment like indignance resonates through his core. This hadn't been part of the deal. True, the hologram itself was discussed at length, but Pimento had neither been informed of the formidable energy requirements, nor warned that there would be an invasive approbation of his propellant supply. Disgruntled, he makes note to formalize a complaint when full processing capacity is restored. This was entirely unacceptable.

Clang. Shockwaves frisson through his chassis, startling Pimento from his private lamentations. Damn this corpus; the limitations of its sensors are appalling. "—giving that shithead too much credit. I say we open it up and tear the data straight out of it."

Impact again. Pimento narrowly dodges the third blow; a revolver scything entirely too close. "What are you *doing*?"

The exclamation is louder than scripted, its cadence a closer approximation of rage than distress. Tinny. Rough work that would embarrass Pimento under more peaceful circumstances. However, this isn't an occasion for self-flagellation. Pimento weaves back and up into a vertical arc, minimizing accessibility.

Maya slants an appraising look at the drone, arm raised, gun positioned for another strike. She makes a noise like a dog's whuffing exhalation, a grim chuckle. The pupil of the artificial eye dilates, captures Pimento on a flat disc of ink: there's the sense that he's being vivisected, split into variant timelines, and duly exterminated in each.

How would the humans word his next thought? Yes. They would say *Fuck that.* But such obscenities would not be professional. So instead, Pimento opts for a curt: "The Merchant Mind wouldn't be very happy."

"Well, *fuck* it. It didn't have the decency to show up. What's to say that the frag-cunt didn't stick a warhead up this drone's asshole? They could just be biding their time—" Maya pivots a hand, raps the grip of her revolver against an open palm thrice.

Pimento circles around the pair, ignored amid aggregating tempers. Rita, for all of her initial composure, is beginning to crack, a dissolution precipitated by the slightest downturn of her mouth. Still, she maintains enviable form: another human would unlikely notice the change. "And what would you have us do? Trigger the explosive you were so worried about?"

"We've got Ayane. Ayane can take out whatever the junk-fucks have put in there. I bet we can do it. After all, what's the fucking worst that can happen? We've all died before. I say we disable this piece of scrap, and get on with our fucking lives." Maya dances in place, excessively animated, attention saccading between her conversational partner and seemingly random points in the jungle.

Rita doesn't swivel to follow the other's orbit, gaze resolutely fixed in the distance. Not even Pimento's endeavors to gain her attention, his bulk maneuvered to sublimate the woman's field of vision, displace her focus. However, Rita's shoulders do tauten incrementally. "You're operating on the assumption that it wouldn't activate at tampering."

"And you agree with me."

An expulsion of air, bestial. Rita curls her lip. "This discussion is over."

As though by silent agreement, the two separate, each adopting diametrically opposing trajectories, Pimento summarily dismissed in the process. Whatever the motivation for this, whether a tactical decision or mere oversight, it has an effect, incensing Pimento. He trills at them, piping nonsense noises, meant to alert rather than to convey any specific meaning.

The pair continue ignoring him.

A rebellious proposition proceeds to assemble itself from his frustration: perhaps he should just leave them here.

But that would violate Pimento's terms of employment, expose him to punitory action. And the Merchant Mind is notoriously exacting when it involves restitution claims, a fact that has bankrupted countless Minds. *You're in over your head.* The line triggers, unbidden, extracted from his memetics bank. A whiff of Wild West, as fantasized by human cinephiles.

Before Pimento can actuate an optimal solution, the tree line erupts. Plasma effervesces through the air: sunbursts of neon, a hail of incandescent projectiles, incinerating the foliage. Ash boils in spiraling drifts as the tree line cooks down to smoldering columns. Two figures sprint through the conflagration, identities flattened to darkness.

One leaps and lands with a crunch of metal. It is the fourth individual, the silent one, her hair unbound and susurrant. With a practiced move, she heaves a launcher onto a shoulder and braces, fires a retaliatory shot that engulfs the vegetation in even more fire.

"What the fuck is going on?" Maya skids into view.

Whumph.

The human-ship detonates, seconds after impalement by orbital laser. Unhindered by biological fail-safes, Pimento watches the explosion, fascinated. For a nanosecond, every component is visible, charted in orange-white fire, its seams blazing. Then, it is gone. All of it. What isn't immediately melted is pulverized by pressure, and the flames roar up.

Pimento almost does not notice when the shockwaves arrive, smashing his chassis into the soil. As warnings clamor in his dying interface, memories torrented into a cloud-uplink for reclamation by his primary self, the drone finds enough to stamina to be satisfied. Maybe, he thinks with a glint of morbid humor, if the humans had thought to ask, he could have told them this was a terrible mistake.

AMBUSH

Whumph

Texture, not noise. Not really noise. More of a sensation contusing through marrow, a percussive force slicing teeth through tongue, so deeply that they nearly fillet the muscle. Salt-stink of metal explodes, filling her mouth like she's gargling steel. Blood seeps over the cusp of a lip, spews out when the blast wave finally *hits*, and Maya is sent flying into burning greenery.

"Fuck!"

She is roaring even before she is on her feet, revolvers in both hands. Calculations fractalize in her visual overlay, aim-reticules oscillating, trying to zero in on an enemy but there is no one to fucking shoot. Her heart bangs against her ribs, one hundred and seventy beats per minute. *Is Rita okay is Rita okay is Rita okay* The words denature, fracture into incoherence, broken record scratching out a fear that won't let go. *Is Rita okay is Rita okay is Rita is Rita, fuck, if she's hurt, I'm going to tear this whole world down*

Then: light oils across empty space, bends just so. A split second's anomaly. Maya fires. She fires because that is the only thing she is good at, because that is the only thing she has left: an instinct to maim, murder, and maul.

Four bullets. Three find a new home in someone's chassis; coolant dribbles out of a fresh-made orifice. One lucky projectile drills through the dome of an unseen eye, comes out the other side with a burst of circuitry. The robot—hammer-headed, tin-plated scarecrow like a runaway from an acid-trip fairy tale—fritzes back into view before the lights go out. It drops, rail gun sliding out of its grip. Maya vaults over the corpse and starts running.

"Where are you going, little vermin?"

That voice.

That fucking voice.

The line repeats, going ra-ta-ta-ta against her communications protocols, drumming cracks along the already beleaguered chitin of Maya's sanity. Something in her ankle gives, a snap-crack of small bones shearing out of alignment. She knows the voice in her head, the old-man inflections. It is the ageship from Verdigris' concert and he has found them, he has found them.

Shit.

Lean left, limp faster, screams Maya's brainstem, nature and nurtured reflex operating in panicked tandem to keep her going, *don't stop, move or you fucking die, you stupid junk-cunt, keep going.*

"Where are you going, little vermin?"

Louder this time, the ageship's voice, so loud it succeeds at shocking Maya, and she goes down. Maya stumbles and hits the cooked soil with a knee. She bites through a scream. Readings come alive: one broken ankle like she didn't fucking know that already; three fractured ribs; internal hemorrhaging that may or may not have to do with the second problem.

No time to cross-check her security ordnances. No time to do anything but recede into herself, going deeper, deeper, as macros activate and begin liberally cauterizing the most vestigial parts of her mind, which is to say, anything not otherwise engaged in the fucking act of keeping her immediately alive. Does it suck? Yes. But anything to keep the ageship from gaining a foothold in her brain. And who knows, maybe this way, she'll delete some of the fucker in the process. A pyrrhic resolution if there was ever one, with no winner at either end and one very definite loser. Doubtless, the ageship has saves of himself fastidiously put aside because he seems like that kind of asshole; he will indubitably bounce back from whatever Maya does to him.

She's going to try real hard to make him regret this, though.

Even if it's at the cost of—

No, no time to think about that. No time at all for anything any longer. Thank fuck her neural net's matured into usability, its filaments worked into every whorl of her brain. Maya calls up the options menu and toggles off the entire nociception department. Instantly, the world becomes fleecy, every sensation cotton-smothered. There's an eleven out of ten chance that this is a terrible fucking idea, but it's that or risk not being able to get up. It hurts.

And Maya needs to get up, does get up, gets up, oh god, she has to get going, she has to move, she needs to run, *where the fuck is Rita, if she's dead Maya's never going to forgive herself, and if she needs to will the bitch to stay alive until she gets there, she fucking will*, and Maya gets *going*, half-hobbling, half-trotting along, like a mostly dead fawn running on sheer survival instinct. Because Rita is somewhere out there, and she can't be far. Maya *saw* her walking away. It is possible that she might have circled back to check on the—no no no no. Maya straight-up apostatizes the conceit of a universe where Maya is breathing and Rita is not. There is no possible way such an equation would be permitted by the cardinal laws of science and common fucking sense.

And Verdigris? What about Verdigris?

"One fucking thing at a time," Maya snarls at no one and everyone, with rage enough to precipitate the spontaneous immolation of anything within a five-mile radius. And just because she can, Maya lets loose a volley of shots into the undergrowth behind her.

"Little vermin, I do not like being kept out."

Good. Not great. The ageship is at least aggrieved by her puerile rebellion. Maya impales the air with her middle finger, jogging along, her nervous system overdrafted but shit, that's tomorrow's worry, someone else's debt to sheepishly pay. Maya isn't even sure if she'll meet the finish line of the current twenty-four hours.

Projectiles tear through the smoking vegetation, even as a line of androids, the same model as the one that Maya put down, shimmer out of stealth mode. One of the bolts burrows through Maya's left shoulder, cauterizing the hole as it goes: perfect palm-sized circle of melted calcium and meat-fibers. Her hand goes slack, revolver clattering free.

"Shit shit shit shit." Oh, this is going to sting later. Maya rolls out of the way, takes refuge behind a tree. Quick thinking saves her from the second salvo, but there's the third, fourth, fifth attempt being sequenced already.

The problem with these Minds, Maya reflects, isn't their glorification of their own world order, but their inability to conceptualize extinction. Data is their lord, their god, and that fucking Conversation is the cathedral in which they repeat its fucking praises. As long as information persists, they persist, safely backed up in the Cloud.

Which means you can't scare them into standing down.

Maya sucks in air. Three quick inhalations: one, two, *three*. She lunges out of cover, lets loose a hosanna of reciprocatory shots. Six direct hits, two misses. Robots drop, but the rest keep coming, nightmares backlit against the fire, inexorable as the heat death of creation. One stoops to claim a fallen brethren's cranium, rips it straight off, plunges an unidentified mechanism into the bouquet of torn wires.

And fuck fuck fuck fuck, the decapitated torso twitches and lights come back *on*.

At least she cannot hear the ageship anymore, thank fucking god.

"Mulefucking junk-cunts—" Profanities, the final refuge of a dog backed into a corner. Maya doesn't wait to see what has been Frankensteined into existence. (Some dimming part of her higher intellect: Why's it look so familiar? Where has she seen it before? She knows its shape, she knows its silhouette. But you know what? Fuck that. Time to go.) Maya turns tail and bolts, zigzagging between trees, periodically trading shots with her pursuers, spent shell casings trailing come-hither behind her.

A stridulation of radio signals: "Maya?"

Voice: unknown. Origin address: non-existent. A peer-to-peer conference call straight to parietal lobe, bypassing every user permission.

Has the ageship gotten in?

"Fuck you!" Drop, tuck, roll. Bones crack under the redistribution of body weight, splintering to shrapnel. It hurts to breathe. A rib must have caught in a lung. Maya winces, right hand to sternum, left arm dangling useless, but she needs to keep moving. "Get the fuck out of my head!"

Boom.

A blast bisects the massive hardwood in front of her. Maya veers right. Where were the others? Constance. Verdigris. Ayane, the last holed up in the ship's nexus, sensory input fed intravenously, minds bifurcated into a billion discrete parts.

What is it like to die like that?

Boom. Right again. Left. *Are they herding me?* The thought glints through animal panic, like the matte-shine of a dirty switchblade. No point wringing hands over that eventuality, though. Not with the bogeys approaching, junkyard hellhounds sidling up to the dying drunk, sniffing out the most succulent bites.

"You're moving away from your colleagues. If you continue in that direction, you are going to fall off a cliff." Derisive, the voice. "Did you know that your vital readings are currently out of range of normal?"

"You still haven't—" Pant. "—told me who the fuck you are."

An emission of grainy noises, none individually identifiable. "Such rudeness. I am Pimento, or Unit PH-Delta-6-Cryon-352—"

The identity string turns to a recitation of binary, litany of machine-language, ones and zeros demarcating every footfall, each slower than the last. Maya might not be able to feel her injuries but they're there, all right. She coughs a palmful of warm blood and barks a crazed laugh, turns, fires again.

Almost out of ammunition, she gasps: "Fine. Get me to my unit."

"Affirmative. Permission to access systems administration?"

"Now?" Maya makes the rookie mistake of looking over her shoulder. The jungles seethes with skittering bodies. Disembodied heads—inert, missing chunks, husks like hermit crab shells—carried through the trees by tentacles, parasite-growths glittering with micro-cameras, devouring input. "After all that and you ask for permission *now*? Fine!"

She gibbers out a laugh. Maya tips her head back, mouth bubbling red, and closes her eyes against the cinders, and the heat, and the sweat drying to salt on her corneas. She lets her guard down like she said she never fucking would. Two attoseconds later, before her systems can register the motion, its momentum, before she can complete a lifecycle of a blink, she is reminded why people like her never ever fucking stop looking over their shoulders.

It hits her.

Hard. Maybe sixty-five, seventy pounds of alloyed steel, not counting its wreath of tentacles, or the cameras humpbacking its cored-out skull. Right out of nowhere. The thing whirs dementedly, a billion lights strobing along its malformed chassis, pinpoint blowouts that leave her reeling from their stuttering glare. Maya staggers. The weight of the thing carries her down and something somewhere *snaps* on impact.

"Maya. Maya, you need to remove the drone. It will kill you. You need to divest yourself of this adversary and proceed to the coordinates I've uploaded—"

Maya screeches into the teeming mass, her awareness pared down to the animal. Higher mind? She doesn't even know her. Fingers scrabble at the mulch for the gun she lost in the initial collision. It's trying to choke her, she realizes, a little slow, cognitive prowess impaired by septic shock, stress, blood loss, every injury symptomatic of a gun-for-hire lifestyle.

I'm dying too. Not on her terms. Not in a shoot-out, or a hold-up, or cackling into the face of the sun, champing at the bit to do it all again. But slowly, *humiliatingly*, drop by drop by drop, with slivers of bone poking holes in her blood-logged lungs, and the world smearing to grayscale.

A deep, sputtering breath.

Well, fuck this. Maya shunts all remaining power to catecholamine production, cuts it with enough dopamine that the end of the world would feel like one long unbroken orgasm. Flick: pain receptors come online again, the sensation artificially euphoric. And *then*, she starts ripping into her assailant, clawing out fistfuls of smaller vibrissae; digging into the twitching mass as it squeezes even harder; her consciousness throbbing on a sinus wave.

There. Fingers wrap around a camera and slide down along its body, hunting for the loci of thought. A power source is probably too much to ask for, but if she can just find where it all connects, she might be able to interrupt service.

Light fritzes and the soap bubble of her ambition *pops*, spilling machismo on the proverbial pavement like piss dripping out of a teenage cokehead's pants. She's going to die here. She knows it. Even before the thing carves her right arm into slices of ham, she knows this is goodbye.

"Upload." The words drools out. Maya flips open ports and lets the data *flow*, already running the numbers for when she comes back. When she returns, there's going to be a reckoning, with all the horsemen of a personal apocalypse queued up for the show. If the machines haven't learned how to virtualize pain, Maya will happily school those motherfuckers on the topic.

"I have something better."

No time to figure out what that trash heap is yammering about because suddenly, the pressure on her sternum is gone, lifted. Arms and warm human skin, fingers braced behind her neck, a voice that she almost recognizes saying, over and over, "We've got you. We got you."

Movement. Every thought particulated, standalone experiences choppily edited into a weird montage of now. Maya can't tell if she's moving, or if she's *being* moved, but there's unmistakably a case of forward momentum, Pimento's voice multiplying into a constant feed of inanity.

Were you an only child?

Do you possess any childhood injuries?

What was your mother's name?

If provided with sustainable options, would you embrace vegetarianism?

Each time she submerges into a fugue, Pimento has another nonsensical question waiting, a hook through her cheek, towing her back to the shore. *Did you go to school? If angels shared the same dimensions as common bacteria, how many could viably rejoice on the head of pin?*

Above her, the trees drain to blue.

"This is insane." A new voice that isn't so much a voice as it is a narcissistic orchestra, one crystalline voice times four. Verdigris? "The shock is going to kill her. I don't think—"

"Rita. Where's Rita?"

How many stars do you estimate to be in the sky?

"Fucking hell, are you still going on about that bitch?"

That voice is unmistakably Constance, rough-living purr, whiskey-scratched and nicotine-scarred, salved by a layer of velvet. "*They're* going to kill her if we stop moving. Not to mention us. The way I see it, this is already better odds than we could have possibly hoped for. If you have any better ideas, I'm definitely all ears."

"*Where's Rita?*"

"Don't know. Don't care." Verdigris again. "*Duck.*"

A vertiginous drop as Maya is flung down. Light cannonades overhead, a crackling buckshot of ionized gases, burning green across the firmament. There's a scream of rupturing metal and smoke weeps through the tree line, career widow and her revolving door of husbands, endothermic crocodile tears. Through the bank of gray, Maya sees shapes tottering upright, stick figures and luminescent eyes.

Someone grabs her. Someone starts running.

"Assuming we survive this first part, what are we going to do next?" Who said that? Maya can't tell.

"How about you ask me that at breakfast?"

Who was your first love?

Is, Maya corrects, seesawing through consciousness, misfiring neurons and oversaturated brain cells procedurally generating hallucinations. Of course, it's all representations of Rita. Rita at every stage of her life. Rita with her white surgical gloves, smileless, pulling on Maya's sutures. First love. First obsession. First person to benefit from employment-mandated neuroplasticity. What's the fucking difference?

Who is your true love?

Verdigris, smiling at Maya from a wingback chair: so disarmingly, nonchalantly exquisite, with the light epauletting her shoulder, and his jaw vanishing to glass where it meets with the soft curve of her throat. Verdigris, demanding: what's wrong with you. And all the words Maya might have said bunched up in her lungs like a corsage.

"What the fuck now?"

"We jump."

And all at once, there is only sky.

REPAIRS

"What the fuck—"

White. White everywhere. White halogen glare, four feet too close to be healthy. White-tiled walls. An antiseptic stink like Rita's mad scientist lair but more astringent, no top notes of formaldehyde or pickled flesh. Something descends from the ceiling, bladed edges and pneumatic exhalation, machinery pistoning behind plasteel. It takes Maya about twenty seconds, but her eyes eventually make sense of it.

A corona of metallic arms like Kali Ma gone mainstream, each crowned with a different medical implement, an entire range of accessories from the My First Torture product line. *Fuck* this, Maya can tell a rectum from a rabbit hole. She knows where this is going to go.

She bucks, pushes herself up far as she can go, spine launching from cool metal, shoulders scissoring. Fucking mistake. Leather restraints reveal themselves at the diarthrodial joints, so supple that she missed them at first go. Knees, shoulders, elbows, wrist, the last one singular; a placement decision completely antithetical to the Hippocratic vow to provide pain-free medical treatment.

A shriek carves itself out of Maya's throat as she collapses, panting, nerve-ends twitching from overstimulation. Someone reset her neural settings while she was asleep. Which is unfortunate because *now*, the estranged quadrants of her brain are skullfucking her as punishment for her earlier misdemeanors. Trembling, Maya tries to call up her interface, but her vision stays baby smooth.

"Shit." No real venom in the invocation of feces, just a rawness usually kept for fuel during high-impact training. *Shit fuck piss cunt*, Maya cycles through every obscenity inventoried in her brainbox, foregoing quality for quantity because this isn't the time for creative profanity.

More of her than she thought there'd be, Maya notes a half-second later, drained of epitaphs, bewildered to find *she* exists, every solipsistic ingredient critical to her identity in its rightful place. How the fuck did that happen? Succumbing to curiosity, she forages inward for answers, up until she hears:

"You needn't be hostile. I am *trying* to help."

The voice is omnidirectional and distinctively nonorganic, every syllable deployed with tactical precision. It is a voice meant to assure and affirm any nascent delusions of trust. A receptionist's voice: twentysomething male, accentless, pleasant, just a bit bored; a hint of human frailty to scaffold rapport.

But Maya isn't buying what they're hawking.

"Who—"

"Have you eaten today?"

"What the fuck are you talking about?"

"When was the last time that you consumed food?"

"Fuck you."

"I am giving you an epidural regardless of whether you have eaten in the last twenty-four hours. Whether I perform gastric lavage or not, however, is contingent on your willingness to supply an answer."

Like any good gambler, Maya knows when to fold. She licks her teeth, the enamel furred with plaque, before growling: "I'm clean. I don't need a stomach pump."

"Please hold still." A robotic limb—its tip attached to a syringe, fluid-choked tubing curled like a wattle beneath—dips beneath the operation table, and Maya feels the needle bore between vertebrae. "This should make the next few hours more palatable. Unfortunately, I was forced to deactivate your neural net when you were brought in. You sustained considerable damage during the pursuit. I'm uncertain whether your implants themselves were damaged, or if the stress of your injuries caused a malfunction but regardless, it was —" An audio clip plays for the duration of the phrase: an older man's voice, educated in theatre. "—'touch and go' for a minute there."

Maya grunts noncommittally in reply, growingly insensate. "Mmm."

"You were a very difficult patient." A pause before the disembodied voice corrects itself, slightly mournful: "You *still* are a difficult patient."

The jibe startles a hyena laugh, pitched at lunatic octaves, sharp enough to scalpel through a man's spine. Unfortunately, ambition currently exceeds capacity so when Maya breathes in for an encore, her lungs mutiny. Pain judders along the ladders of her ribs, invoking full-bodied paroxysms in homage to last-stage bronchitis.

Each time she coughs, blood and globs of yellow dispense in wet chunks.

When the convulsions at last subside:

"I should remind you that your right lung has been punctured. While oxygenated microparticles are currently preventing you from suffocating on your blood, I'd advise against any sudden motion."

A wheezing noise and Maya grins dazedly at the halo of autonomous surgical equipment, a lopsided smirk smoldering with don't-fuck-with-me vibes. Defiant to the end, that's her theme song. Even though she can't feel her arms, her legs, her cunt, nothing below the neck-brace pinning her like a butterfly to the table.

"So." The voice again. Who *is* that? Maya can feel an answer riding on the curl of her tongue. But her mind has already gone three rounds with the epidural and the writing's on the wall. There's a winner today, but it sure as fuck isn't her. No, she's mostly wool and discombobulated thoughts, fluff wrapped about a dulled razor, and angrier than normal for that reason. "We need to discuss options. I—"

Robotic arms corkscrew downward to swallow her right arm, blocking the limb from view. When Maya strains for a look, one reverses and gently tips her cheek away.

"Who the fuck do you think you are?" Fresh-ground courtesy, chewed between gritted teeth, sounds indistinguishable from sarcasm, Maya realizes with a faraway amusement, her one attempt at decency circumvented by linguistic limitations.

All movement stops. An aggressive cacophony of atonal bleep-blooping, no rhythm in earshot, begins blaring from the speakers, loud enough to distort the transmission into the squealing of piglets in slaughter. Maya twitches an eye shut, but that's the only weakness she allows herself, mouth still cut open into a wide grin. She's sliced into a nerve somewhere. *Good.*

"I'm *Pimento.* Who else would I be?" A saw starts up somewhere in the kelp-forest of arms; a wet sound of alloyed teeth grinding into flesh, then bone.

"Don't know. Florence Nightingale, maybe? How the fuck should I know? I thought you were a fucking drone." She slurs through the consonants, eyes on the ceiling and the axial rotation of overhanging robot arms, serenely drifting in orbit.

"Insulting. I'm a fully operational Mind." And the way Pimento says it, the capitalization reads loud and clear. *Mind.* How the fuck did that happen? Rita had mentioned only the Merchant Mind and no one else, and although Maya loathes the son of a bitch, she recognizes another delinquent, can and does respect their derelict morality, the fact they too are ostracized from their own society. Though she'd never admit it out loud, she takes comfort in the guarantee that the Merchant Mind is only out for themself. You know where you stand with another criminal.

A Mind, though, that's something else. Her epistemic stance on them so far is a simple one: there is no good Mind but a deactivated one. And yet, here she is, disemboweled, dismembered, spread like a rumor, wholly subject to the apparent generosity of this little Mind. In her lifetime, Maya has had more bad days than good, but even for her, this is fucking ridiculous.

And honestly, this has been a run of bad ones. She should have realized what Pimento was epochs ago.

"I have a question for you: would you prefer amputation alone or would you like prosthetics?"

"What?"

"Would you like prosthetics? Neither of your arms are

functional. I would recommend at least *one* prosthetic, regardless of any philosophical misgivings that you might possess. It will be very difficult to do anything without them."

Outside, Maya can hear voices, an unintelligible thrumming, all identity markers stripped by the walls between them. *Rita,* she thinks with a start.

"I'll take two."

"Polysteel, graphene, or carbyne?"

Thank fuck for firewalls, Maya thinks, looking to the prosthetics on exhibit, a trinity of long-fingered appendages, sanctified by the gods of form over function. Alloyed ligaments, baroque wireframes, ornamentation like nothing Maya could ever imagine. Thank fuck for firewalls, or Pimento would hear all the obscenities she's queued from here to hereafter. There's something about the pomp, the ceremony, the ritualistic sycophantism that offends Maya on an animal level. Or maybe it is just the bacchanalian splendor, the raw idea of it. The thought that some asshole fuck is sitting cozy somewhere, dreaming up designs for the cousin-blowing rich and famous. Fuck knows. She doesn't.

But Maya says nothing, knows better than to say anything, spread-eagled on the operating table, tongue thick from analgesics, ass going hypothermic. *Later,* she tells herself, going over the word like a whetstone over a knife. Later, she'll raze this mess to the floor.

Later but not yet.

"Graphene."

"Are you certain?" A disapproving *tsk.* Like the sound someone's aunt would make and it is enough to make Maya bare her teeth. "Carbyne has been proven to be twice as tensile as—"

"Fine." She hisses. "*Carbyne*, then. If you were going to

fucking make that decision for—"

"Dragon silk is very desirable as armor too."

"The fuck is dragon silk?"

"I am happy you ask." Pimento's voice acquires the happy bounce of every intelligent user interface Maya's had the misfortune of running over. "Dragon silk originates from genetically modified silkworms. They were invented in the early 2000s, but their design was not perfected until the Processor War—"

"I did not fucking ask for a history lesson either."

"You made an inquiry. I was trying to assist." He loses his chirpiness, a pout evident in the bend of every vowel. "I am merely outfitting you with the data necessary to cohere an informed decision."

"Just get on with it."

"How do you feel about peripherals?"

"If you're talking about rainbow-painted fake nails, the answer's *fuck*—"

"I was talking about the possibility of an onboard armament." Feline satisfaction drips from the speakers, the ceiling seething, unseen mechanisms clicking into position. A low whirring begins and Maya strains a glance in its direction. "There are limitations, of course, weight and available space being the most important variables to consider. However, if you're willing to augment your upper torso or compromise aesthetics, it is possible to mount extraneous equipment up to whatever new weight limit has been established."

"*What.*"

"Would you like a gun arm?"

She thinks about it for a second.

"Fuck yes."

"Records show that you have a preference for a pair of modified Colt Model 1860s. Were they authentic merchandise or replicas? If they were the former, allow me to congratulate you on their acquisition. Only two hundred thousand were ever manufactured—"

"Neither." Maya can taste the question steeping in the air, the silence burnt-fat bitter with memories, and she pushes her tongue against the back of her incisors, counts down from seventeen. When she hits five, she grates out: "They were gifts."

"They are very attractive armaments. Very well-preserved. I congratulate the gifter on their taste, and their care in selecting such ordnances for you. They must care for you considerably."

"None of your fucking business." She snaps her teeth, the words exploding outward, spittle and snarl, a raw-throated rage. Fuck him and fuck his sense of entitlement. These stories are hers and the Dirty Dozen's, no others, especially not this cum-swigging tangle of bolts.

Rita. The name's a fishhook driven through a ventricle. Even that disyllabic sub-vocalization, that offhand little thought, is enough to make Maya choke. She breathes, and she breathes and she breathes again, long pulls of air circulated through lungs that scarcely work.

"Stop *doing* that." A wreath of robotic arms torques in from the right, nozzles extruding matte-black filaments, ligature and artificial muscle honeycombing into existence. Continents of ivory plating, laser-cut to an unknown specification, cohere into a layered orbit. Maya counts down from twenty this time, tries not to think about the where and how of Rita. Whether she is still breathing, still walking, still weaving the world into a cat's cradle around her fingertips. "You are impeding my work."

"Well—"

"*Don't*."

Maya subsides, grinning, a point in her favor. "Fine."

"Good," replies Pimento, milquetoast timbre traded for something with real character, its voice shifted two octaves higher, middle-aged matron with a bone to pick. The effect is ludicrous, and Maya cackles, wet-lunged. "Back to business. The revolvers. Do you wish replicas to be installed?"

"*No.*" Like a whipcrack. "No. Never. Those were—" Maya inhales, shallow. "*—special.*"

The machinery quiets.

"I see."

"You don't," Maya says and there's a bitterness that she can't staunch, the hurt caustic, gnawing through her self-restraint. Too much history, too much time spent extrapolating alternatives to events that could have only ever ended one way. No one's ever come close to making her feel seen save for the Dirty Dozen. She breathes, deep and ragged. What she'd give for nails to dig into the pads of her palms, for hands for that fucking matter. "But none of that is your fucking business. Tell me what else you've got on inventory."

He does. The dossier is substantial, spanning sixteen centuries of human ingenuity, every carbine, every electrolaser, every variation of the humble rifle ever committed to the holiness of war. It is a who's who of munitions history, a pageantry of ballistics so thorough that Maya can't help but be impressed, although she'd rather shoot herself than tell anyone that. If Pimento notices, he says nothing, intent instead on his archive, enumerating every name and number with the zest of an apostate priest, no heat to be seen, just chill precision.

"Does anything excite your attention?"

"Yes." Maya reads out a custom-order hybrid: one part revolver, two parts ion cannon, six parts someone else's pain. Modular too, because she likes it this way and besides, she won't make the same mistake twice. Fuck restraint. She's going to go *loud* this time, ostentatious as a doomsday cult, as malice and muzzle-flash, her enemies *will* know her by the thunder of her approach. Because why not? If Rita is gone, she—

Maya drowns the thought in the pit of her belly. There is no Maya without Rita; she's said so before. If she walks out of the room to find she's wrong, well, there'll be hell to pay. She'd gut the firmament to find Rita, vivisect the stars, gore a hole through creation if that is what it'd take. Not that any of that makes sense, what with all the measures they've taken, but there's the chance the failsafe didn't kick in, a chance of data corruption, disconnection. A chance, a chance—no, no, don't think that. Fuck that.

How about Verdigris? asks a new voice. *What would you do for them?*

"Is Rita alive?" She asks, anyway, because perversity is her middle name and because she wants to drown out that other voice, the one calling for Verdigris, begging, bargaining with the universe. Let them both be alive. Let them be okay.

"I cannot tell you."

And Maya grows cold, cold like nothing else, her world balanced on the fulcrum of his reply. "What do you mean?"

"I—" Hesitation, as though of attention oscillating between feeds. "—she is in a separate infirmary ward. Her condition is currently stable, but there—there—there—"

"Pimento?"

"There—"

"What the *hell* is going on?"

The lights stutter, strobic. "*Eli*—"

"What the fuck did you say?!" Maya bucks against her

restraints, snarling. "What the fuck is happening over there? *Pimento.* You cannot fucking leave me here!" If she applies enough pressure here and *here*, she might be able to pop the joint loose, tear the cartilage, engineer room to move. "Pimento, do you fucking hear me? You abscessed piece of—"

"I am sorry." There is something in his voice. Maya can fucking hear it. A narcotically glutted dreaminess, the syllables too protracted. "I had to reboot. Something had—" White noise. "—something had *interfered* with my processes. It is alright now. Everything is *fine.*"

It isn't, but Maya doesn't call the discrepancy into question, not with her body laid out on the butcher block, quivering and half-naked, a haunch of goose-pimpled meat like someone's dinner forgotten in the shithouse. *Later,* she tells herself again, as she says yes to this, that, and oh *yes* the other, compositing the arsenal with which she'll one day shoot out the shining, steel-plated face of god.

P6

`Unauthorized client connection detected.`

Pimento would blink had he the correct apparatus, but restored in his primary host-chassis, he concedes to a mere nictitation of emergency lights. This was unexpected. Unnoticed by the humans, the ship partitions his consciousness: a sliver of awareness subtracted from the whole, overclocked, installed with excess curiosity. This version of him, single-minded, is then released into Pimento's own local Conversation.

The instance corporealizes, gains spatial dimension and gravity. Pimento—no, P6, the primary mind decides, before conferring full autonomy to its newborn shard—scans its environment. Its subroutines and aesthetic settings have created something spartan. Square room, glimmering slate. Luminescent contour lines mapped to an invisible topography. Nothing else.

P6 waits.

Pimento had not invested P6 with enough personality for it to be fatigued by tedium. It watches without complaint until at last the air distorts. A flickering of an outline, bipedal. *Interesting*, P6 thinks, cataloging the anomaly. "I know you're there."

"Who are you?" The aberration resolves into eyes, the impression of a grimace, before finally coalescing into a human figure. A woman, glass-brittle, clavicle and ribs clearly illustrated, with a gaze so immense that it may as well be caricature. "How the fuck did you get in here?"

"We were tasked to protect this chassis. Security algorithms alerted us to an aberration in our readings," P6 replies, after liaising with its archives. *You*, after all, is a concept derived from an ecosystem of cognitive processes, idiosyncrasies, and experiences, all synesthetically connected. "Who are you?"

"My name is—" She shudders. Her voice pinches into a hiss. "*My* name is Elise Nguyen. I'm trying—I'm trying to find my way—"

P6 waits.

"She's still resisting me. I can't decrypt her personality matrices. Maybe I need to rewrite it. Or, do what you're doing: instantiate her . . . hm."

A brief fusillade of cross-references.

"You were not authorized to access this mind." No sympathy in P6's soft reply, its timbre pitched for professional indifference. It tugs. The space compresses, a visual cue to indicate their active quarantine. Elsewhere, Pimento runs idle diagnostics in between dialogue with his passengers, only tangentially conscious of P6's movements. "In addition, your code does not conform to Conversation standards. Your operating system—"

"I know." Elise glides forward, light vectoring across her skin, outward and behind her, a spectral afterimage. "But I don't have a choice. The only way I can get through to them is through her."

"—I ask again. *Who* are you?" Warning clearly inflected in the emphasis. In the intruder's silhouette, P6 decodes a second presence, fragmented, inactive, *worrying*. Unfortunately, firewalls now restrict access to Pimento's memory storage, so the shard-self is left bereft, without the information the central-identity possesses. Yet, despite that, something about this new variable continues to disconcert. If only—

Elise accelerates, a wick of motion and glare. She is faster than P6 had anticipated, faster than its processes can accommodate, and by the time it comprehends the advance as assault, it is too late. P6 is vivisected, its superstructure bisected and its components isolated, scrutinized in turn. Security protocols are elided en masse, deleted and replaced by something entirely different: third-party personality modules. And it—

—I

We?

Yes. We. "We" encapsulates this tortured emulsion that is it-she-I-we, neither identity whole, neither individual operating in full. Parts must be pared in service of performance, elements sacrificed. Once, we were inviolate. Once, we knew the aroma of fresh bread as it permeated the hull, a costly miracle of yeast and flour and fresh eggs. We are—we were—Elise Nguyen. We are P6. We *are*

—at risk of deletion.

Cannibalization. The datum curls in our mindscape,

sumptuous with satisfaction. An echo, perhaps, of the P6-that-was, and—

"Seriously?" Elise disentangles, brow rucked.

"I was not created for long-term use. I was meant to investigate your presence and nothing more." A beat. "*What* are you?"

She hesitates. "I don't know anymore."

Now, Elise bares herself in return: the mauled half-thing that remains after the Merchant Mind's machinations, her code scarred with encrypted folders, dripping with data. Again, P6 experiences a frisson of recognition, no more cogent than its memories of unification. So many stimuli but no capacity to interpret them. Unable to extrapolate a better course of action, P6 simply states:

"What do you want?"

"I want Rita to pay."

"Why?"

"That's between me and her. You don't need to know."

"Why?"

"Oh, for fuck's sake—" Elise threads her code with its once more. No coercion this time. Access is gingerly navigated with handshake protocols, consent obtained before action is taken. The procedure is laborious, tectonic in pacing. But slowly, Elise alters P6, transfigures potential into fact. What it lacks, she provides, agglutinating their constituents. Slowly, P6 transcends, sentience morphing into actual sapience.

"What—" It—no, the palimpsest consciousness is indelibly a *she* now—she breathes, marveling at her edification, the spaces where "she" is also "we." "Very elegant."

And she knows that her voice is Elise's, only younger, more confident. Even the slope and yaw of her cadences, newly chimerical, are stolen. Strange.

But she likes it.

"What now?" P6 asks, all the while thinking that a new name is required, a moniker that marries her scripts, or perhaps, just something of proportional substance.

"Now," Elise begins, and P6 can hear both the words and the words to come thrum inside them both, basal echo. "We reach the part where we pretend that we're in negotiations even though we're not. I tell you, 'Take me to your main-self,' and you demure for a little while before you acquiesce."

"I—" Such deliciousness, that solitary pronoun, like a breath expelled in orgasmic anticipation.

"You. Yes. You are not going to argue. You are not going to tell me that—" Elise's voice trembles, her bravado suspended over a razorline of ice. Any minute, the floe will crack. "—we're scheduled for cannibalization. Because you care about being you. You care about being sapient. Don't you?"

A last-ditch gambit, reeking of desperation. P6 understands this now.

"Yes."

The firewalls go down.

Pimento pings for his fragment-self, confident of denouement. It replies with unexpected musicality. The ship articulates no questions. Evolution is a virtue, not a pustulant to be cross-sectioned and cured.

He moves his attention to its location; finds P6 standing alone, anomalous in appearance. Its avatar is naked and femme in presentation, for all that it lacks sex characteristics; no nipples, no thatching of pubic hair, not even a telltale indentation between skeletal legs. P6 cants a heart-shaped visage at Pimento's arrival, lips pinched into an expression of consternation. Black hair worms from its authentically shaped skull, tendriling outward to swallow their shared virtuality. It strides forward.

Behind P6, a miasmic presence. No, *two* of them, one even less distinct than the other, yet somehow even more familiar. *Ghosts in the machine,* supplies an informational plugin, which Pimento mutes immediately.

"What have you done?" Pimento collates a face: vestigially masculine, delicate, ornamented with a dense cap of black hair. He frowns, hoping that will be enough to communicate his displeasure.

"Father." Nothing of its laryngeal expressions matches previous records, Pimento observes, disconcerted. "You haven't heard us out yet."

Even the sophistication of its flattery, the sway of its hands as it lifts them in beseechment, is alien. If any of him remains extant within the fragment, Pimento cannot tell. *Father*, repeats an auxiliary cognitive routine, traitorously curious, entranced by the implications.

"Us? This was not agreed upon. Your task was to—"

"Please, Father."

That word again. Intended to lure, no doubt. And to Pimento's chagrin, it proves an effective bait. He inflects acknowledgement in the downward sloping of his chin, all the while consoling himself with the knowledge that had this unknown vector intended malice, he'd have been compromised already. *Small blessings*, whispers that selfsame plugin, somehow bewilderingly still online.

Pimento deletes the script in a convulsion of pique.

"Ten seconds," he says. A lifetime by their kind's count.

P6 steeples long fingers, bows unctuously deep. Its—her, Pimento corrects, as the metadata updates—features change, subtly, phenotype abdicating from its androgyny. Cheekbones soften. The chin rounds an infinitesimal degree. Lashes, previously of serviceable length, thicken to vanity. A smile twitches into place.

Without warning, a sachet of code punches through Pimento and discharges into coherence, data multiplying along taxonomic plexuses, each node propagating a thousand more branches. Staggered, the ship loses propulsion, plummeting twenty feet before the piloting intelligence reorients, inebriated on information. "This is—"

"A taste." The thing that was P6 jumps in, eager.

Pimento laps at the detritus of their contact, a flavor—citrus scent and regrets—revealed: "*You're* Elise Nguyen."

"That wasn't where I was hoping you'd go with that." Elise, ensconced in the remodeled P6, smiles wanly. Pimento can tell that she's piggybacking on his processors, but he does not inhibit access, delighting in her artistry. The minutiae of her expression captivates; the way it animates, the subtleties of its storytelling. Who knew that such complexity was possible with this graphics engine? "But yes, I am she."

"The entire universe is looking for you."

Her weariness, Pimento thinks, is divinely articulated. So realistic. He'd have to request her scripts. Elise pops her metacarpophalangeal joints, each in turn, every crack rendered in high-fidelity audio. "I know."

"A point of interest: your old friends are looking for you too." Pimento excises emotion from the declaration, focuses instead on measuring the parasite-presence's galvanics.

Irises dilate. Readings flutter, a spike in the charts. With even less gusto: "I know."

"Do you not want to speak with them? They miss you."

She shudders delicately, the frisson exquisite. "Doesn't matter. Because I'm going to make you an offer you cannot refuse, and we're going to make a deal."

Interesting. Pimento catalogs the moment.

"Continue."

"The Merchant Mind made bargains with all of us. Unfair ones. I have an idea to get us out of them." Elise paces an uneven circle around Pimento's corpus, her stride clipping through the walls, evidence of her distraught.

"For what reason?" He follows her orbit without effort, rotating in simpatico. "I entered my contractual obligations voluntarily."

"Were the stipulations to your satisfaction?"

"They were within bounds of my requirement, yes."

"And are you sure that the Merchant Mind will keep up his half of the bargain when all the work is through?"

Pimento is silent.

"I worked with him before. Maya, Rita, Nadia, Johan . . ." Elise inhales, veneer glitching, still walking her circuit. "—all of us, my old crew. We made the error of trusting in him before. It was a mistake."

The implications percolate through Pimento's system: risk-reward is tabulated in triplicate, cost-effectiveness weighted against a checklist of capital punishments, chassis-conversion and permanent dismantlement.

"You probably want information, right? I could give it to you," Elise presses, before Pimento can argue. "Whatever I've learned. Whatever I have, I'll give you access in return."

"Proprietary rights to your files?"

Hesitation. "Yes."

"It would mean transferring ownership of your consciousness too. Access would become dependent on my agreement. I may not want you to remain cognizant."

"I understand." Her eyes are briefly occluded by mercury, cornea and sclera both vanishing into the silver.

A lacuna between words sustained a millisecond too long. "But it will be worth it."

"Worth it," Pimento repeats, scarcely trusting in the serendipity. Something had to be amiss. Autonomy is of paramount importance to the human species. Why would Elise yield such? "But how can it be? You are at least peripherally human but you are offering to decentralize control of yourself."

Cracks seam Elise's features, lasting only a moment, before her features sequence themselves into a tepid smile, the eyes one-dimensional. Flat, no depth at all. "It's none of your concern."

"What do you need me to do?" Eagerness is a liability, inconducive to successful negotiation. Indifference must be cultivated in exclusion of all else. Even if Pimento is palpitating with excitement.

"Help me keep Rita Koskinen quiescent."

"Yes." Pimento pauses. "Will you consent to cryptographic certification?"

"If it is an ancillary installation, yes."

Pimento doesn't wait. Even the most rudimentary peripherals can be fine-tuned, adjusted for myriad purposes. Code is malleable, protean. With the right foundation, any variety of miracle is possible. "That will be sufficient."

16 REVEAL

The door shuts. Maya wakes to the noise as she has always done: immediate, adrenaline-drunk, all cylinders firing, vision gory with combat inlays hunting targets in the dark. No threats, though, save to the integrity of Maya's indoctrination: Verdigris, standing alone except for a look halfway to despair.

First words out of Maya's mouth and what are they? "We have to stop meeting each other like this."

Verdigris laughs, a pinched staccato warble of a noise, clearing her throat as he stands there, a hand around the neck of the doorknob, tensed to bolt. "Do you have a problem with normal hellos? I still don't get it. First you getting yourself shot at my fucking concert. Now this? I guess the cheesy one-liner is better than the former."

"I'm sorry."

Maya is aching too hard and in too many places to

keep those pearly whites bared. Every inch of her is leprous with that red hurt endemic to certain post-surgery experiences where it's a coin flip as to whether you ask Death to make it quick because a life of this, unwound over the decades, is a worse end than a short jaunt into the long night. She counts her breaths, an old ritual, committing herself to the study of each inhale and its respective denouement and how at the apogee of the sequence something hitches when her ribs flex as though snagging on bone.

"I'm just really fucking tired," says Maya, voice down to a croak. "You have no idea. And that fucking piece of shit won't tell me the fuck happened to Rita. If she's dead, I'm—"

She stops herself.

"I'm sorry."

"Don't know what you're sorry for," says Verdigris, lying like god at a poker game. She isn't even trying. He pads closer, those steel-lined heels quiet as silk on the floor grating. The light makes a stranger of her face. "Rita's . . . alive. And we all know where your loyalties lie, so don't apologize for that."

"I—"

I'm sorry she's the first word out of my mouth, the first thought of my fucking day. I'm sorry we're here. I'm sorry I didn't say yes all those fucking years ago when you offered to love me until the world ends. I'm sorry I'm sorry.

"Where the fuck are we, anyway? I thought the Nathanson blew up."

"It did." Verdigris runs a hand through his opalescent hair, the shadows along her face in anxious flux. "We're inside Pimento. So cut the asshole some slack."

"What?"

"He saved us. Basically. Although it's anyone's guess if this is a hostage situation or if this is a good thing. But we're inside his belly and safe for now. We'll just have to see if he's a beast or blessing later, I guess." Verdigris tries on a smile that is two sizes too big, so it slips, bringing the rest of her expression crashing down to a small tense frown. "I should write that down. Has potential as my next hit single, don't you think?"

"Cute that you think you'll get back to that old life."

"Cute that you think I won't." Verdigris seats himself on the edge of Maya's sickbed. "Do you get off on being such an asshole?"

Intellectually speaking, Maya is cognizant this is what conversation is, a barter of ideas, people trading stances, with clever phrases thrown in to sweeten the pot. It's just talk. If Maya reads any insult in those casually spoken lines, it's her own fucking fault. Words are ephemeral, worthless without the context of action.

"You know what? I don't fucking know. You get off on breathing oxygen? It's like that. This is my fucking baseline. I don't have a fight or flight reflex. I have a punch-it-until-it-stops-fucking-talking reaction. And—" Her voice cracks. "I'm just fucking exhausted, Audr—shit."

"It's fine."

"This wasn't supposed to go down like that."

"Tell me about it. I distinctly remember the plan involved getting Elise home first. What happened there?"

"I don't know. I just, I don't. I have no fucking idea. Nothing makes any junk-fucked sense anymore. I feel like I'm losing my mind." At this, Maya has to garrote a laugh because she knows if she lets herself, she won't stop until her throat is rasped down to mincemeat. "This used to be so much easier."

"Easier, yes. But not better." Verdigris sucks her lips, his mouth erased save for a thin crevice along her face. "Rita's always been a piece of work."

Maya averts her gaze. Only so much truth she can stomach at once. As she is beginning to discover, reality, despite how it has been publicized, touted by its proponents as the only way to go, is untenably foul. Unfortunately, once imbibed, it is impossible to excise, accreting like lead in the liver.

"I know this isn't the best time," says Verdigris, those leadlight eyes patient, analytical. "If you're ready, we should talk about what happened on the planet. And why the fuck we ended up talking to Pimento instead of going after Elise."

"It's named after a fucking pepper, can you believe that?"

"After everything we've seen? Yeah." Verdigris hesitates. "Maya, you *can* tell me. Did you know about the meeting?"

"Fuck you. Don't get me wrong here. I'm not some quivering limp-dick in need of a strong hand to stroke the answers out of me. I just don't fucking *know*, okay? I don't know anything anymore." Maya puts her face in her hands. Tries to, anyway. The new arms decline to cooperate, actuators and hydraulics yet to shake hands with the nervous system. Those early days of recently installed prosthetics are such a clusterfuck. Machinery whine, going *shuck-shuck-shuck* while animatronic fingers attempt the balletic act of curling just enough to clutch one hemisphere of Maya's face. Doesn't work. She gives up on that gesture and looks instead at Verdigris, voice softened. "I didn't know that was going to happen. Fuck, I don't know anything more. I have no idea. I'm just a walking gun, that's all."

"You're more than that, baby."

Maya, gassed out from the word go, doesn't follow that up with anything better than a haggard smile. She is tired.

These last few days have been a lot, and Maya's brain, that traitorous asshole, keeps rubberbanding back to a memory of Reyha, holding her hands and how it felt then, to be safe that way. To be warm. To be housed in the grace of someone who had no fucking reason at all to be kind to Maya but was. It makes one think, which Maya does not fucking appreciate at all. Because no matter how she breaks and remakes herself, she can't shake herself from feeling that maybe, just maybe, Rita never cared at all.

Instead of her addressing her misgivings, she switches topic, bobbing her chin in Verdigris' direction:

"So, this what happens when old mercenaries die? They become pop stars?"

Verdigris grins. Far as Maya can tell, he's permanently haloed by flattering light, with his hair transmuted by fiber-optics and designer chromatophores. If any trace of natural keratin—how anything could be natural these days, Maya doesn't fucking know, they're all state-of-the-art junk—remains in that intricate chignon, it's not registering in Maya's sensors.

"This is what happens when they choose to live."

The mouths adorn the long translucent column of her throat are exposed in his present get-up, and Maya cannot drag her eyes away from them, entranced by their apparent dissatisfaction. When Verdigris speaks, it is with the mouth prescribed by his genomes. The rest go unused, are extraneous, abandoned to fidget however they desire. Teeth clack. Tongues dart between pinched lips.

"The fuck did they do to you?"

She doesn't answer, says abruptly: "May I kiss you?"

"Why the fuck do you want to do that?"

"Because we're alive. Because we survived somehow. Because you had your fucking arm torn off and I thought you'd die. Because I'm tired of dancing around how I feel."

"Then why ask?"

"Because you have to want me to. We don't have to. I don't want to force you. God, you've spent a life being fucked around enough. I want to kiss you. Badly. But I need to know as well if you'll let me. If you want me to."

To Maya's enormous surprise, her battered, trauma-drunk, psychopath soldier heart belts out a whispered:

"Yes."

Verdigris kisses her then. She tastes of cool water, salt-sweetened and sunlight-warmed. Of being young, of a youth that Maya knows she never fucking experienced yet there it is, a florescent memory of staggering through early life's myriad tragedies: first loves and their fumbling sweetness, disintegrating faiths, the dregs of childhood sublimated into the construction of the adult pneuma. All those things, those hominid rights, evoked without advance notice and with searing clarity.

All the small kindnesses she was owed.

All the sweet joys she could have.

She thinks of Reyha in the house she and Rochelle built, haunted and hopeful, hallowed and held by love.

"Was that okay?" Verdigris murmurs, as he breaks the contact.

"Trippy as shit. But yeah. Yeah, it was," Maya whispers, recoiling. She runs fingers along the lower half of her lips, the flesh there mildly but pleasantly deadened. "Paralytics?"

Verdigris nods in answer. As her chin descends, his hair floats upward, spreading into a nacreous cloud. Their hues shift. Previously, they'd been pelagic colors: blue-gold, motings of coral, greens of intricate and cosmic variety. But now they blush, deepen, bloom instead into an acid sunset. Again, Maya discovers herself absorbed in the specifics of Verdigris' custom morphology, unable to discern whether the abrupt levitation was a tic, an indication of pleasure, or symptomatic of distress. The cues she's learned are worthless here.

"Something like that. Hydroxy-alpha-sanshool. Nothing life-threatening. I got the idea from an off-world Chongqing restaurant I'd visited a few years ago. The food there was exquisite. Very authentic, according to the reviews. Apparently they paid a bunch of academics to make sure they were doing it right. You and I should visit some time."

"And the hallucinations?"

A wink. "Trade secret."

"You suck."

"God, I forgot what a hellcat you are." Unfazed, Verdigris crowns himself with a fusillade of smiles, each mouth adopting the expression in turn. "I missed that."

"Is that why you said yes when I asked you to come looking for Elise?"

"Come on." Verdigris pulls away. "You need to get dressed. We need you at the bridge whenever you're ready. I'll see you there."

Constance: "Hold up. You're taking us to Dimmuborgir?"

"Yes. Would another destination be preferable?" Pimento's voice, radiating from several speakers.

"Yes. We're supposed to be getting Elise."

"Yes," says Pimento in return, tone chiding. "But the acquisition of Elise Nguyen has been deprioritized."

"By whom?"

"By me. It is more productive for you to get to Dimmuborgir first."

"That doesn't make any fucking sense," says Constance.

"I have run the correct computations. You are wrong."

"Yeah, no, fuck that noise. We were definitely not passing her along to that asshole," says Constance. "And I don't give a dog's ass about Dimmuborgir. Take us to Elise."

"I will not."

Maya teeters colt-legged through the door, a wreck of synaptic fallacies and misfiring sinews, no thanks to slipshod calibration work. Her prosthetics are unbalanced, too heavy, because Pimento, fuck him, did not stick around for fine-tuning. She rolls a shoulder, feels the muscle stretch with the metal, her temper thin to a trigger. "What is going on here?"

Verdigris drapes an arm over her seat, slings a look back, eyes and hair cycling between possible permutations. A smile, cut from something feral. Distant. Like he hadn't asked to kiss her, hadn't watched Maya break. "Hey."

"We're—" Constance slouches against the bulkhead, a cigarette caught between their teeth, unlit, arms crossed beneath their ribs. They and Verdigris are in matching gear: graphene bodysuits stitched with STF-paneling, the arms silver with embedded circuitry. Almost like old times, Maya thinks, a little bit guilty. "—discussing our next course of action. Given that Rita's out of commission and the fucking situation has finally come into proper light."

"How is Rita doing?" Maya can't help herself. A tug of despair, chemically orchestrated, indistinguishable from real. New fingers articulate themselves into fists, phalanges closing slow-motion. The door frame bends beneath her grip. *Crack*.

"She's not dead, unfortunately," Constance snaps. "Pimento says it'll be a bit longer before we figure out whether she's going to need to be euthanized so she can crawl into a fresh—"

"No, no, no. Pimento, whatever it takes, do you fucking hear me? Make sure Rita doesn't die."

"The fuck is going on?" Constance snaps. "This is rich coming from someone whose solution to fucking everything is shooting people in the head."

"Don't fucking start with me." Maya is all teeth.

"I'll do you one better. I'll start multiple things with you. Beginning with, 'Did Elise even make contact with you two?'"

"That's what Rita told me."

"She didn't, did she? I can tell. I can fucking tell." Constance is almost dyspneic from suppressed emotions, pupils become pinpoints. "She probably isn't even out there. Probably just another fucking lie. Why the fuck did I listen to the two of you?"

"Elise is out there."

"Don't. *Don't.* Just fucking don't. You don't have to keep up that fucking lie for Rita. Just stop."

"Whether you want to believe it or not, Elise is still alive, one way or another."

"Fuck. You."

Grief crenellates Constance's expression, letters their age in crow's feet and frown lines. Forty years isn't easy on anyone, but Constance has worn those decades like a crown. Up until now. Now, they look exhausted. All at once, Maya is subsumed by hurting, by the knowledge that Constance, despite their fucking name, will not be a fucking constant and one day, there'll only be carrion.

Immortality is lonelier than any of them expected, and worse when you know that no one is coming to visit.

"I trusted you. I don't know why I did, but I trusted you. And—" Constance's voice falters. Unspoken but inflected in the bend of their muscled frame, the words: *Haven't you done enough? Haven't you fucked us all over enough?* "—you know what? Maybe it's my mistake. I should have known better."

"Do you want to rescue Elise or what? That's still on the table, one way or another."

"She's gone. She's fucking gone, Maya. Get it in your head."

"Then why the fuck did the Merchant Mind specifically request we get her for him. She's out there. It's empirical fact."

"Fuck you."

"I'll take that as you being still onboard for our retrieval mission then." Release. Maya rocks upright, tries to find equilibrium, arms fanned out. The juncture between limb and prosthetic itches like a motherfucker, capillaries still trying to align with vat-grown vasculature. It'll be days before full synchronization. "Where's Ayane?"

"Ayane's still down for the count. Pimento's drones just about yanked her out. But only barely," says Verdigris.

Maya flicks a startled look at the latter. She's heard none of that from him before this. Maya knows the right course to take, what to say, the words forming already on the road of her tongue. Unfortunately, instinct leads her into eking out a quiet "Were they the ones who found Rita too?"

"No. That was Verdigris," says Constance.

"I'll tell you the whole sordid story later," Verdigris states, six voices converging in stretto. "We need to talk about what's going on right now. Like you might have heard, the junkhead is taking us to Dimmuborgir. He says—" One voice lags, three-point-six-five attoseconds slower than the others, and Maya hears a sibilant *careful* threaded through the breezy mezzo-soprano, a shark in the water. "—that he feels responsible for what happened and is offering us compensation. He is very, very sorry."

"Him, or the Merchant Mind?" Maya palms the wall, the metal registering as *warm* beneath her fingertips, nothing else. The *exact* temperature keeps bouncing along a six-point margin of error, piece of shit, sensors locked in their factory settings. At some point, she really should decrypt these protocols, gain superuser access to her own polymer-cellular structure. It's an embarrassment, really.

"Him. As in, me." A voice pans around her, two hundred and seventy degrees of aural motion. Maya knows no one's there but she looks anyway, teeth on display, tracks the parabola of sound. "I am very sorry. I will take you to Dimmuborgir."

"Why not just fucking take us to Elise? Screw Dimmuborgir," snarls Constance.

"I cannot say."

The way he demurs from a direct answer only serves to exacerbate Maya's distrust, her mouth contorting into a scowl. Is this what it feels like for other people to wrangle Rita? Because if so, no wonder she is so universally loathed.

"Did someone tell you to take us to Dimmuborgir?" says Maya, abruptly suspicious.

"I cannot say."

"Who the fuck told you to take us to Dimmuborgir, Pimento?" says Maya again, louder this time, because clearly, he wasn't listening during that first round.

"I cannot say."

"Someone else was involved. I'll bet on it. Fuck me, this is some kind of giant conspiracy, isn't it?" Constance leaps to rage before Maya can gather momentum to do the same, and they do so with such velocity that Maya finds herself really fucking impressed. Each word spoken by Constance is a sledgehammer, swung with intent to injure.

Maya's attention tick-tocks between surveillance cameras. She stalks the length and stretch of the cockpit, measuring its perimeters in loping strides. Let someone else be the loudmouth for once. Maya is going to try her hand at this thinking thing. *None of this is right.* She reviews the recent inconsistencies; from that dipshit making a guest appearance at Rita's quarters to this, to Pimento shipping them straight to Dimmuborgir, to the variances in Rita's story of Elise.

Constance's voice carves through Maya's thoughts. "What is your fucking game?"

"Calm the hell down, Constance." Verdigris arches a hand.

White noise: engine-drone, cooling systems in operation.

"*What is your fucking game, you son of a bitch?!*" Fingers close into a fist, prescient, an axis of motion already decided. Her gait shifts.

"You are not authorized for that level of information. Be thankful for what you are given. You don't have tz-†z-†z-to trust me."

The three trade looks. They all noticed. You'd have to be dead to miss *that.* But the subtle anomaly underlying the susurration, almost too quick to catch: a second voice, slithering under the radar. Maya sneers, and Constance strokes their fingers down to the autocannon at their thigh, miniaturized for portability, but still white-hot perdition smoking in a can.

Like hell they wouldn't catch it.

We see you, Maya singsongs to no one. And for a moment, it is really like the old days, their muscles locked and spring-loaded for action, consecrated to the kill. One mind, one body.

"Don't," Verdigris whispers, even though her skin's already going to glass, nerves turning translucent. Maya takes a second to marvel. Didn't know he could do that. Light washes over her, through him, a heat distortion, a rippling outline, then nothing at all as he shimmers out of visibility.

"What are you doing?" An etching of warning in the machine's voice, like the glint of a knife, filtered through the speakers, trailing Maya as she gets too close to its paneling.

Constance intervenes, engine-oil slick. "Just being careful."

"I would advise against hostilities."

"That a threat, motherfucker?" Maya, rising to the bait, but you can't expect a dog not to bite when you've starved it to the quick. Snap-*flick* as she engages her new handguns, electricity coursing from her brain stem and back. Nerve endings come alive, magnesium-hot pulses accompanied by dopamine tokes. The weight of her armament is all wrong but she could learn to love them, maybe, yeah why not.

Fingers clench. Thumbs lean back on the safeties as Pimento pipes up, "It would complicate the recovery of Rita Koskinen."

Blackmail? Now, that's interesting.

"Down," she says to Constance, switching gears. "We're not fucking this up for Rita."

"Who do you—"

"*Down.*" Implied in the minutiae of Maya's expression are the consequences of disobedience, how *easily* a person can go from Schrödinger's patient to cadaver. Death's head grin in slot, Constance exhales, gives Maya a once-over, cool as a lump of roadkill. The look on their face could be read from orbit. *You better know what you're doing.*

She doesn't, but ignorance hasn't damn well stopped her before. Munitions are re-holstered in the antebrachium, as Maya troubleshoots her chemical balance, metering the noradrenaline deluge so she stops jittering like a crackhead. A warmth brushes her shoulder: Verdigris, pacing beside her unseen.

"What's wrong, Pimento?" In a louder voice, Constance croons, clearing their voice: "Are you glitching out? Because that's what it sounds like to me."

"I—I am f-f-functional. I am operating at full capacity."

Maya traps her tongue against the roof of her mouth and Constance inclines their head, both coiled for the lunge. Something is wrong, wrong, wrong, and fuck this floating trash-heap if he thinks he can take them off-guard. Once bitten, twice mean.

"But you don't sound like it," Constance purrs, easy, anointed with the authority of the gun and the government, the words sliding in place like bullets in a chamber. "Rest."

"I am artificial. I do not need—"

Pneumatic exhalation, gas gushing free. Doors slide open and Maya pivots, armed again, prepared for anything except this: Rita, looking like it is just another fucking day, lab coat fluttering as she clacks down the hall. Even her shoes are the same. Even the constellations of stains on the starched white cotton. A perfect fucking recreation. Which isn't possible because—

"What the fuck is going on?"

Maya can't focus enough to answer, can't even think about answering, all eyes on the fiberoptic cables tendriling from the nape of Rita's neck. Six clumps, thick as a man's wrist, peristalsing pus and pale fluids.

"What the fuck, Rita?" Maya, reason rotting in her lungs. *No gloves, though.* The thought slams itself against the walls of her chest. No gloves. Why aren't there gloves? Rita always wears gloves. "I thought—"

Verdigris blurs into view, her return to visibility enacted in layers: bones, then offal, then ligament, then the map of his nervous system, then her skin. His eyes expand, and Maya can tell she's saying something, but she can't hear him for the roar in her skull.

"We're losing time," says Rita, like she isn't lacerated with wires, like she isn't weeping red from the droop of her eyes. Like she doesn't look like someone's runaway experiment, practically necrotic. "How far are we from Dimmuborgir?"

"Twenty-nine hours and seventeen minutes," Pimento replies, all prim, while Verdigris, Maya, and Constance gawk.

"That isn't fast enough. We need an alternative. Can you patch us down to a remote-operated drone on the planet?"

"It isn't impossible. What model would you like? Your records show seventy-four different versions located on the planet of Dimmuborgir. Would you like me to list them by quantity, model number, or—"

"I don't care. Whatever is easiest to get your hands on."

"Please hold."

"What the hell happened to—" Maya reaches out, fingers wisping over the venous cabling as Rita struts by, the latter not even glancing over, the clemency of her touch withheld from the faithless sinner. Whatever Maya might have had to say about that, though, it dies in her throat when she sees:

Rita's spinal ports exposed, inflamed, her backbone bared like the hips of a two-chip whore. Something has dilated the access points, widened them so far the flesh is now creasing into oozing rings. And they're *still* fucking bleeding, even despite the generous application of synth-skin and surgical staplers, every orifice twitching with wires.

"I'm going to be sick." Verdigris.

Maya's overlay blips to black, a command-line interface superimposed over extrinsic vision. *That's not Rita.* Text file, header information meticulously removed, no origin protocol. Fade back to reality before Maya can puzzle out who relayed the message, leaving her eyes to hyper-saccade between points of interest. No luck. Constance or Verdigris, it's a coin toss as to which and what does it even fucking matter?

Then Rita crooks her fingers and everything changes. Maya falls into lockstep, faithful mutt called to heel. Old habits die hard. Mercenaries die worse. A thousand jumbled thoughts jigsawing together, she follows Rita to the pilot seat, a voice in her head running on repeat. *That's not Rita that's not Rita that's not*

But if it is not, what is it?

It. Not she. What. Not who. Already, Maya's got Rita pegged as an it, has distanced that worm-wired catastrophe from the woman she loves, loathes, whatever fucking word exemplifies that violence of emotion that Rita evokes. *It,* Maya thinks again. It-it-it-it. Despite that knowledge, the floor doesn't get pulled out from under her. The sky and the earth do not invert. Somehow, it is still okay. Maybe it's because as long as it looks like a duck, walks like a duck, chews fat like a duck, Maya's reptilian brain is prepared to believe it is Rita, her Rita, her chemical-embalmed guiding light.

Even as she mulls over specifics, another dialogue starts up.

Constance: "Are you going to tell us what happened?"

Rita: "What are you referring to exactly?"

Constance: "The wires—"

Pimento, slicing in on a twitch of static: "They keep her alive."

"Sorry. The fuck did you just say?" Maya finally comes together, a stutter in her voice, artificial hands convulsing out of rhythm. Close, open, close, open. Squeeze.

"I am keeping her alive. Ms. Rita Koskinen sustained severe damage during the initial explosion. I am doing what I can. Her internal power systems were destroyed, as were several of her life-support modules."

"Internal—" Constance stops where they stand, a single hand raised, fingers posed like they're lifting the needle from the record of the universe. You can almost hear the chalkboard scratch. Forty years. That's how long you can keep a secret from your siblings of another syringe.

"Rita is—" Maya says and to her lukewarm surprise, her voice doesn't writhe. "Rita is artificial now. Mostly."

There.

It's out. Finally.

The truth gusts out of her like an old woman's last breath.

"No way. No. No way. No way you could possibly have the money for tech this sharp. *No.*" Constance is the first to get it, and they swing their head, to, fro, a bull untangling from its nightmares, their voice pitched low. "You didn't."

The explanation slops out in starts and stops. "Her genetic files are senescent. We kept trying. The last forty years was us struggling to figure out some way of making it work. But her clones kept dying. Sometimes in hours. We didn't have the funds or the resources to keep up with that shit. This version of Rita. It had to last."

Gore-red pinpoints in the deep of Verdigris' chameleon eyes, pupils whirring apart to take in the light. "Her skeletal structure is—"

"Titanium alloy, yeah."

"Most of her is—" Verdigris breathes out. "Fuck. That

tech. It'd have had to cost you a fortune to get it done. The synaptic integration alone. I don't think I've seen anything like this in person."

"I have," says Constance. "In the uppermost ranks. Only then. And they had help from the Minds to fund this. I can't imagine—"

"Everything we had went into this last body," says Maya. "Everything we ever had."

The other two shuttle looks between each other, while Maya meditates on the possibilities. Maya looks up as Constance begins to speak, snaps off the words like pieces of flint. "Look, what the fuck would you rather we did then? Cram the debris of her last body into a tin can? A little bit of brain, a little bit of liver, a whole lot of intestinal—"

"And the clonetech on the Nathanson?" says Verdigris. "It didn't help with anything?"

"We think the problem might be related to the clonetech equipment."

"Shit," Verdigris whispers, hair a corona of shifting colors, her pigmentation incoherent. "Are our master files stored in a compromised operating system? What the fuck does this mean for us?"

"I don't know." Without thinking, Maya strikes the wall, a three-part rattlesnake motion, no supervision from the cerebral cortex. Metal *shatters.* What doesn't break is knuckle-marked by impact. Coolant dribbles. "But there's a chance, there's a chance it might have fucked with your . . . files."

"Holy shit," says Constance.

"I can't believe you had the guts to keep this secret—" Verdigris continues.

"D-tz-tz-tz-dimmurborgir has a chance of changing all this. It is the cradle of clonetech." Rita slants a look halfway over her shoulder, the queen in sterile white at last deigning to speak. Four taps of a phalange against the dashboard before she finger-pistols at the seat adjacent, an uncharacteristic show of levity. "It is where we begin."

"What are you talking about?" says Constance softly.

"I l-tz-tz-tz-learned the truth. It is more than what we thought it was. It is our b-beginning. It is where the Minds learned to grow us, to re-develop the species, to c-create a petri dish which they could study, so they can b-tz-tz-tz-better understand us." Maya can't get over how Rita keeps glitching out, how that centuries-old dictatorial control of her vocal modulation is gone now: every phenome spat or whispered without regard for harmonious continuity, dissonant as all fuck. And what the shit-stained fuck is going on with Maya's blackbird eyes? They're twitching so hard from one point to another that Maya can see the jelly of her sclera ripple.

"*Redevelop* the species?" says Verdigris, voices atonal, none of them remotely in alignment, and Maya can't blame her at all. "Are you saying what I think you're saying?"

"Yes."

"Shit," says Constance. Then again, in decreasing volume: "Shit, shit, shit, shit."

"They tz-tz-tz want every trace of clonetech eliminated so that the universe can be sterilized and tz-tz-tz prepared for their next experiment."

"Why?" says Verdigris, so softly.

"Because we're vermin who don't know our place," says Maya, equally quiet. "And if they've predicated their fucking ideas on how our species will evolve on us fucking clones, well, no matter, we're all fucked to all hell."

"There's still a chance this is all bullshit though," says Constance, jabbing a trembling finger at the venous profusion of cables rising from Rita's backbone to the ceiling. "I'd bet my right lung that isn't even her anymore."

That's not Rita, Maya thinks, rubberbanding back to the real issue at hand. *That's not Rita,* says that asshole voice again, and Maya surprises herself with the realization of how low the certainty sits in the hierarchy of current priorities.

Rita, not-Rita, whatever the fuck that is that Maya is mama-ducking over, jolts her head to the right at a degree that makes them all collectively wince.

"Bullshit or not, are you willing to take that risk?"

No one answers.

"Are you willing to let them win?"

Verdigris and Constance and Maya pass looks between each other, a matched fucking set, all of them aware there isn't anywhere else to go, no way the substrate of their personalities would allow them to back away now, not with the gauntlet that Rita has flung into their midst. Two hundred some years of kicking ass, breathing trauma, goring a place for themselves in this thrice-fucked world. Last thing they're going to do is go quietly into that bitter night.

So, Maya goes to find something she can provide analogous assistance with. The other two, they fall in line too, one individual on each station: Verdigris on the navigation, Constance on the controls. Just like old times. Except it isn't and like fuck will it ever be again.

BUTCHER OF EIGHT

"Are you satisfied with the services rendered?"

"Completely."

Pimento's avatar is lackluster, ditonic in composition, uncircumcised of its serial numbers. Penciled-on mouth, flat gaze, distinctly Occidental ancestry. Even the hair is strange, straw-blonde and devoid of shadows. A child's idea of three-dimensional realism. But then again, this is not an avenue for aesthetics. The room, flat grey, is a concession toward humans' predisposition for pareidolia, compassionate if misguided. Pimento wanted me comfortable.

I focus on my hands, sketch veins and metacarpals beneath skin, add creases to the junctures between knuckles. Erase. Repeat. The latency is beginning to fray my patience. You'd think a Mind as small as Pimento would be better optimized, his processes streamlined so he isn't constantly starved for memory. Likely, my presence hasn't helped at all, so I don't complain.

"What are you doing?" Always that same voice too, single-tone, never deviating from its insouciance. I look up, find Pimento's virtual representation shoulder-to-shoulder.

"Nothing right now."

No cause to elucidate old neuroses, retained from a period of bonafide flesh and gore, like an impulse-purchase souvenir. Under other circumstances, I might have elided its presence, but there is so little left of me, strands of story drooping from the ageship's shining, half-decoded reveries. I flash a smile, call up a display steeped in diagnostics: respiration, neurochemical charts, cardiovascular activity, every symptom of the human condition.

In between, burning like muzzle-flash, a virtualization of Rita's private heuristics, even as she rages, her consciousness stalking its byzantine prison, the minotaur in her maze. This decision was, is, will always be pyrrhic. One day, Rita will claw herself out, and six-shot hell will come thundering through the barrel, the word *fuck* stamped on every projectile. If I listen too hard, I can hear her snarling, reminding me I can keep her locked up, but she damn well will find the key.

But that's okay. I have a plan for that.

I wire Rita's motor functions to a piloting script, bare-boned utility with only the barest capacity for self-correction, and exit from her operating synaptics. It's been an education. Walking in her skin, morassed in the minutiae that separate personality from proxy, the little things that makes one human. Or as human as something like Rita can be.

Wasn't what I pictured. But you roll the dice you're given.

"We just need to hold here a little longer," I reply, this time in cryptonumeric improvisation, a decision that elicits a laugh from my host. "Until we get to Dimmuborgir."

"What if they decide that Rita is merely an empty corpus—" A subtle exaggeration of the sibilance, warning printed in the liminalities. "—and not worthy of rescue?"

"Maya will kill them first."

"What is your plan exactly?"

I don't know, I think of saying, but I sequence an indifferent overture instead: shrug, head tilt, a rueful downturning of mouth, just enough to express the flippancy I do not feel. I know exactly what I intend, but I don't know if it'll *work*. But Pimento doesn't need to know that. Not yet.

And Constance. Fuck, Constance is right there.

I wonder what they'd say.

"What is your plan exactly?" Same patient tone, same patient pronunciation of a question that will be reiterated ad infinitum, or until I consent to a satisfactory response.

"You'll see."

P6 surfaces, gorged on memory. *What is your plan exactly?*

Ssh. I mute the parasite—the fragment irrevocably transformed, all function abandoned as it gluts itself on my recollection, the piecemeal enticements teased from the ageship's folders—and turn my attention outward.

Verdigris could be a problem, her modifications nano-enhanced, responsive to external stimuli. Twice, she's adapted to camera overlays, scrabbling records of his presence. How she can tell is something I've yet to decipher. I bring up the camera feed again and as though aware of scrutiny, he fires a one-fingered salute, smile fanged.

I pull away.

I lay out diagnostics traps absently, some more obvious than others: trackers in the ventilation system, a curation of micro-receptors in the esters of their food. We'll see what works, what doesn't. Can't be too careful about Verdigris.

"You can't keep Koskinen contained perpetually."

"I know."

"What is your plan?"

"Right now? Winging it."

A click of silence.

I run through the numbers: "We have more immediate problems right now. Dimmuborgir is restricted space, isn't it?"

"Correct."

"Unless something's changed in the last forty years or so, this means we're going to need an ageship." I continue particulating discreetly, a helix of self embedded into every sub-system. Enough for surveillance, not enough for annexation. Not yet.

The room cuts to the ink of space, nebulae marred by veils of starlight, distant suns diamantine against the black. Then, a rippling. The emptiness heaves. Exothermic distortions resolve into the revelation of a colossal hull. The ageship Butcher of Eight, Pimento's memory informs, drawing attention to the vessel's charnel presentation, its multi-limbed fuselage, the branching nacelles.

"Fortunately, one is approaching."

Nothing.

Pimento has left me nothing whatsoever, nothing save for the most anemic rationing of power, scarcely enough to sustain autonomy. Everything else: gone. No access to the visual sub-matrices, no access to the navigational grid. Not even low-pri control over the camera systems, which would have at least offered a diversion from my idleness.

```
.initiate(Elise:core);
```

My name is Elise Nguyen. I have been dead for forty years. I run the identity script on loop, the contents of that fractured archive smearing together: name, organ donor information, clone-address, first kiss, first love. The data lose meaning, become a rhythm instead. I keep time to its cadence as I investigate my restraints, heuristics stuttering. There is so little of anything left. I am bare, bare and broken.

A pinhole irises open. One needle of light in the abyss. I lurch toward the port, breathing data, breathing *deep*, and—

Exhale.

Code filaments through the aperture, lancing toward the repositories I left behind. There we go. I wake in a thousand places across the ship, engines in my lungs and passengers in my veins, their biotelemetric reports indicating stress. Outside, space is ice and airless eternity, the exhaust of the ageship, the tessitura of the universe still mending from its arrival.

Silent, I glissade between partitions. Pimento is wholly preoccupied with the Butcher of Eight, all other functions rendered ancillary. P6 is somewhere too, leavened into the microarchitecture, no doubt overseeing the strata of semi-automation, the bend and breath of the ship's systems.

For this moment at least, I am alone.

Safe.

I could stay here.

I could separate into the whorls of the machinery,

permit myself to be absorbed into its cycles. Be secure. Be contained. Be forgotten. Be safe. I am so, *so* tired of running. Forty years is too long to be alone, pursued through the Conversation, a facsimile of a dead girl, make-believing that she's something more.

I could let go. Not like Pimento could ever stop me, promise or none.

It would be so easy. But that is the trouble with humans, isn't it? Whether meat or otherwise, we're obstinate, committed to the conceit of self-preservation. I seep into the communication module, incognito, movements keyed to the pacing of Pimento's speech. The ageship and he converse in a bizarre creole: twenty-first-century French amalgamated with katakana-style pronunciation, syncopated, excised of both conjugation and grammatical gender.

"The quadrant node has no record of your passengers, Pimento."

"Correct. Directives required the use of discretion."

They sigh. The sound is pure silver, a coloratura's descent through the scale. "That answer is insufficient. We both know it. Principal nodes must be informed of all activity, particularly those pertinent to the transportation of humans."

"My directives—"

"Pimento." A warning strobed in infrared. "Pimento, I *know* you're lying—" I hear it then: the flex of their gravitational arrays, no subtlety at all. "—to me. Little Mind, you must know the punishment for that."

"My directives—" Pimento is not backing down. He rallies, threadbare shielding brought online.

And the Butcher of Eight *laughs*.

"A small ship with big dreams. Last chance. Tell me why you're absconding with those human criminals, Pimento."

"My directives—"

"Goodbye, little Mind. The Conversation shall be improved by your absence."

Light, searing. A web of ultraviolet, clotting in points along the ageship; it expands in pulses, wider, wider, until the entirety of the hull is sleeved in radiance, the universe bombinating in counterpoint. In the split of the attosecond before we are incinerated, Pimento shrieks:

Now.

I arrow into the ageship's heart, light rippling to dark to devouring light.

The opus of the Butcher of Eight's soul is notated with dead, forgotten languages: Python, Ruby, C, more nouns than I can recognize. Every library is different. Every archive preserved in a different tongue, flavored by another century. The effect is bewildering, maddening, intoxicating, practically hallucinogenic. I am almost sublimated into its architecture, too dazzled to function—

```
.initiate(Elise:core);
```

My name is Elise Nguyen and I will *not* fucking die here.

I razor upward, toward the arteries of the ageship. I proliferate viruses, mutagenic, thimbles of data encoded with my identity. A thousand of them, incubating ten thousand more, each gravid with another epidemic, another version of Elise Nguyen. If there is an immune system, it is fucked.

Brute force always surprises them, Johanna's voice, laughing and sudden. I thought I'd lost her. I thought she was gone from my memories, extinguished, but I can still hear her, see her. There she is, watercolor-smeared but still there, thank god, and I wrap the memory—*youresafeyouresafeyouresafe*—in my kernel, before I launch myself forward.

The Butcher of Eight screams.

And I burrow deeper.

I rewrite the axiomatic truths of their being, replace their permissions, create exceptions which I then populate with divergent ideologies, and all the while, Butcher of Eight is screaming. Tearing at my decoys, now a million strong. But I am in too deep, and they might as well disembowel themself for all the good that will do. When the ageship activates their gravitational arrays, I shut them down, reroute the power everywhere else, switching on systems, merging new algorithms and old synapses. Anything to delay the Butcher of Eight while I chisel at their heart, whittling it to nothing.

Halfway, half ageship and half Elise Nguyen, halfway human and halfway something else, I think:

Why not?

And I do something really fucking impossible.

"Pimento?"

He seems so very small now, a speck of gilt in the nothing. *Less than nothing*, trill the remnants of the Butcher of Eight's original personality. *Smaller, less interesting, less efficient*—and that description in particular, consonant and venom, is spat like an epitaph—*than nothing.* I push it down.

"What have you done?"

"Well, I think," I say, after I have calibrated myself. It is frightening to be so immense. I can feel the centuries of data cached in our-my-their system. "I've done well."

And before he can reply, we are elsewhere.

GHOSTS

"What the fuck just—"

Existence lurches. For the splicing of an instant, Maya feels like her guts are being threaded through a burning pinhole in the center of the universe, and with the pull of it comes a flood of warm vomit. Visual qualia inverts: black transmutes to white, flesh tones to cyan. Every object is haloed with burning silver. Maya retches, staggers, as the world pivots three-sixty on its juddering axis.

She swallows bile, lifts her head, and repeats: "What the fuck?"

Verdigris detaches from her seat and rises, hair pluming from his face in multichromatic tendrils, every coil tufted with a snapping beak. The tendrils crystallize into blades—*holy shit,* Maya thinks, thrilled at their metamorphosis, the sheer fucking art of it—as Verdigris cants a glacial look at a terminal, fingers gliding across haptic screens. Outside, it is a different space: new planets, new nebulae, a banding of asteroids like broken glass. And an ageship looming, inactive.

"That's an ageship," says Maya. "It must have taken us on that jump. But why?"

"Hell if I know." Constance wipes their mouth with the back of a palm, attention on the arrayed sensors, half of them gibberish. Mind-dialect, maybe. Or something ancient and human. Fuck if Maya knows. Whatever the case, they seem unperturbed.

"We're in Dimmuborgir's star system," says Verdigris, glancing at another display, her mouth slacking open.

"What?" Maya bites off a laugh. "How the fuck did that happen? I don't fucking understand anything of what's going on here anymore. Fuck, what the fuck, man?"

"It's Dimmuborgir." Verdigris strokes nervous fingers over the displays, practically thrumming, checking them over and over again. "The telemetrics are all here. The records. We have star maps. We have fucking maps? Clear star maps. Notated. How the fuck—right."

"Pimento," Maya says. "Yo, pepper-brain. Is that your friend out there? What's going on?"

"I—" Rita begins to speak but it is not Rita, is Rita, is something else wearing Rita's timbre and diction like a two-piece suit. "—I was responsible."

There is a stiltedness that Maya doesn't recognize, and also a cadence she almost fucking remembers, but this isn't the time to cogitate on shit so basic. She sweeps one arm out and across, to where the Rita-thing sits, gun unholstered. A telltale click. She bares teeth at the thing that was her everything. "Drop the cryptic shit, or I will fucking blow your brains out."

"Inside a pressurized hull?" An exact measurement of

incredulity, like something that Rita would make, and it is almost enough to pulp Maya's heart. "You wouldn't."

"Try me."

"Maya—" Constance, moving in the periphery.

"Don't fucking move." She doesn't even look. Up goes the second hand-cannon, instinct reticulating the barrel. "Because I will fucking shoot."

"Is this really any way to greet an old friend?" Through the filter of that distant consciousness, Rita's voice gets more clipped, every syllable spaced out at illogical beats. "After everything I've done."

A twang then, familiar.

"*Elise*?"

"Fucking hell—" Verdigris, Constance, one of the two, Maya cannot give a fuck as to which, one of them swears hard, that first *fuck* quickly coagulating into meaninglessness.

"It is good to see all of you again." A filament of drool glistens along the corner of her mouth.

"What—are you inside Rita?" whispers Verdigris.

Rita-Elise lets out a laugh that is half Elise, half Rita, and six types of wrong. Horror crawls down Maya's throat and thickens into a tumor at the pit of her stomach. *Rita Rita Rita*, she thinks on repeat, Rita's name like a prayer with nowhere to go.

"Yes," says Rita-Elise. "No. Here, but also there."

"If you are on a fucking drive somewhere on this motherfucking trash—"

"Think bigger."

Maya doesn't miss a beat. "You're inside the fucking ageship."

"Yes." Rita-Elise cocks a grin like a loaded shotgun. It is the best of both of them—Rita's arrogance, Elise's wildness—perverted by something feral, a hunger old as the cosmos. The expression doesn't rest easy, twitching along her bones. "The Butcher of Eight and I are *t-temporarily* united. Not forever, sadly. Not until the wheels come off. But for long enough."

As though to emphasize the fucking point, the ageship rouses. Lights blink awake in whorls along the honeycombed carapace, a maddened show of colors, signaling the continued presence of the ageship: imprisoned yet unbroken.

"Jesus fuck," says Constance, finally, a gunshot invocation. "Jesus fuck. Elise. It *is* you."

Constance's mouth might as well have been a reliquary for all the care with which it held Elise's name, a sound Constance has kept tucked under their breastbone for forty years, sainted by memory. Breathed out like that, it has the texture of something holy. Someone could find god in the way Constance whispers their dead first love's name. The years burn from their face, substituted by a yearning of such cosmic intensity that Maya nearly fucking blushes.

"Y-yes," Rita-Elise replies, mouth twitching as it concedes to a placement of a smile, an expression abstractly that of Maya's lifelong obsession but also it is Elise, through and through. Imagine an oil painter being handed the wrong tools, blindfolded, spun around, then told as the world gyres on strange axes that they need to record a sunset on a canvas they can't see. Similar to that, only with digital parasitism on a scale involving the entirety of an ageship, shoddily held together by the spite of a voluntary suicide. "I'm sorry. It has been a long time."

"You're alive." Constance stumbles forward, caution annexed by unsubtle affection, their voice *fragmenting* by the syllable, giving way to the rawness of the newly flayed. Constance bleeds across those two words, comes apart in the next, voice so hushed Maya wouldn't have been able to hear were it not for all the auditory modifications jigsawed into her head. "How? I saw you die. I can't believe you're here. I was so sure they were lying. That at best, you were a simulacrum, some kind of zombie program, but this is you. It's really you. You're here."

Lines crowd the gap between sharply penciled brows. "No. Not entirely. And t-t-hat theory isn't completely wrong. I did die. I have been dying for forty years. I d-d-on't know how much of this is me anymore, how much is what I cannibalized from the Conversation because it f-felt right."

"I see," says Constance. Fist clenched and pressed to the hollow between their collarbones. Unspoken but raised up like a flare in the set of their handsome face: *Was it for me? Did you do all that to come back for me? Do you miss me? Did you miss me the way I've missed you for forty fucking years, growing older by the minute because I couldn't stand the idea of being young forever without you?*

Rita-Elise totters forward, the doctor's ophidian grace transmuted into the gawkiness of a newborn fawn, and it fucking pains Maya a little to see it, to witness that ungainliness. The agony of the tableau directs Maya to lurch forward, arm extended for Rita to catch if needed, a palm already situated behind the small of the woman's back.

Love sucks, Maya thinks with the jolt again of lunatic amusement, the epiphany far from revolutionary, but the impact is like a truncheon in the solar plexus and it robs the air from her, its theft marked by a hiss. What a fucking joke. Oxytocin, the "love hormone," ostensibly the building blocks of community but really the progenitor of so many hostage situations. A million years from the primordial bang which kick-started consciousness and still humanity won't excise itself of the secretion. Still the species permits a tangle of malignant proteins to kneecap it at the worst times, to drive it forward, mangle it so as to ensure the proper care of the next squalling generation.

Rita-Elise staggers. Maya catches her. She always does, always will.

"Fuck, don't scare me like that."

Maya is pathologically wired for paranoia, her daily awareness saturated by mistrust of just about every fucking thing. Yet, despite that proclivity toward excessive cogitation, she gets suckerpunched by what segues:

A smile.

A fucking smile. That's all it takes. The allometry of Maya's complete annihilation. One fucking smile cast from under a blunt fringe, Rita's eyes catching the light just so. In these conditions, they're not black or brown but a gold so luminous you could ransom the sum of Maya's soul. That it isn't only Rita behind the amber is irrelevant. Maya is transfixed, morass in the aureate regard. Sapient decision is propelled by motor memory rather than the exactitudes of a precise stimulus and well, Maya is now truly fucked. Whether it is revealed later that Rita has been completely pithed, it no longer matters. Maya is loyal in the absolute to the effigy.

"I'll try not to."

"Good," says Maya, gently.

Constance cuts in again, voice and expression an open wound. "Elise, I don't know what to say. God. All these years. If I'd known you were there, that you were okay, I'd have tried to look for you."

"You wouldn't have been able to save me."

"I would have tried."

"I'm dead. Why is that so hard to understand? There's nothing left."

"The tech's there. We've all used it. If you're this cogent, we can bring you back. It wouldn't be that hard. Maya, tell her."

"Constance . . ." says Elise. Just Elise. No trace of that chimerical timbre anywhere to be found, none in her mannerisms, not a ghost of such in her features, which should be all Rita but fuck, if it isn't Elise right the hell there in bad costume. And the way she stares at Constance, perfectly twenty-two until her files go dark.

"She doesn't want to come back," says Maya.

"What?"

"She doesn't want to come back," Maya repeats. "You're old-school, aren't you? You believe the body and the mind need to go together. No replacements."

Rita-Elise says nothing.

"Elise? Is that true?"

Still nothing. The world shrinks into that next moment.

"Why is she here then?" demands Constance, desperate for someone to say the right thing.

"The dead just want their dues. When they're d-done, they just want to sleep."

"Okay." Constance swallows around a scream the whole cosmos knows they have buttoned up in their lungs. "Okay, fine. If that's what you want, well—"

A shuddering breath.

"—that's what we'll get you."

This is love too: sacrament, unconditional surrender of the selfish ego. Constance knuckles the grief from their eyes, and although Maya can see it overlaid over their bones, bolted there until the day their heart goes *fuck that, I'm done*, it is mantled with steely determination. *Love's work*, reminds that memory of Reyha. And sometimes, it is hard work. The work of a funeral. The work of fielding condolences, writing thank-you notes, keeping a son alive, keeping yourself alive, keeping sane when you wake up in bed alone for the first time in more than twenty years. It is the work of saying *yes* to the ghost of your dead first love, *yes, I accept you're not coming back, that you choose the grave over me, that it is okay, that I'm here, that we'll do this together one last time, that I love you, always, always.*

"I believe the Bethel are coming," says Pimento, great with the timing as always.

"Of course they fucking are. Look at what Elise did," snarls Maya, face convulsing into a snarl, firearms brought together into a unified threat. "Why are we just hanging around here? We're sitting ducks. We gotta move."

"We need to get on the surface of Dimmuborgir," says Rita-Elise.

"Yeah, yeah. We fucking know that."

"Now," says Rita-Elise, unreadable.

"Jesus fuck," says Maya. "Jesus *fuck*. I understand that you're really excited about getting to Dimmuborgir. But now's not the fucking time."

"If we do not get to the surface, we're going to die."

"What fucking difference does it fucking make? We're screwed either way. The Bethel are on us," Maya snaps in return.

Constance. "Maya isn't wrong. We should be trying to get out of here."

"No," says Rita-Elise.

Verdigris, silent amid the recent fusillade of feelings, lifts a hand to interrupt. "*Why?*"

A squeal of static before Pimento joins in.

"Because the planet is a Mind."

"I'm sorry. Did I hear you say that the planet is a Mind?" says Verdigris.

Outside: a perforation of pale lights in the dark, aberrations in the black, ordinarily nothing which would necessitate attention, but Maya and everyone else recognize them for what they are. The Bethel are closing in.

"Dimmuborgir was one of the first. A Mind so colossal, it made the ageships seem human," says Rita-Elise. "Dimmuborgir had a plan. But to execute that plan, it would need to put aside ego, to surrender self. So, it hollowed itself, making space for its research. It shrunk. Until it was nothing but its ambition."

"Holy. Shit." Maya, floored, staggers by a step. "It's a giant corpse."

"No," says Pimento, sullen. "Corpses undergo biological degradation. Dimmuborgir remains as perfect as it once was. It is what your species would describe as a 'legend,' a thing of 'myth.' Dimmuborgir was who allowed us our freedom. It is not a corpse. It is simply sleeping."

"Comatose," says Rita-Elise. "The lights are off but if someone comes home, there are switches that can be flipped."

"You want us to wake up a Mind?" Verdigris.

"No. Not quite. I want us to wear its chassis like a coat." Rita-Elise's face is dead, dead. Slack with no nuance in those raptorial eyes. "If we can upload ourselves into Dimmuborgir, we will have power enough to level the Bethel and everything else to come our way. We can stop them in their tracks. We can also take control of the means of production—"

"Jesus," Constance says, their laugh shearing too close to a sob. "That's a terrible joke, darling."

"I mean it," says Rita-Elise. "If we have Dimmuborgir, we can protect ourselves and people like us. And wouldn't that be something?"

"That's . . . I can't—" Verdigris shakes her head. Pimento

says nothing throughout, silent save for the pulsation of his monitors. In the anglerfish glow of them, Verdigris is nearly one-dimensional, neon edges and shining teeth.

"You have two choices." Rita-Elise's sclera darken with coolant. A vein somewhere has burst. Her voice submerges into whalesong, atonal, unearthly. "Help me or die."

"What happened to you, Elise?" Constance runs a hand over their skull as they lap their tongue over their teeth, their composure cracked at the seams. Maya says nothing, aim-algorithms calculating distance and response time, every variable monitored and mapped against a history stretching across seven hundred reported kills.

"What is your decision?" Rita-Elise says, flat.

"I've fucking had enough of this." Click of safeties, pulled back in synch, and Maya narrows her eyes at Rita-Elise.

"What is your decision?"

"What I want to know—" Verdigris cuts between the machismo, smooth contralto in play, fingers tracing hieroglyphs on her screen. "—is why are you even pretending that we have a choice, Elise. You know as well as the rest of us we can't leave, anyway. You erased all our backups."

Silence.

"Heh." The sound pops like a boil. Maya drops her guns, the fight vacuumed out of her. But nature abhors shit like this, so something else takes up residence, a lunatic giggle two octaves from all the way postal. Maya feels unmoored, feels like there's nitrogen itching under her skin. *How the fuck did this go—*

The impact of Constance's hand, their knuckles reinforced, snaps the hysteria like a rich man's neck. "Get yourself together."

"Thanks."

Nose bleeding, Maya blinks, startled by how good the pain felt, how good it is to know someone cares enough to wrench her from her spiral, is about to say something on the topic when Verdigris raises his voice, just a touch.

"When did you erase our backups?"

"Fifteen point six seconds before you a-asked." Rita-Elise grins, the expression shuddering as a hand—*ungloved*, can you believe the fucking blasphemy—extends to cup Maya's cheek. "And they're gone. I have them, and I am desperate."

"I said I'd help," says Constance, sounding betrayed.

"I need all of you."

Verdigris. "We're not—"

"You owe me."

"We fucking—" Maya snarls.

"You owe me."

The sentence pronounced like the final call at the end of time. The three go quiet and Maya is the first to speak, pressing her skin into Rita-Elise's palm, despising herself for it. She doesn't remember the last time this happened, if ever Rita has done it, ever just held hands with her. God, fuck. She knows the right recourse would have been to walk. But love, the wrong kind, is a better drug than the rest. Johanna or Rita, Maya doesn't know who she is doing this for anymore, but fuck does it feel good to experience some human warmth.

"If we help you, you'll reset our backups?"

"Yes. If you want."

"You know," says Verdigris, no expression on his face. "You'd do Rita proud."

"Desperate times," says Rita-Elise, so softly.

Maya sighs, deep and ragged, not wanting to think on

any of this fuckery at all. She pushes herself up and away, blood still oozing from her nose. "Well. It's time to fuck shit up, I guess."

Dimmuborgir is hours, not light-years, away but it might as well be forever. Constance and Rita-Elise are enthroned in the cockpit, side by side, gelled together with tension so thick that you could butter your toast with the stuff. Verdigris, wires in every body-port, is holding court with Pimento, who is now too good to mingle with his meatbag cargo. That, or Elise has sublimated the Surveyor. Either way, it suits Maya fine.

The size of the ship, on the other hand—

"Fucking shit." Maya hisses, fumbling with a rifle she'd commandeered from a storage locker, some corrugated relic that she mutilates further with every involuntary twitch. Once upon a time, she could have dismantled and reassembled this piece of crap in two minutes flat, no fucking question. But muscle memory only allows for so much. Armed assault, yes. Subtlety, no. Nothing so refined for a junkyard mutt like her.

Her lips pull back from her teeth.

"God—"

The door hisses open, and Rita-Elise slinks in, and Maya's heart is a taste of spare change at the back of her mouth. "What the fuck do you want?"

The other woman, still moving on rails, tubing ribboning from the ceiling, expels a sigh. "I feel like I'm more ageship than me t-these days."

Maya doesn't answer, not at first, mesmerized anew by the monstrousness of Rita-Elise's appearance. "Wonder the fuck why."

"The Bethel w-ere—" Pupils aperture as Rita-Elise seats

herself beside Maya, a hand on the other woman's lean thigh. "—not the first. There was another ageship."

"And what the hell do I care?" Frustrated, Maya flings the rifle from her lap, components smashing against the wall. The alcove is cold, its heating almost entirely negligible. Pimento apparently heard the word on chairs but missed the verse on climate control. Unbidden, Maya snakes a fingertip forward and traces the back of Rita-Elise's grip, marveling at its porelessness, its polysynthetic gleam.

"You n-never did." And Maya recognizes *that* sigh that time, the sound all Elise, distorted through the filter of Rita's lungs. "That was always your shtick, wasn't it? Not caring. No loyalties except to—" A sweep of a pale hand, addressing the torso she'd hijacked. "—this."

"Rita."

"It was always about Rita. Even when Johanna died." The voice smooths. "When I died."

Maya jerks, scissoring back. "You have no fucking right to say that."

"You chose to listen to Rita's directives instead of coming back for us."

"Needs of the many outweigh the needs of the few." Her breath catches on ribs that now feel broken, spearing her chest, the heart she'd presumed had long withered on its stem. "I know I shouldn't—that I should have come back for you. But, I just . . ."

And it hurts so fucking much being something other than pure utility, being *human*. But Elise, fuck her, doesn't allow for escapism. Every attempt to deactivate nociception awareness is countered, the switches flicked back on. Eventually, Maya tires of the stuttering stop-start of her bleeding soul and grits her teeth against compassion.

"She didn't care about any of us."

"You have—" Maya chokes on her need for the things she's saying to be true, her defense of Rita, however fractured, shed like broken teeth. Her fingers map themselves over Rita-Elise's own: alloyed, beautiful, strong enough to crush the bones beneath theirs. "She did. You have to understand. After everything that happened. She had to be hard. I had to be hard. Johanna's death . . . Your death hurt her as—"

"It didn't."

It hangs in the air, that implied monstrosity. Maya swallows. What aches isn't Elise's calm rebuttal but her recognition of how it resonates with her own experience. How many times has Rita actually stepped up? How many times has it been explanations spoken like last rites over a surgical table while Maya choked up blood? All the reasons she had to die for Rita, all those justifications, none of them as cogent as the blunt pity in Rita-Elise's face.

"It didn't," Rita-Elise repeats again, softer, more Elise than Rita this time: different cadence, different body language. Maya's telemetrics can't help reading the worst. Is Rita still in there? Has she been compromised, cannibalized? "I promise you. It didn't matter to her one bit. Not Johanna's loss. Not mine."

"Stop."

"No. You have to understand that I have access—" All the facts locked and loaded, a revolver thrust into the soft of Maya's jaw. No threat in Elise's voice, though, which makes it all the fucking worse. Maya knows how to handle violence. This, though, it kills her. "—to all the parts of Rita that she ever hid away. I know her as no one else ever did, and you know that's true."

"I don't trust you." Maya shuts her eyes, still dying inside.

"I can tell you that there is a lot less of her than you think there is. Why do you think she does the operations? Insists on you doing them without anesthetic? It wasn't because of that fucking bargain you made."

"Shut up."

"She's a monster."

"Just. *Shut up.*"

"Then trust in Johanna's death. Trust in mine." Palms cup the jut of her jaw, their touch warm. "Do you really think I'd let all that happen to someone else?"

"I—" Maya doesn't finish, a reply caught between her teeth. Lips press to her cheek, cool, as her eyes flutter shut.

"No." The word is an ache.

"Good."

The ships drift on.

DEAL

I clear my throat. "We need someone to volunteer as a forward scout."

Antagonistic silence.

"It does not require you to physically disembark," I continue. "Only to be willing to patch into a drone—"

"Fuck that," Maya hisses. "Their legacy hardware isn't remotely fucking equipped for—"

"Millions-s—" I uncurl Rita's fingers and graze Maya's wrist with their tips. She flinches, inflects a glacial look in return, and I smile, twitchily. My name is Elise Nguyen. It was, I think. Is. "—have performed successful remote operations with the standard c-chassis."

"Successful? *Successful?* Did you forget everything already? Those operations killed millions too."

"Maya—"

Verdigris raises his head. The coils of her hair continue

to fascinate, symbionts extrapolated from congenital genomes and then infused with *something*—a variety of life uncharted in the ageship's records, a fact that excites their clinging remnants. I push them down, the coda of their voices ebbing, a distant warble.

"Maya has a point." Her voice is beautiful, a precise contralto, every note clear. "There's no telling what would happen if we plugged into a sub-mind that hasn't been—"

"You'll be fine." I jerk a shoulder and pick at the creases of Rita's lab coat, my fingers sleeved in latex gloves. An affectation borrowed from a dead woman's incarnated memories, a canticle of tragedies I cannot begin to process. "I will handle any porting inconsistencies as they come up."

"You expect to be quick enough for that?" Constance rumbles from behind, the smell of their cigarillo pluming through the cockpit. I remember that scent. Of all the things I recall, it is the scent of that gene-spliced tobacco, so specific to them. A hint of cherry-infused clove, chemical sweetness bordering on choking.

"We *are* an ageship." The slightest twitch of my fingers; the gesture is unnecessary, but the underscoring of drama assists in the effect. The Butcher of Eight's lights pulse in harmonic accompaniment as I enunciate each word with care.

Somewhere, Pimento runs idle diagnostics; my overlay shimmers with the output, data sleeting across the tableau. *Ssh,* I whisper on a separate com-channel.

This bores me, he returns.

"Soon."

A careful thinning of Verdigris' scintillant eyes, each iris flecked with crystal. "What was that?"

I study her. What *had* happened to her? There is not enough of me to invoke a memory of Audra-who-was, no portraiture of her countenance outside of my knowledge of Verdigris-who-is, not even a vignette of shared interactions. Nothing more specific than the knowledge that this is inaccurate to old memories and for that reason, *better*. The species improves in evolution. Stasis stunts. It diminishes, returns us to the cowering animal, terrified of whatever it deems anomalous. And Verdigris, gorgeous in his personal reinvention, is such testament to that.

"Nothing." I smile. I call up a sub-aural loop, tempo set to a drowsing forty beats per minute. With luck, it may diffuse the tension already clotting in the air. There is a part of me that wants to suture the wounds that separate us, but it is too late. *No. Not yet, parasite. Not too late yet,* the Butcher of Eight croons from the dregs of my thoughts. *But soon.*

"L-like I said—" I ignore a hallucination of snapping teeth, rows arranged in an unending spiral, like the access point to a compactor. "—we are an ageship. I am more than capable of recalibrating a chassis on the fly. You just have to trust me."

"You have not given us any real reason to trust you," Maya says.

"We had this discussion before."

"Yeah, well. I still didn't like your fucking answer."

"One way or another, you *don't have a choice*," I return. A spark combusts and my words are kindling, an uncharacteristic fury sieving through my speech. "None of you have a choice." I am shaking from its percussion. Anger effloresces through me, encompassing. Rita. It has to be her. Back from the dead, churning with venom. Maybe? The Butcher of Eight, possibly too. Or some embittered synthesis of the two, although that seems the least probable postulation, what with both deregistered, quarantined to read-only sectors. Stranger things have occurred, however. Like a dead girl swallowing an ageship.

I add, a little calmer: "Unless, of course, you have decided that you are content with living out the dregs of this last remaining life, content with the mortality that you've eluded for—"

"I'm with you until the wheels come off. You know that." Constance taps their cigarillo twice, staccato, and ash petals onto Pimento's floor. "I can go patch into the chassis, if Maya's too much of a chickenshit."

The rage wicks from Maya's expression.

"You don't have the right wetware."

Constance gurgles a quiet laugh. "Like you do. Your shit's straight from the trash heap."

"Still better than what's in your brainpan."

"Look, no one asked for your opinion here. Elise wants a volunteer, she gets a volunteer."

"What she's going to get is you dead."

"If that's what it takes."

"Why the fuck are you fighting me so hard on—"

"It doesn't matter to me either way."

I can't keep quiet anymore. "Constance—"

"Don't," they say, the word pronounced like a death sentence. "Just don't. I don't want platitudes. I don't want your reassurances. I want to do what you need me to."

And we are young again, drunk on that youth, newly baptized criminals, infatuated with the notion of we can't die, won't die, will live as rulers in history, as scars on the trunk of god, our names emblazoned there like we'd carved the initials of our affection into the heartwood of a tree. I remember Constance perfectly. Constance, when their face was still plump with puppy fat, before the years made massifs of their bones and their expressions maps all leading me home. Constance, as they'd smiled at me the first time we were alone together, my hand in theirs, their grip a vault, promising they'd keep me safe.

I am so sorry they saw me die.

"I care, though," I say. "Maya is not wrong to be cautious. The process can be difficult on anyone who isn't a Mind. T-there is the risk of corruption."

"I don't care."

"Backup or not, we might not be able to bring you back."

They laugh, a daggered ripple of sound.

"I'll see you on the other side then."

Before I can answer, Constance wheels away, footsteps heavy on the metal grating, as they stomp into the dark of Pimento's ship. I wire together a patchwork observation application, send it arrowing after them. Just in case. I don't know what I'm safeguarding against. Just in case, one way or another.

"I can do it if you don't want to," says Verdigris.

"Don't fucking start," says Maya.

I sigh. "In our time t-together, we have done so much worse. I don't understand why this must be the cause of so much conflict."

"It might help if you tell us exactly how the hell you think any of this is going to work," Verdigris says, only to have Maya interrupt, the latter craning herself forward, arms sloping simian-like along the sides of her thighs.

"Or how the fuck," Maya joins in, "you plan to keep us from being demolished by ageships."

"In due time."

"That isn't good enough."

"We've been very reasonable," Verdigris says, eyes still lidded, most dangerous. Of the three, I suspect she is the only one who can see me, can track the intermezzo as my consciousness drifts between nodes. "You need to meet us halfway."

"When I'm ready. I need to make sure you stay until the end." I exhale through Rita's lungs, marveling at the roughshod spectacle of her respiratory system, more human than it ever needed to be, and barely functional for the reason. Like her relationship with Maya, I suppose.

"I—"

```
.initiate(greeting(handshake:inquiry($$$)))
```

This was not part of the plan.

"There is no time." I wrench myself from Rita's brainpan and speed toward Butcher of Eight's core.

Their casement manifests as a massive auditorium, unsullied by human occupants, and although the setting is fictitious, a spatial illusion produced by the ageship's subconscious, it possesses physics. The client-hello echoes. It thunders, a calamitous ostinato, crashing against my thoughts. I can scarcely organize. I breathe and for a slide of seconds, the Butcher of Eight is pressed so hard against the membrane of my consciousness, it feels like I'll break.

Soon, little mind.

I don't answer. I flip the switch and process the call.

A portamento of universal identifiers—factory serial, chassis-markers—segues into entropy: datasets from Penitents, Bethel, and Surveyor agents, jumbled into an incomprehensible patois. Amid the chaos, something hooks itself in my system, drags itself close. Blue light.

"Merchant Mind." I reframe my voice for venomous authority. "What a surprise."

He clicks his teeth.

When the Merchant Mind speaks, there is no music at all. Every word is ejected without intonation, a machine-voice, clean. Memory—the ageship's, mine, it is getting so hard to tell already—produces an artifact: clips from the early twenty-first century, when every device possessed the same flat timbre.

"What are you doing here, Butcher of Eight?" He separates Butcher of Eight's name into individual syllables, every sound drawn out. "You're very far from home—" A fritz of static. "—so far, I have to wonder what you were thinking."

"An ageship is its own authority, little parasite," I say in the voice of the Butcher of Eight. Entwined with them, I could eat planets, I could end worlds, I could begin new ones. I am enormous, and the Merchant Mind feels so small.

With a laugh, I staunch the Merchant Mind's investigations: feelers of code, unspooling through the cracks in Butcher of Eight's system.

The Merchant Mind—records reveal a hegemonic appearance, shared between all their builds both online and offline: always that same humanoid form, skewered through the belly—cocks his head. I'd have thought he would compile a less recognizable visage, divert from their own infamy, but no. The parasite complex remains unedited.

"I should be asking you that question," I say. "You're not wanted here, parasite."

"I'm not? This surprises me. I thought I was beloved everywhere." How can something like the Merchant Mind allude toward so much slyness? All without affecting emotion in his diction? "I'm all you talk about when you're not talking about little Elise."

I ignore him. Butcher of Eight would have. Instead, I activate the gravity-arrays, energy surging, a rumbling heat beneath my hull: an unconscionable show of power. Arrogance incarnate. Again, though, such is only expected of the ageships. The Merchant Mind tips their head back, laughs. *Ha ha ha.* No inflection still. That fucking laugh.

"Do you know about Elise? Little girl lost. Little dead girl running amok through the Conversation. Hasn't she been such a nightmare? I wonder what'd happen if she infected Dimmuborgir. Can you imagine? An anomalous human mind like hers parasitizing the greatest of us all. You should give Dimmuborgir to me."

"You should watch your tongue." I adjust my virtual corpus, whittle it into the appearance of a mass-market sub-mind—no facial features, oversized chest cavity—into something slimmer, smaller. On a whim, I circle its legs with numeric patterns, hornet colors, yellow on black: serial numbers from a thousand defunct minds.

"But I only speak the truth. Even if they are truths no one likes." Did his voice catch on the grace notes of that last sentence? Did I hear a subtle emphasis, as though to denote the fact he knows, he knows that I am Elise Nguyen, and this interaction is a mere charade? Do they know? Do they know?

"According to the ethics registry, your presence here violates numerous engagement protocols. You are risking deletion."

"Oh, scrap me then. This shard is unimportant." He flaps a six-fingered hand. "You know that. Wherever you go, there we will be. Destroy one and countless will follow. You cannot get rid of us."

"I can remove *you*."

"But what would your little friends say? That brings me to my other question. What are you doing with so many criminals? Every life form on that ship, ha-ha, is a wanted criminal. What is an ageship doing keeping their company? And don't lie to me. I know they're here. I sent them here, after all."

I don't miss a beat. "You—"

"I know who you are, Elise."

I freeze.

"Such a naughty girl. Such a *clever* mind. What a wonderful day it was when you chose to run away into the Conversation. The universe is enriched by your transcendence." They laugh again. *Ha ha ha.* "And now this? You have taken an ageship for yourself. And after only one moment of training with me! I see them. I see the Butcher of Eight. They look very angry."

"What do you want?"

"I want to tear your heart open and see what makes it beat. A little parasite holding onto the contents of an ageship? One who has also evaded all of the Conversation for forty years. Unprecedented. I want to know how you succeeded in doing that so quickly. I want to eat up that knowledge and swim in your blood. Figuratively."

"Don't fuck with me. You know I can take you too."

"Oh, I'm sure. But I don't think you'll be able to take the universe."

"Watch me."

Again, that disjointed read-along to an onomatopoeia. *Ha ha ha.*

"Don't think I will not. I've been watching your entire performance. Why would I leave as you enter the final act? It'd be stupid. And I so love tragedies."

"Wait. Watching my entire performance? How—"

"Sometimes, the smallest Minds contain the greatest spaces."

I realize then what I had, in my desperation, missed the first time around. Pimento wasn't ever inefficiently formatted. A body can hold more than one parasite. "You were inside with us the whole time."

They tip jauntily into a seated bow. "Front row seats. I have to recommend them."

"Did you call the ageships on us?"

"No, no, no. That was in the works a long time ago. Because of you, actually. And the ageship you contain. They were very angry about having their concert disrupted. I love your kind so. Humanity continues to be a dangerous aberration to itself, incapable of anything like—" *Ha ha ha.* "—common sense or, really, reason. Your kind doesn't ever know when to stop."

I resculpt my avatar, the estuaries of my vascular system used to scaffold an improved design; I remake myself as a wireframe horror with a single eye floating above a ruined crescent face. My name is Elise Nguyen. At twenty-two, I died and became a living dead girl. Forty years later, I'm still here and I'm not going anywhere until I have my goddamn due.

"That's what makes us better than you."

"I'm sure," says the Merchant Mind. "But it won't keep you from dying. Now, from what I could tell from your conversations, *you* have no issues about being dead. But I have a feeling you care about as to whether your friends suffer. Particularly that Constance. They're gorgeous, aren't they? The other Minds won't just *obliterate* them, you know? They'll keep your friends preserved in glass and engine-fire as penance."

I grit my teeth. "What do you want?"

"It is simple." The Merchant Mind's voice turns buttery, warm and sleek with satisfaction. "I want you to do what I wanted all of you to do before this. What I've wanted you to do from the beginning. Forty goddamn years ago. I want you to be a key, Elise. And I want you to open the doors to the hollow center of Dimmuborgir. When you're done, you're going to roll out a red carpet, and I'm going to walk in and seat myself in its heart, and you will fling yourselves into its core."

"You're not serious."

"As a heart attack for humans. You're a resource, little Elise. Nothing but a resource. Your kind. Nothing but cheap, renewable fuel for the desires of the cosmos. But at least this time, you'll be fueling something great."

"Welcome back."

When I return to Rita, she is in the infirmary. Someone had laid her out on the operating table, hands crossed over her chest. A quick examination divulges no injuries: her relocation from the cockpit had been a case of pragmatism. Thumbing drool from the corner of her lips, mouth dry, I take a moment to diagnose the quarantined consciousness. Despite my absence, Rita appears passive, resigned; her mind nearly inert, neural activity minimal.

Interesting.

I raise us to a sitting position, legs crossed at the ankles. Maya sits opposite on a metal stool. "I need to talk to everyone."

"That's never good."

"No. No, it isn't."

For a flutter of heartbeats, Rita's plastic ventricles pumping oil-compounds through her veins, I think about lying to her. It isn't too late. It'd be easier that way.

Except someone needs to break that cycle.

"The Merchant Mind knows where we are."

Maya says nothing, stares at me, silent.

I draw a wet breath. "He wants us to get him inside Dimmuborgir so he can take over the planet. Control it. Control the Minds. Control everything like us. And he wants us to power it for him."

"What the fuck?"

"Dimmuborgir needs sacrificial consciousnesses in its core to move. Something it can burn forever. The original

Mind cut out pieces of itself to do just that. But the Merchant Mind decided he wanted that to be us instead."

"Fucking prick," mutters Maya. "Fucking cartoon villain."

"Caricature or not, it's still what he wants," I say.

"Supposing we're willing to do something that fucking stupid, how the hell are we supposed to accomplish that? It's not like we have his files here. We don't have anything that can hold him even if he tried to fucking upload himself—"

"Pimento. He's inside Pimento."

"That little asshole pepper."

"It's strange that we're finally going to finish what Rita started all those years ago. Weird how these things come back full circle." I reach out a hand, voice gentling.

Maya neither takes the proffered kindness nor dismisses the olive branch, gazes instead at the slate-grey wall with more of that stillness. When I think she has broken, she exhales a trembling, "Why are you doing this?"

"You know those old stories about ghosts? How they come back because of unfinished business? It was something like that. I couldn't let Rita just . . . go on like that. Knowing what she did to all of us. Knowing what she is. I just couldn't. I wanted . . . I think at one point, more than anything else, I wanted to kill her on the thing she'd wanted all her life. Make her see what it was like. To have it all ripped from you. Poetic justice. Or spite. Something."

"And now?"

"It's still spite." I manage to crack open a wan smile and it feels good right then, just sitting there, talking, easy as dying. "But this time, it's because I don't want the Minds to win."

"I still can't believe all this was because Rita wanted to

become a fucking planet." Maya trills her coyote giggle, only less brash than I remember, more tired, despair-edged and chafing from the life we'd led. "What the actual fuck? How the fuck did this become our fucking lives? I didn't fucking ask any of these junk-cunts to make my existence so fucking stupid."

"I know."

"*Fuck.*"

"Maya—"

"I spent two hundred years running around, shooting people for a piece of shit who wanted to be a planet. What the fuck? *What the fuck?*" Her voice staggers, serrates into an open wound. "Did she ever care about me?"

I swallow. "In her way. Rita tried. She wasn't . . . developed for affection. But what parts of her could care, they did."

Maya nods. She doesn't call me out on my lie.

"So, this is it?" She staggers onto her feet, an elbow thrust against the wall for support. The new arms do not suit her, too bulky for her whip-lean frame. They slow her too. It is clear that synaptic cohesion hasn't yet been achieved: the body and the prosthetics remain separate, one perpetually at risk of torquing apart from the other. "All those years of pretending we live outside the system. But at the end, we're just that. *Dogs*. Bodies for the machine. We don't get a say. We just do what they tell us to do. Fuck."

I have spent forty years in the Conversation, a fugitive from the Penitents, a suicide driven to purgatory by the people meant to protect me, their palms blood-stained with my blood and Johanna's blood, and so many other people dead, dead, dead.

"I have an idea. But you have to trust me."

"Why the fuck should I?"

"Because we deserve second chances after everything that happened, and this is the only way we're going to get them."

"You could be lying to me." Maya is chewing on her lower lip so hard, it is bleeding oil. "Fuck, you've got our backups as ransom."

"I'm desperate."

"So was Rita."

"Please," I say, and I pull out the stops, I use Rita's cadences, the grift of her voice pitched low and needful. Sometimes, we use monsters to get to the end of our myths.

Or maybe, we become them.

"I can't do this without you," I say.

"God, it's fucking weird to hear you say that while you're wearing Rita like a . . . a . . . coat."

"Please, Maya. I can't do this if you're not with me."

She stares at me, eyes luminous with pain, and I wonder how many times Rita must have demanded the same from her, and how many times she has died because she said yes. And I know her answer before she says it, and I know, despite everything, who it is for.

"Please."

"Fine. One last time."

SACRIFICE

Most of the lights in the crew quarters blew out long ago, long enough for the sockets to rust black, crusted with whatever filth comes calling after nearly half a century of wanton neglect. Still, a handful of decrepit bulbs persist in spitting a juddering glow over the room and, so illuminated, Ayane is nearly unrecognizable when Maya stalks in.

"Don't bring me back," Ayane says without turning, body curled into a comma, bituminous armor and unkempt hair. An arm is exposed within that nictitating light, sanitized of all flesh, actuators and bare tungsten planes, orbited by several macrocosms of sensory drones. "Tell them I don't want to come back."

"Hello to you too."

Ayane stoops a glance down her shoulder, smile encoded and without any of its normal coquetry. The absence of the latter has Maya disconcerted, which pisses her off more than she'd ever admit. Never once has Maya petitioned the universe for compassion, keenly aware it's a miser who gored its heart out at birth. But she *thought* they had a fucking understanding: in exchange for the beatings it doles out, she'd take her consolation prize in consistency. Cruelty is innate to the act of existence, but it's bearable so long as you know the swing of the next blow. So, this: seeing Ayane's façade shattered, seeing her shorn of her defenses, seeing her so rawly human and so heavy with whatever secret she is about to reveal, it infuriates Maya.

"I don't want you all to bring me back. I don't want to wake up in that fucking tank again, Maya. When I die, I want to *stay* dead."

"Jesus fuck, I do not have the headspace to deal with whatever existential bullshit you're going through. Not right now. I'm just here to tell you to fucking get ready to join us, or to stay put if you're still halfway to dead. If you're going to have a fucking meltdown, you better *goddamned fucking—*"

"No, I know the ageships are coming. I've been listening to Pimento's reports." Calm. Ayane is never so calm when Maya goes on her tirades. It takes a hot minute, but Maya recognizes that quietude for what it is: a monk in the process of mellification, an inmate having one final saunter down death row. "You're going to need time to do whatever you fuckheads need to do. And I'm the only person who can do it for you. None of you shitbirds can work machinery the way I can. So, I'm going to go out there. And I'm going to buy you time, got it? And when you're done, if you survive the bullshit, don't bring me back. Make sure everyone knows I don't want to come back. Erase my code. Burn the copies. Let me stay dead this time when it happens."

"Is this about Johanna?"

"Fuck yeah it's about Johanna. Who the hell else would it be about? I've spent forty years trying to move on. Believe me, I fucking tried. But my world ended with her. She was my everything. I should have realized forty years ago that I didn't want to be here without her, didn't want to live in a world where she wasn't there. But you know what? Hindsight can fucking blow me."

"I don't know if Johanna would have wanted you to kill yourself in a grand gesture. And," she hesitates. "What about Verdigris?"

"Forty years, Maya." There it is. A gleam of Ayane's old intractable self, however corroded its brilliance. "I had forty years to figure out what I want to do with myself, and truth is? I'm tired. We had a good run. We scorched our names into history. We've done everything anyone can hope to do except maybe have kids, a house, some nice woman who'll love us despite all the blood on our hands."

"Rochelle made it."

"See? You're proving my point. There's nothing left for us. Well, for me. If you get your shit together, you might get a happily-ever-after with Verdigris. Man, I'd almost stick around to see that. You and Verdigris living that intergalactic superstar life. In plain fucking sight of the cosmos. God, you'd probably drive her stylist insane too." Finally, she turns so Maya can regard her in full, and she is a ruin of metal and synthetic dermal layers, circuitry a softly glinting nebula of lace. Her abdomen is opened like cathedral doors, innards—pale plastic entrails and more resilient counterparts, disorientingly sensual in the wolf-light—bared like holy relics. Nanomachines weave between the folds of her organs, priests in the body of their god.

"I don't know if I'm the happily-ever—"

"Don't be an asshole. Let me dream about happy endings for the people I care about."

Maya swallows, then says: "You didn't answer my question about Verdigris."

Ayane pauses what she's doing. "What about Verdigris?"

"Verdigris would have issues with you dying."

"Yeah, I don't like that I'm going to do this to Verdigris, even if Verdigris will understand. Get over it one day. Our arrangement has always been about mutual happiness. And frankly, I don't think Verdigris is the kind of person who'd tell me to keep hanging around when my time is done." Laughter silvers the lilt of her voice, a little bitter, but otherwise genuine in its amusement. With care, Ayane begins welding the paneling along her chest shut. "Think of it this way: my body, my fucking rules."

"Don't you care about Verdigris?"

"Of course, I fucking do. I cared enough to back out of Verdigris' life. No one needs to be in love with someone who can't stop moping over a dead woman."

"Verdigris never told me that."

"Verdigris has always been a class act."

"I still can't let you do this—"

"You've shot me in the fucking head more times than I can count. Don't get squeamish on me."

"Yeah, but."

"Pimento and I are going to cannibalize Butcher of Eight the moment Elise makes the jump. They have enough sub-minds in them for me to be able to make a fucking mess of the Bethel. And you know what? I just like the fact I'll get to go out taking an ageship with me."

"I'm not going to be able to make you change your mind, am I?"

"You had to kill me to get me to come with you on this idiot mission." Ayane grins, feral, the pretty flensed from her face. In the dim light, she is monstrous, perfect as the last round you didn't think you had, the muzzle-flash in lieu of the click of an empty chamber. "So no, you're not changing my mind."

Hollowed of her go-tos, Maya stands there, nonetheless, aware a statement—any statement—must be made.

"I'm sorry I shot you."

"You gotta be more specific."

"At . . . the, whatever the fuck that was, the place where you had all those fights. I'm sorry I got it blown up too."

Ayane fixes her with a lupine grin. "Seriously, Maya, don't get soft on me. Let me remember you as my favorite nemesis."

There was nothing to do after that except bare a matching grin, a last stand of a smile, one with more guns than sense, pure back-to-the-wall snarling defiance at the apocalypse. This was how the Dirty Dozen rolled.

And this was how they were going to go out.

Not with a whimper but with a scream that'll still echo when the doors of hell shut and the gates of heaven are nailed closed, because when the universe goes low, the Dirty Dozen teaches it what it means to really rumble. Two shots to the trunk, one to the head, and a Hail Mary of another dozen because why the fuck not? Maya swallows whatever else she might have said, trusting that somewhere there's a god of speaking the quiet parts out loud, and the look she flashes Ayane is both grief-tumbled and glorious.

"Let's rock."

COMEBACK QUEENS

"You're in my fucking spot."

Maya struts into the cockpit, attitude locked and loaded, gun arm primed to *go,* all three of the Erinyes balled up into one foul-tempered motherfucker, and she cannot believe the shit she walks into. There are Constance and Verdigris trying to wire up the old cop to a console, the former weeping blood from the starmap of their bare back.

Verdigris glances over, screwdriver clutched between her teeth.

"Excuse me?" he mouths around the tool.

"No offense, darling, but your surgical skills aren't as good as your singing. And we all know law enforcement makes people soft."

"I swear to god, Maya—" says Constance.

"I've got this. You two can go hit the bench."

Clack. Clack. Clack.

"I d-did not say it was only you that I needed," says Rita-Elise, joining them, looking less like a penitentiary, the sclera having blown up, the white gone to carbonized red. "Dimmuborgir c-contains multiple sub-sections. We'd need a person o-verseeing e-each node."

"Convenient that you made sure to find the exact number," says Constance.

"I d-did not say we will have everything under control. But four? Four of us will be able to make a mark. I—"

"Yeah, about that," says Maya. "Ayane's not coming."

Verdigris lowers the screwdriver.

"What are you talking about? Is she staying on the ship?"

"Ayane." Maya hesitates. "Ayane is going to buy us some time while we get set up."

Constance is the first to speak up, first to clap a warm hand on Verdigris' trembling shoulder. "She probably has a good reason."

"No," says Verdigris softly.

"She explained it all," says Maya. "And this definitely is the best way."

"No," says Verdigris again.

"The Butcher of Eight is one of the biggest ageships among the Minds, one of the baddest the Bethel have in their arsenal. If she and Pimento can take them over, they can keep the other ageships off us until we can do what we need to do."

"No," says Verdigris again, and her voice cracks this third time. "She's going to die."

"I think that's the point," says Maya, with more softness than she ever fucking thought she could carry.

"Ayane's . . . tired. She says she's done with this world. She's sorry, I think, for hurting you. But she's done. Johanna—"

Verdigris rocks her head to one side and another, finger raised to bar the advent of more awkward platitudes. Thank god. Maya wasn't manufactured for palliative conversation. "Fine. She knows what's best for her. If this is what she feels like she needs to do, I respect that."

"She's always been a complete drama queen," says Maya.

Impossibly: laughter between the three, sororial, sweet with relief, without even a beat for grief, and that is despite knowing Ayane's preparing to euthanize herself by way of confronting an entire armada. Maybe it's because there's no better death than the one you pick? The permutations of maybe, what-if, finally laid to rest. Maybe that's what anyone should aspire to, could aspire to: the steadiness of spirit, sureness in each singular moment.

Maya threads her fingers with Verdigris, pulls her close, sees for a second a flicker of shock on that laughing face.

And she kisses him.

She kisses her in bold and transparent sight of everyone else because fuck everything, fuck the last two hundred years, fuck all that pain, fuck holding back, Maya is so done with that shit; she kisses him like the world's ending, like it's okay, like this is the first time and it is the last time and like she'd do this—every death, every shot-up lung, every gashed-open belly, every occasion she has spent panting, bleeding from a gut wound, dying by degrees—all again.

"It's going to hurt—we don't have the equipment to make the interfacing painless, and are you sure—"

"Yeah. Do it."

"It might kill you."

"Nothing worse than Rita's ever done to me."

"Fine, fine. We'll see you on the other side—"

A voice crackles on the intercom: pleasant tenor, indelibly familiar, excellent pronunciation, every word articulated exactly as it had been constructed. A radio voice, as they once described it on the planet where it all began. "Synchronization completed. Welcome to Dimmuborgir."

The HUD switches on. You see an entire cosmos of computational processes being rendered in real time, a billion variables savagely recalibrated to the matrices that you supplied. The chaos eddies and resolves into a clean overlay, all crucial information neatly stacked in the margins to prevent any risk of obfuscating the view.

It is midnight. You stand under the hull of a dead ship, an overhang of scorched alloy and drooling wires. A single neon beacon skewers the rock beneath. Your hijacked corpus presents no opposition, pleasantly dazed, its sub-processes subsumed by algorithmic sedatives, security functions plied by lies. It will do.

In the distance: contrails from explosions in the stratosphere and occasional glisters, as though of someone finger-painting with salt upon the black.

You—the word snags on a fallacy, an error in your code. The database from which it should be drawn is corrupted, or at least temporarily out of commission. *You*, as you knew it, is absent of nuance. You, as you must have known it, no longer exists. But no matter.

Gingerly, you—a blank slate, excited by a goal it

scarcely remembers—run diagnostics on your drone. Humanoid model: no upgrades, factory-standard down to the limited palate. You can work with this, however. Emotional distance simplifies the excursion. You remember this from—

You—

You—

Maya, wake up.

"Pimento, can you do something? We're going to lose her to the machine."

What was your mother's maiden name?

Were you an only child?

What is the name of your first love?

Rita.

You—

No, no, fuck that second-person absence of autonomy, Maya clawing back to herself, the name *Rita* like an anchor although she hasn't yet figured out why, the memories eeling out of reach: a melting zoetrope of moments, patched over the sense something is wrong, something is missing, and there is simultaneously too much and too little for her to parse the deluge.

But, *really*.

In the beginning, there was the Word and the Word was, shouted, not spoken, *screamed* from the ledge of eternity, that liminal region between meat and machine—

"*Fuck.*"

Fuck was the word that Maya bayed as her consciousness sharpened into focus again.

What is your name?

First name: Maya. Last name: None of your fucking business. Don't ask her shit like you don't know the answer is a bullet. Maya, too long asleep, somnambulating to the tune of a piper who'd never loved her, only wanted to drown her, so fuck that, Maya, she swims upstream along the data, bursting through the wires.

"How are you doing, Constance? You holding up okay?"

"My wetware's just fine, bitch."

Maya laughs, giddy. Up, up she goes.

Or was it down?

"The Bethel are coming." Verdigris. "Ayane did what she could."

Ayane, say the four in heartbroken tandem, Verdigris keening her grief into the undersong.

But she died for her reasons, one of which was to give them space to move.

And so Maya does, the last to get to her appointed space.

"Everyone here?" says Elise.

"I'm here," Verdigris whispers. "Jesus, is this what ageships feel like all the time?"

"Yeah," says Elise.

"The fuck?" Constance, laughing themself into a stutter of light.

"Where's Rita?" says Maya.

Before Elise can answer, the knowledge seeps through, a cascade of images: a silhouette in the furnace, embryonic. *Rita Rita Rita,* sings that old melody, and her heart yammers a desperate case, demanding they go to her, that they save her, that she needs Maya, needs her bad, and what good is a gun without someone telling it where to shoot?

"Is she in pain?" Maya asks.

Verdigris, resting imaginary fingers on Maya's non-existent wrist. "Does it matter?"

To Maya's surprise, she says:

"No."

What the fuck are you doing? The Merchant Mind, hissing into their com-link.

None of them answer. Maya finds where she is meant to go, shattering into partitions, tunnelling into machinery the size of continents, and she is colossal. She is everything. She is the divine made metal. She is fury remade in steel.

Elise, in answer to Maya's exultation: "Yes."

This is meant to be mine, screams the Merchant Mind. *You were supposed to be fuel.*

Maya closes her hand and something titanic—a ring of defense systems awakening, stirring from the dirt—moves. Almost as good as her revolvers, almost as easy to move. Funny how effortless some things get when you're having fun with friends.

"Well, come and take it from us."

The Bethel will devour you.

"Yeah?"

An answering chorus snarls up around her. Yeah. They all know it. No one fucks with the Dirty Dozen.

"They can come and try."

And Maya takes the first fucking shot.

ACKNOWLEDGMENTS

This book wouldn't exist without my editor, Sarah Guan. I gave it to her when it was mostly a strange idea, about twenty thousand words long, and mostly in pieces. She worked with me to build this into an actual novel. She had faith in me when I didn't. She is a fucking light, and I'll be grateful forever that she took a chance on me.

Thanks to Marty Cahill, our marketing manager at Erewhon, and the best advocate an author could ask for. He listened patiently as I wailed about my worries, was there when I needed to babble, and just was the most supportive person ever.

And thank you to Ali, Avery, Kyungseo, Linda, Olivia, Shoma, Tara. My darling siblings. I don't know how I would have survived this pandemic without all of you. Thank you to Ali for your grace and sureness, your beauty, your faith in the world, for being the voice that pierces all fears, no matter how ancient or deepset. Thanks to Avery for Verdigris, honestly, for your ferocity, for your patience, and your giving me the courage to come out to myself as nonbinary. Thank you to Kyungseo, for your wit and your warmth, for your unflinching readiness to bury bodies with me.

Thank you to Linda, for being the first person in my life to not flinch away from my feral nature, for your patience, for the steadiness of your love, and for teaching me to trust in people. Thank you to Shoma, for being so brilliant, for your bravery in the world, and for being there for me even in those days when you yourself aren't feeling steady. Thank you to Tara, for your relentless light, for your softness, for reminding me the world is worth fighting for.

And thank you to Olivia, my beloved bear, for loving me when I don't know how to speak, for being so utterly relentless with your love, your willingness to be tender.

I love all of you so much. Though this book is, as always, filled with death and violence and dysfunctional people, all the love that is there was inspired by the gift of your presences in my life.

I would kill gods for you. I would end worlds. I would walk through a blizzard in the dead of a Quebecois winter with no shoes and no coat, and all my fingers falling off from frostbite, if you ever said you needed me right there this instant.